Masters
of Atlantis

ALSO BY CHARLES PORTIS

Norwood

True Grit

The Dog of the South

Masters
of Atlantis

A NOVEL BY

Charles Portis

THE OVERLOOK PRESS
WOODSTOCK & NEW YORK

First published in paperback in the United States in 2000 by
The Overlook Press, Peter Mayer Publishers, Inc.
Lewis Hollow Road
Woodstock, NY 12498
www.overlookpress.com

Library of Congress Cataloging-in-Publication Data

Portis, Charles
Masters of Atlantis / Charles Portis.
p. cm.
1. Secret societies—Fiction. 2. Atlantis—Fiction. I. Title.
PS3566.O663 M3 2000 813'.543—dc21 99-0086846

Manufactured in the United States of America
ISBN 1-58567-021-9
1 3 5 7 9 8 6 4 2

Masters of Atlantis

1

Young Lamar Jimmerson went to France in 1917 with the American Expeditionary Forces, serving first with the Balloon Section, stumbling about in open fields holding one end of a long rope, and then later as a telephone switchboard operator at AEF headquarters in Chaumont. It was there on the banks of the Marne River that he first came to hear of the Gnomon Society.

He was walking about Chaumont one night with his hands in his pockets when he was approached by a dark bowlegged man who offered to trade a small book for two packages of Old Gold cigarettes. The book had to do with the interpretation of dreams. Corporal Jimmerson did not smoke, nor did he have much interest in such a book, but he felt sorry for the ragged fellow and so treated him to a good supper at the Hotel Davos.

The man wept, overcome with gratitude. He said his name was Nick and that he was an Albanian refugee from Turkey. After supper he revealed that his real name was Mike and that he was actually a Greek from Alexandria, in Egypt. The dream book was worthless, he said, full of extravagant lies, and he apologized for imposing in such a way on the young soldier. He apologized too for his body odor, saying that nerve sweat or fear sweat made for a stronger stink than mere work sweat or heat sweat, or at least that had been his experience, and that he was always nervous when he spoke of delicate matters.

Perhaps he could repay the kindness in another way. He

had another book. This one, the *Codex Pappus*, contained the secret wisdom of Atlantis. He could not let the book out of his hands but, as an Adept in the Gnomon Society, he was permitted to show it to outsiders, or "Perfect Strangers," who gave some promise of becoming Gnomons. Lamar, who was himself an Entered Apprentice in the Blue Lodge of the Freemasons, expressed keen interest.

It was a little gray book, or booklet, hand lettered in Greek. There were several pages given over to curious diagrams and geometric figures, mostly cones and triangles. Mike explained that this was not, of course, the original script. The original book had been sealed in an ivory casket in Atlantis many thousands of years ago, and committed to the waves on that terrible day when the rumbling began. After floating about for nine hundred years the casket had finally fetched up on a beach in Egypt, where it was found by Hermes Trismegistus. Another nine years passed before Hermes, with his great powers, was able to read the book, and then another nine before he was able to fully understand it, and thus become the first modern Master of the Gnomon Society.

Since those days the secret brotherhood had seen many great Masters, including Pythagoras and Cornelius Agrippa and Cagliostro, but none greater than the current one, Pletho Pappus, whose translation this little book was. Pletho lived and taught in the Gnomon Temple on the island of Malta, with his two Adepts, Robert and a man named Rosenberg.

Lamar was embarrassed to say that he had not heard of this Society, nor was he aware that flotsam of any description, literary or otherwise, had ever been recovered from Atlantis. What was the book about? Mike apologized again, saying he was bone tired. Could they continue their discussion another time? He could hardly keep his eyes open and must now find himself a dark doorway where he might curl up and try to get a little rest. But Lamar would not hear of this and he arranged for Mike to be put up in the Hotel Davos.

Their friendship flourished. They had many meals together and many long talks. Lamar paid for Mike's food and shelter and cigarettes, and even bought him a cheap suit of clothes. Bit by bit the truth came out. Mike confessed that his real name was Jack and that he was an Armenian from Damascus. He was here on a mission. Pletho, with an eye to expanding the activities of the secret order to the New World, had sent him here to Chaumont, disguised as a beggar, to look over the Americans and determine if any were worthy of the great work. So far he had found only one.

Lamar was embarrassed again. But Jack insisted that yes, Lamar was indeed worthy and must now prepare himself for acceptance into the brotherhood. Lamar did so. First came the Night of Figs, then the Dark Night of Utter Silence. On the third night, a wintry night, in Room 8 of the Hotel Davos, Lamar Jimmerson folded his arms across his chest and spoke to Jack the ancient words from Atlantis—*Tell me, my friend, how is bread made?*—and with much trembling became an Initiate in the Gnomon Society.

This work done, Jack said that he was at last free to divulge his true Gnomon identity; he was Robert, a French Gypsy, and he must now hasten back to Malta to report his success to the Master, the success of the American mission. He would leave the *Codex Pappus* in Lamar's care, for further study, and as a kind of token of good faith, or surety, and he would return in a month or so with more secret books, with Lamar's ceremonial robe and with sealed instructions from Pletho himself. There was a $200 charge for the robe, payable in advance. This was merely a bookkeeping technicality, one of Rosenberg's foolish quirks, and all rather pointless, seeing that Lamar would begin drawing $1,000 a month expense money as soon as his name was formally entered on the rolls. Still, Robert said, he had always found it better to humor Rosenberg in these matters.

Lamar saw no more of Robert and heard nothing from Malta. He wrote letters to the Gnomon Temple in Valletta but got no answers. He wondered if Robert's ship might have been torpedoed or lost in a storm. There was no question of his having run off with the robe money because he, Lamar, still had the *Codex*, along with Robert's "Poma," a goatskin cap he had left behind in his room. This Poma was a conical cap, signifying high office, or so Robert had told him.

The Armistice came and many of the doughboys set up a clamor to be sent home at once, though not Corporal Jimmerson, who remained loyally at his switchboard. He even volunteered to stay behind and help with all the administrative mopping-up tasks, so as to replenish his savings. In May 1919, he received his discharge in Paris, and went immediately to Marseilles and got deck passage on a mail boat to the island of Malta.

On arrival in Valletta he took a room at a cheap waterfront hotel called the Gregale. He then set out in search of the Gnomon Temple and his Gnomon brothers. He walked the streets looking at faces, looking for Robert, and clambered about on the rocky slopes surrounding the gray city that sometimes looked brown. He talked to taxicab drivers. They professed to know nothing. No one at the post office could help. He managed to get an appointment with the secretary to the island's most famous resident, the Grand Master of the Knights of St. John of Jerusalem, but the fellow said he had never heard of Gnomons or Gnomonry and that the Grand Master could not be bothered with casual inquiries.

Lamar found three Rosenbergs and one Pappus in Valletta, none of whom would admit to being Master of Gnomons or Perfect Adept of Hermetical Science. He tried each of them a second time, appearing before them silently on this occasion, wearing his Poma and flashing the *Codex*. He greeted them with various Gnomon salutes—with his arms crossed, with his right hand grasping his left wrist, with his hands at his sides and the heel of his right foot forming a T against the instep of his left foot. At last in desperation he removed his Poma and clasped both hands atop his head, his arms making a kind of triangle. This was the sign for "Need assistance" and was not to be used lightly, Robert had told him. But Pappus and the Rosenbergs only turned away in fright or disgust.

Was he being too direct? A man who wishes to become a Freemason must himself take the initiative; his membership cannot be solicited. With Gnomonry, as Robert had explained, it was just the reverse. A man must be *invited* into the order; he must be *bidden* to approach the Master. Perhaps he was being too pushy. He must be patient. He must wait.

Just at that time, at the sidewalk café outside the Gregale, with the cries of sea birds all about him, Lamar met a young Englishman named Sydney Hen. Sydney was Keeper of the Botanical Gardens in Valletta, and as such had been exempted from war service. He too was curious about things. Not only was he a student of plant life but he also collected African artifacts—spears and leather shields and such—and he read strange books as well, and speculated on what he had read, hoping to piece together the hidden knowledge of the ancients.

The two young men hit it off fairly well, particularly after Lamar had let slip the fact that he had in his possession a book of secret lore from Atlantis. They walked along the quay together, sometimes arm in arm, though Lamar found this European custom distasteful. They talked far into the night about the enigmas of the universe.

Sydney kept after Lamar to show him the *Codex Pappus*, and Lamar kept putting him off in a polite way, saying he was not sure under what conditions he could properly show the book to a Perfect Stranger. Lacking immediate guidance from his superiors, Robert and Pletho, he was not sure just what he could and could not do. He would have to think it over.

"And quite right too," said Sydney, who did most of the talking on these dockside rambles. He had strong opinions. The Freemasons had gone wrong, he said, through their policy of admitting every Tom, Dick and Harry into the Lodge, and the modern, so-called Rosicrucians were *not* the true

Brethren of the Rosy Cross, far from it. And this stuff from India, this Eastern so-called wisdom, was a complete washout. He had looked into it and found it to be a quagmire of negation. It looked sound enough and then you thumped it and it gave off a hollow ring.

On Sunday afternoons Sydney presided over a kind of literary salon at his hillside villa, which was ablaze with flowers the year round. Lamar, told that he would not feel comfortable with such people, was never invited. Then one Sunday he was invited. Sydney said, "Come on up and meet the gang, Lamar!" Lamar was not favorably impressed by all the slim, chattering young men at the gathering, nor they with him, but the food was good and Sydney's sister, Fanny Hen, a crippled girl, was kind to him, very attentive.

When he returned to the Hotel Gregale that night he found that his room had been ransacked. Nothing, as far as he could tell, had been stolen. His Poma and *Codex* were still safe behind the loose board in the linen closet. Probably children looking for war souvenirs, he thought, and he was careful to stuff his puttees and some other things behind another loose board. The next morning, just as he stepped out into the street, something came whipping past his ear like a boomerang. Careless kids, throwing a marlinspike around. Later that same day, at dusk, he was assaulted on the street. He was walking around a corner when a man struck him full in the mouth with a long wooden oar and knocked him flat. As he lay there in a daze two or three men were suddenly all over him, handling him roughly and ripping his clothes in search of something. Waterfront thugs, he later decided, who had taken him for a rich American. The laugh was on them.

The sunny days passed, and the warm nights, and Lamar ran out of money. No word came from Robert or Pletho. Time to take stock. He was a Gnomon Initiate with a hidden Master, a book he couldn't read, some thirty-odd stitches in his lips and no robe. He did have his Poma. But when to wear it? He looked about town for work. Sydney said he might be in a position to make a personal loan against the *Codex Pappus*. Lamar said it would hardly be fitting to mortgage the Codex.

The only job he could find was one cleaning boots and emptying chamber pots at the Gregale. There was no pay but he did get his meals and the use of a cot in the basement. The Gregale guests, mostly English poets and Greek honeymooners, were poor tippers. Now and then a poet would fling him a threepenny bit. The Greeks, when they left anything at all, left tiny brass coins in their broad shoes that could not be exchanged. But these Greeks—brides, grooms, chubby merchants—were quite generous in another way. They translated the *Codex Pappus* for Lamar, a page or two at a time. He allowed no single Greek to see much more of the book than that, being fearful lest the entire text be exposed to a Perfect Stranger.

The pages of handwritten English accumulated. At length the work was finished. Lamar bound the leaves together with a shoelace and began his study. He sat on the cot at night, wearing his Poma, and labored over the hard passages, reading a sentence over and over again in an effort to wrest some meaning from it, as he brushed away on the high-top yellow boots of the poets. In later years, in his introductory remarks to Gnomon aspirants, he was fond of saying, "Euclid told the first Ptolemy that there was no royal road to geometry, and I must tell you now, gentlemen, that the road to Gnomonism is plenty tough too."

He committed the entire work to memory, all eighty-eight pages of Atlantean puzzles, Egyptian riddles and extended alchemical metaphors. He knew every cone and every triangle by heart, just as he knew the 13 Hermetical Precepts, and how to recognize the Three Secret Teachers, Nandor, Principato and the Lame One, should they make one of their rare appearances before him in disguise. Soon he began to wonder if he might not be an Adept. He became sure of it one afternoon when he overheard a remark in the street—"Don't worry about Rosenberg." That is, he did not become sure of it at that moment, but only a little later, as the words continued to ring in his head and swell in volume. This, surely, was what he was waiting for. The sense of the message was obscure but there could be no doubt that the signal was genuine. This was Pletho's oblique way of communication.

As an Adept he now felt free to put the whole business before Sydney, with a view to bringing him into the brotherhood. Sydney had come to doubt the existence of the book from Atlantis and he could no longer receive Lamar, a bootblack, socially at Villa Hen, but the two young men still managed to see one another on occasion, behind the giant ferns at the Botanical Gardens or at one of the low waterfront cafés. So it was, at a sidewalk table of the Café Gregale, that Lamar told Sydney the full story of Robert, the *Codex*, Hermes, the Poma, the translation, the voice in the street.

Sydney heard him out, his skepticism giving way to excitement. He looked through the two booklets, one Greek, one English. He read Greek, though with difficulty, forming each word slowly with his mouth and on the bilabials blowing little transparent bubbles that quivered and popped. Then he turned in impatience to the English version and read hungrily. "This is marvelous stuff!" he said, in a fairly loud voice. "I can't make head or tail of it!" He had to speak up over the shouting and scuffling that was taking place in the street. It was some political disturbance that did not concern them. Sydney wanted to take the books home and study them at leisure, but Lamar said he could not, at this time, let them out of his hands. Trying to soften the refusal, he pointed out that the *Codex* was largely incomprehensible without the keys that Robert had revealed to him. These keys were never to be written. They could only be spoken, from one Gnomon to another.

Sydney became agitated and demanded to be given the keys and taken into the Society at once. Then he sighed and asked Lamar's pardon. He took Lamar's hand between his two hands and begged that allowance be made for his short temper. He had been a very naughty boy. The only thing now was for Lamar to move into Villa Hen, where he could live in that comfort and peace so necessary to the scholar, and give instructions in this great work in the proper way.

Lamar accepted the invitation and the next day he carried his bag up the hill to the villa. Fanny Hen, the crippled girl, was not around. He asked about her and Sydney said he had moved her into a boardinghouse down the way so that Lamar might have her room. But Lamar would not hear of this and the girl was soon restored to her room. Lamar slept in the library.

Fanny had made no very distinct impression on him before, apart from her kindness and her game leg. Now he began to notice other things about her. She was small and dark like her brother, but there the resemblance ended. Where Sydney was moody Fanny was sprightly, and where Fanny was open Sydney was sly. She had been an army nurse and her right knee was stiff from shrapnel wounds received in the final Flanders offensive of September 1918. She wore billowy shirts with striped neckties.

Sydney was an apt pupil, much quicker than himself, Lamar had to admit. He cut short his work at the Botanical Gardens and came home early each evening, flinging his black cape carelessly from his shoulders and quickly slipping into his red silk dressing gown, eager for another long session with Lamar in the locked library. He smoked black Turkish cigarettes and sipped Madeira. From time to time he rubbed his hands together. When he had grasped a Gnomonic point he would say, "Quite!" or "Quite so!" or "Just so!" or "Even so!" and urge Lamar to get on with it. The progress slowed somewhat when they came to the symbolic figures. Sydney found himself in a tangle with these cones and triangles. He often confused one with another and got the words slightly wrong.

During the day Lamar enjoyed the company of Fanny

Hen. They discussed their war experiences. He expressed regret that he was not free to tell her, a woman, about Gnomonism, except in very general terms, but there it was, he was under certain vows. She said she understood and that, after all, women had their little secrets too. He told her about Gary, Indiana, carefully pointing out that his people had nothing to do with the steel mills. She talked about girlhood escapades at The Grange, Little-Fen-on-Sea, which was her home. They sat at the piano and sang "Beautiful Dreamer." They went to the harbor and watched the boats and ate Italian sausages. She made light of her "silly knee" and apologized for being such a slow walker. Slow or fast, he said, he counted it a privilege to be at her side and would consider it a great honor if she would take his arm.

In little more than a month of intense study Sydney became an Initiate in the Gnomon Society. Within another month he was an Adept, and then, as a peer of Lamar's, he began to speak out on things. He suggested how the course of study might be organized along more efficient lines. The ritual of investiture could be improved too. A processional was needed, a long solemn one, and more figs and more candles, and some smoldering aromatic gums. Lamar agreed that such touches were appealing. The innovations seemed harmless enough and might even be useful, but how could two Adepts presume to do such things without direct authorization from Pletho Pappus or some other Master?

Then Sydney Hen uttered the thought that had been troubling Lamar for some weeks. It was a wild thought that he had often suppressed. "Can't you see it, man? You're already a Master! We're both Masters! You still don't see it? Robert was Pletho himself! Your Poma is the Cone of Fate! You and I are beginning the New Cycle of Gnomonism!"

So saying, Hen produced a Poma of his own, one he had had run up in red kid, and then like Napoleon crowned himself with it.

Thus boldly expressed and exposed to the blazing light of

day, the thing could be seen clearly, and Lamar knew in his heart that it was true. He was Master of Gnomons and had been Master of Gnomons for perhaps as long as six weeks. He had not, however, suspected for one moment that Sydney might be a Master too, and this news took his breath away. What was more, Sydney said he believed himself to be a "Hierophant of Atlantis." Lamar was puzzled by the claim, there being no such title or degree in Gnomonism, to the best of his knowledge.

Over the next few days Sydney outlined an Alexandrian scheme whereby he and Lamar would take Gnomonism to the world. He, Sydney, would be responsible for Europe and Asia, and Lamar would establish the ancient order in the Americas, in accordance with Pletho-Robert's plan. There was no time to lose. He all but pushed Lamar out of the house, saying he was terribly sorry but an unsecured personal loan was out of the question. He must make his way back home as best he could.

Lamar, as a veteran in distress, was able to get a hardship loan from the American consul, upon surrender of his passport, just enough to pay steerage fare to New York in the sweltering hold of a Portuguese steamer. Fanny kissed him goodbye at the dock and so the rough accommodations bothered him hardly at all.

2

L amar was hardly noticed as he passed through New York with his *Codex* and continued on his journey home by rail. In Gary he picked up his old job as clerk in his uncle's dry goods store. He took his meals and his baths at the YMCA down the street, and slept in the back of the store. Here, in the shadowy storage room, with the drop light and the cardboard boxes, he established Pillar No. 1 of the Gnomon Society, North America.

He was unable to recruit his uncle, who said he didn't have time to read a lot of stuff like that, much less memorize it. Nor did Lamar have any luck with his old school chums. His first success came with a traveling salesman named Bates, who set up Pillar No. 2 in Chicago. Bates was followed by Mapes, and Pillar No. 3, in Valparaiso, Indiana. Mapes was a football coach, ready to try anything. He hoped that Gnomonic thought might show him the way to put some life into his timorous and lethargic team. Mapes was followed by—nobody, for quite a long time. Three Pillars then, and three members, all told, and that was what Lamar had to show for almost two years of work.

By this time he had made a typewritten copy of the *Codex*. The string-bound manuscript version was getting dog-eared and did not make a good impression. The typewritten copy did not make a much better impression but it was easier to read. Lamar could see that many men did not accept this as a real book either, judging from their hard faces as they flipped through it, pausing over the triangles and recoiling, and then giving it back to him.

What was needed was a properly printed book. Bates told him about a Latvian newspaper in Chicago, where, in the back shop, English could be set in type and printed without anyone there understanding a word of it. Lamar went there and ordered fifty copies of the book and asked the Letts not to break the plates but to keep them readily available for reorders. The books had blue paper covers and were bound with staples.

Some years were to pass before the first printing was exhausted. The 1920s were later to be celebrated as a joyous decade but to Lamar it was a time of the grossest materialism and of hollow and nasty skepticism. No one had time to listen. Fanny Hen's letters kept him going. Her monthly letter, lightly scented, was the one bright spot in his gloomy round. She was now in London with Sydney, or Sir Sydney, he having become the fourth baronet on the death of his father, Sir Billy Hen, the sportsman. Sydney was disappointed in his patrimony, which amounted to little more than a pile of Sir Billy's gambling debts, but he had pushed on with that energy characteristic of the Hens to set up his Gnomon Temple on Vay Street, and, according to Fanny, was doing quite well with it. Lamar kept Fanny's current letter in his inside coat pocket, where he could get a whiff of it with a slight dip of his head, and where it was handy for rereading over his solitary meals. In his replies to her he always enclosed a money order for fifteen dollars and said he hoped she would use the small sum for some little personal luxury she might otherwise deny herself.

In the spring of 1925 Lamar went on the road as a salesman, working out of Chicago under Bates with a line of quality haberdashery. It was a good job and at first he did well with it, so well that he was able to make a down payment on a small house in Skokie and a transatlantic proposal of marriage.

Fanny accepted, against the wishes of her mother, who was worried about Chicago gangsters, and of brother Sydney, who stood to lose an unsalaried secretary. She arrived at New York on the *Mauretania*. Lamar took her to Atlantic City, where they were married in a Methodist chapel. The honeymoon was delightful. From their hotel room high above the beach they could watch the battering waves. They took rides together on the Boardwalk in the ridiculous rolling chairs and had late suppers at Madame Yee's with tiny white cups of tea. It was the last carefree time the young Jimmersons were to know for several years.

Fanny Jimmerson was fond of her brick bungalow in Skokie, which she fancied to be in the exact center of the continent, and she might have kept it had she not unwittingly stirred up the embers of Gnomonism. Lamar no longer talked much about the Gnomon Society. Repeated failure to interest others in the secret order had worn him down. He no longer bothered his fellow drummers in hotel lobbies with confidential talk about the Cone of Fate. Now here was Fanny telling him of Sydney's great successes in London. He had brought hundreds of men into the brotherhood, including some very famous members of the Golden Order of the Hermetic Dawn and the Theosophical Society. His building fund for the Temple was already oversubscribed.

Lamar, stung, turned on her one night and spoke sharply. The two situations were hardly comparable, he said. Sydney was dealing with a class of men who had a sense of the past and a tradition of scholarship. How well, he asked, would Master Sydney fare with the 13 Precepts on a smoking car of the Illinois Central? How far would he get with his fine words on the streets of Cicero, above the din of careening beer trucks and blazing machine guns?

Fanny said she was sorry, that she had not meant to goad him. She just thought he might be interested in Sydney's work. After all, they were, were they not, brothers in this secret order? Lamar said she was absolutely right. He asked her to forgive him for raising his voice. It would not happen again. He was, of course, pleased to hear that Sydney was doing well and she was right to remind him of his duty.

Once again he set about in earnest to find recruits, to the neglect of his clothing sales. He told his buyers that he had something in his sample case more beautiful than painted silk neckties and more lasting than Harris tweed, and the best part was that this thing would cost them nothing more than a little hard study at night.

Bates too pitched in anew. Through a friend at the big Chicago marketing firm of Targeted Sales, Inc., he got his hands on a mailing list titled "Odd Birds of Illinois and Indiana," which, by no means exhaustive, contained the names of some seven hundred men who ordered strange merchandise through the mail, went to court often, wrote letters to the editor, wore unusual headgear, kept rooms that were filled with rocks or old newspapers. In short, independent thinkers, who might be more receptive to the Atlantean lore than the general run of men. Lamar was a little surprised to find his own name on the list. It was given as "Mr. Jimmerson." His gossiping neighbors in Skokie, it seemed, had put him down for an odd bird. They observed him going into his garage late at night in a pointed cap and had speculated that he was building a small flying machine behind those locked doors, or pottering around with a toy railroad or a giant ball of twine.

He and Bates wrote letters to the seven hundred cranks, with questionnaires enclosed that had been run off at the Latvian printshop. They waited. They sorted out the replies. Those men who seemed to have the stuff of Gnomons in them got second questionnaires, and such of these as came back went through a further winnowing. The process culminated with Bates or Lamar appearing on the doorsteps of the worthy few, *Codex Pappus* in hand.

"Good morning," Lamar would say to the householder at the door. "I am—*Mr. Jimmerson.*"

It was during this period that Lamar, still a young man,

became known to all and sundry, young and old alike, as "Mr. Jimmerson." He and Bates, with Gnomon gravity, had always addressed one another as "Mr. Bates" and "Mr. Jimmerson," and this form now took hold in the wider world. Fanny continued to call him "Lamar," as did Sydney Hen, and much later, Morehead Moaler, but few others took that liberty, not even Austin Popper.

Mr. Bates and Mr. Jimmerson worked long hours for the Society and even bagged a member now and then. When they were fired from their sales jobs they hardly noticed, and they used their final commission checks to pay for a new line of printed study materials. The loss of the little brick house through foreclosure was more troubling. Mr. Jimmerson could see that Fanny was upset and he promised to make it up to her one day. Good soldier that she was, she made no fuss. They packed their goods and left Skokie, and when they were gone, the neighbors, peering from behind curtains, spilled out of their houses and went for the garage at a trot to see what they could see, with any luck a small airship.

The Jimmersons moved into a rented room in Gary, where Fanny prepared budget meals on an electric hot plate. It was a cheerless winter. Mr. Bates often shared their dinner of baked beans and white bread spread with white oleomargarine. Neither of the two Gnomons paid much heed to the Pythagorean stricture against eating beans and the flesh of animals, although they did feel guilt in the act until Austin Popper came along and explained that this rule was never laid down by Pythagoras, but was rather an interpolation by some medieval busybody, and that in fact there was nothing Pythagoras liked better than a pot of Great Northern beans simmered with a bit of ham hock.

The new members of the order, to be sure, paid certain fees, and the Society's bank balance at this time stood at around $2,000, but Mr. Jimmerson was careful to keep that money separated from his personal funds, lest there be any breath of scandal. Fanny thought he should pay himself a small salary as Master of all the Gnomons in America, or at least take some expense money. Sydney didn't stint himself at his London Temple. He even had a full staff of servants. Mr. Jimmerson said that Sir Sydney could do as he pleased, but as far as he, Lamar Jimmerson, was concerned, the great work was not for sale. She must understand that his position was a fiduciary one, one of trust.

Fanny saw there was nothing for it but for her to take a job. She found work as a nurse's aide at Hope Hospital, in the physical therapy ward, where she soon became a great favorite with patients and staff alike. After completing a brief refresher course she took the state examination and received her license as registered nurse, along with a supervisory position in the therapy ward that paid $150 a month.

Mr. Jimmerson knew nothing of this. He had noticed that they were eating better, pork chops and such, and living better. They seemed to be living in a different place, in a clean new apartment just down the street from Hope Hospital, but he was so preoccupied that he had not bothered to inquire into these new domestic arrangements. Fanny was reluctant to tell him about the job. With all his quirky principles he was sure to have objections to working wives. He would put his foot down. As it turned out, he didn't mind at all, and as he became swamped with paperwork he even encouraged her to take courses in accounting and hectograph operation, and lend him a hand. She did so, and, with an hour snatched here and there from her busy day, she also prepared the typescripts of his first three books, 101 *Gnomon Facts*, *Why I Am a Gnomon* and *Tracking the Telluric Currents*. These works, written for the general public, contained no secret matter, nor were they indexed or annotated.

Things began to pick up toward the end of the decade, and then in 1929, with the economic collapse of the nation, the Gnomon Society fairly flourished. Traders and lawyers and bricklayers and salesmen and farmers now had time on their hands. They had time to listen and some were so desperate as to seek answers in books. By the summer of 1931 there were more than forty Pillars in six states, and in January of the next year Mr. Jimmerson went to his Latvian printers and placed an order for 5,000 copies of the *Codex Pappus.*

The Letts were in serious financial trouble. Their newspaper had already gone under and the printshop was just barely afloat. But Mr. Jimmerson was not one to forget his friends. True, they had garbled important passages in his books and left pages uncut and bound entire chapters upside down, but they had also extended credit to him in those dark days when it could not have been justified in a business way. He was now in a position to return the favor. The firm was to be reorganized as the Gnomon Press. No one would be fired. The production of Gnomon tracts and books would have priority but the shop would be free to take in outside jobs as well. When this announcement was made, and translated, amid heavy Baltic gloom in the back shop, the printers at first were stunned, and then they cheered Mr. Jimmerson and threw their paper hats in the air.

With success came the inevitable attacks. There was the usual sour grapes disparagement and mockery of outsiders looking in. Pagan nonsense, said the bishops. At best a false science, said the academic rationalists. An ornate casket with no pearl inside, said the Masonic chiefs. A foolish distraction from the real business of life, said the political engineers. A nest of cuckoos who like to dress up and give themselves titles, said the newspaper writers.

None of these gentlemen could say just what Gnomonism was—the Archbishop of Chicago had it confused with Gnosticism—but they all agreed it was something to stay clear of. *Why the secrecy? Who are these people? Whatever it is they are concealing must be evil. What are their long-range plans? Do they claim magical powers? What are they up to with all their triangles?*

Lies were spread about the Gnomons. They were said to carouse in their meeting halls, which had painted windows like mortuaries, dancing the night away with much chanting and tambourine shaking, following their ritual meal of bulls' blood, lentils and smoked cat meat. There was at least one physical attack. A young man from Northwestern University tracked Mr. Jimmerson down and demanded a refund of the dollar he had paid for a copy of *Why I Am a Gnomon* and an apology for foisting it off on the public. He said the book was "not any good at all" and "just awful stuff," and when Mr. Jimmerson hesitated in his reply the young man ripped the little book into two pieces and flung them away and then punched the Master in the face. Fanny did not know about the fracas until the next morning, when she noticed that her husband's lips and nose were stuck fast to his pillow with dried blood. He told her it was nothing, that he believed the young bruiser had assaulted him as a writer rather than as a Gnomon, and that in any case all this abuse was contemptible, not to say futile. Their enemies were much too late. The Gnomon Society had taken root in the New World and was here to stay.

This became clear for all to see on April 10, 1936, when the Gnomon Temple was dedicated in Burnette, Indiana, the most fashionable suburb of Gary. It was a mansion of Bedford limestone, which, with grounds and outbuildings, occupied a good part of the 1400 block of Bulmer Avenue, the most fashionable street of Burnette. An iron-and-steel tycoon, lately deceased, had built it, with little regard for expense, and his widow, eager to be off to Palm Beach, sold it to the Gnomon Society for $180,000. Mr. Jimmerson was uneasy over the prospect of moving into so grand a house and he had to be persuaded by the Council of Three, Bates, Mapes and Epps, that it was necessary for the Master to live in the Temple, at the center of the web, just as it was necessary for the Temple to be monumental, have great mass, be gray and oppressive to every eye that gazed upon it.

3.

Sir Sydney Hen cabled fraternal congratulations from London. It was another wonderful day for the Society, he said. He regretted that he could not attend the dedication but his health was such that he was no longer able to travel. He was suffering greatly from fevers, fluxes and the dry gripes and could hardly get away from the bathroom for an hour at a time. He suspected that he was being given a debilitating poison by Rosicrucian agents from France. The cable was dated "Anno, XVII, New Gnomon Cycle," and was signed "Hen, Theos Soter, Master and Hierophant, C.H., F.S.A.," with the letters standing for "Companion of Hermes" and "Far-Seeing Arbiter." Thus had the advanced degrees of Gnomonry begun to proliferate.

Mr. Jimmerson quickly became adjusted to the comforts of Temple life. The Council had been wise to insist on his living here. He particularly liked the Red Room, with its big fireplace, the bookshelves that rose to the ceiling, the wine-colored carpet and the wall coverings of wine-colored silk. Here he settled in. In the Red Room a man could study and think. Here he could get down to business on his new book, *The Jimmerson Spiral*.

Fanny liked the oversize bathtubs and the canopied beds and the rose bower and the splashing fountain. She had a number of servants at her disposal, these including a cook, a gardener, two maids and a butler-chauffeur named Maceo, a quiet Negro man who had the additional duty of sweeping out the Inner Hall of the Black Throne, into which neither Fanny nor the maids, as females, were allowed to penetrate.

Mr. Jimmerson's office was fully staffed too, and overseen by one Huggins, whose title was editorial advisor. Huggins was a journalist, an irritable, alcoholic bird of passage who brought certain professional skills to bear on the production of Gnomon printed matter. Austin Popper was the mail boy. That was the job description but he was not really very boyish at the age of nineteen—or maybe it was twenty-four, or even thirty. Even at that time Popper was coy about his age, and his origins, and no one could pin him down on these things.

Popper was quick in every sense of the word. His physical movements were quick and sure, and he could learn a new task in short order and execute it with confidence. He had a ready fund of information gleaned from newspapers and popular magazines. He kept his eyes open. He remembered names. His charm was effective on both men and women, and even the misanthropic Huggins became fond of him. Mapes and Epps thought him just a shade ambitious but they too found his company pleasant, against their will.

When Huggins was drunk, Popper covered for him, and when Huggins had editorial disputes with the Master, or printing disputes with the Letts, it was young Popper who stepped in to smooth the ruffled feathers and suggest a sensible accommodation. Huggins soon found himself working for Popper, and still they remained friends.

But Huggins was bound to be left behind anyway since he refused to become a Gnomon. Out of a natural perversity and a newspaperman's terror of being duped, he refused to join anything, and so remained a P.S., or Perfect Stranger, while Popper answered the summons with alacrity and went on to become a power in the great brotherhood. Soon he was writing speeches for the Master and helping him with his books. He talked and wrote with facility, seldom at a loss for a word, or an opinion. He was never Master of Gnomons, nor even a member of the Council of Three, but the common perception that he directed the organization was not far off the mark.

What Popper did was transform the Gnomon Society. Having gained the confidence of the Master, he was able to persuade him that they must broaden their appeal. The way to do this was to relax the standards. The *Codex Pappus*, for instance, was much too difficult for most beginners and should be revised. There was too much memory work for the ordinary man; the staggering volume of this stuff must be reduced. Only in this way could the Society expect to grow and become a force in the world.

Mr. Jimmerson said, "And how would you go about all this, Austin?"

Popper was turning through the pages of the *Codex*. "The first thing we must do, sir, is get rid of some of these triangles."

"You would do away with the symbolic forms?"

"Oh no, not all of them. I would keep the Cone of Fate. Under no circumstances would I tamper with the Jimmerson Spiral."

"But you think there are too many triangles? The simplest of polygons?"

"Far too many, sir, for the people I have in mind. Do you remember in school how hard it was to get anyone to join the Geometry Club?"

"I don't believe we had a Geometry Club in our school."

"Neither did we but you see what I mean."

"The ordinary man, you say. Why should we concern ourselves with ordinary men? Pletho tells us that most of them are pigs or children."

"Some of them are pigs, certainly, but I need not remind you, sir, that it is our ancient business to transmute base matter into noble matter."

"The great work."

"As you say. All I want to do, sir, is prepare a simplified version of the *Codex* for use at a new and elementary level of our craft. Then, step by step, we can lead these men on to the *Codex Pappus* itself and pure Gnomonism."

Popper spoke of thousands of new members and at last the Master came around. He took the proposal to the Council of Three, or T.W.K.—Those Who Know. Mr. Bates liked the idea. Mapes and Epps conceded that it might have some merit —but was Austin Popper the right person to direct such a program? He was willful, erratic. He was vain in his personal appearance. He was sometimes facetious in a most unbecoming way. In his writing he had a vulgar inclination to make everything clear. He had not yet learned to appreciate the beauties of allusion and Gnomonic obfuscation—that fog was there for a purpose. He couldn't see that to grasp a delicate thing outright was often to crush it.

But in the end, under pressure from the Master, they gave way and Popper was authorized to proceed. An abridged *Codex* was prepared, and a new teaching syllabus. A new probationary degree called "Neophyte" was created.

Popper went on the road with his mission, due east, to Toledo and Cleveland, where he placed small, mystifying notices in the newspapers, and then met in hotel rooms with those men of Ohio who responded. It was a period of trial and error. There was no shortage of idle men on Lake Erie but the wisdom of Atlantis, clarified though it now was, still did not hold their attention. Popper had to grope about for ideas they could hearken to. Little by little he worked things out. Most of the triangles and a good many of the oracular ambiguities had already been pruned from the *Codex*, and Popper went further yet. The Cone of Fate was not exactly abandoned but he no longer talked about it except in response to direct inquiry. The Gnomonic content of his lectures diminished daily as the Popper content swelled. Soon he had a coherent system, one with wide appeal, and he had to book ever larger rooms and halls to accommodate the growing number of men who came to hear his words of hope.

For this was what he gave them. Through Gnomonic thought and practices they could become happy, and very likely rich, and not later but sooner. They could learn how to harness secret powers, tap hidden reserves, plug in to the Telluric Currents. It was all true enough. Popper plugged them in to something of an electrical nature and he bucked them up with the example of his own dynamic personality and they went away thinking better of themselves.

The Gnomon wave was cresting, and it was at this high point that Morehead Moaler of Brownsville, Texas, became a Gnomon, perhaps the most steadfast of them all. But little notice was taken of him at the time, or of his remote Texas Pillar, what with all the national excitement. There were articles in the press about "the mysterious Mr. Jimmerson" who remained concealed in his "Egyptian Temple" in Burnette, Indiana, while his spokesman, Austin Popper, went about teaching "a lost Egyptian science." *Look*, the magazine, published an account of a Popper rally in Philadelphia, with a striking photograph of a roomful of solemn men standing with their hands clasped atop their heads. Popper appeared on a network radio show in Chicago, a breakfast show, and was received with whistles and sustained applause from the friendly oldsters in the audience. He marched around the breakfast table with them, and one jolly old man, whose name he failed to catch in the hubbub, presented him with a talking blue jay. He caught the bird's name, Squanto, but just missed catching the name of the old gentleman, whose smiling red face he was to see often in his dreams, the face saying its name, but just out of earshot, never with quite enough force.

Mr. Jimmerson, at the urging of the Council, called Popper in off the road and said, "This has gone too far, Austin. I want you to stop playing the fool. I want you to show some dignity. They tell me you have a Victrola now and a talking bird."

Popper was contrite. He promised to conduct himself with restraint in the future. Then he went back on the road and resumed his old ways. He led his followers in cheers and he played bouncy tunes on a windup phonograph, marking the beat with wildly swooping arms. He engaged in comic dialogues with Squanto. He continued to court the press and he even had his picture taken with politicians. These were two of the Four P's that all Gnomons were under orders to shun, the other two being the Pope and the police. He continued to weaken the membership requirements until admittance to the order became almost effortless. The two nights of initiation were reduced to a token twenty minutes, with no insistence on figs, and the Pledge was no longer eight densely printed pages of Hermetical mystery lore and bloody vows of faith to the Ten Pillars of Atlantis—all to be recited without stumbling once—but rather one short paragraph that was little more than a bland affirmation of humility before the unseen powers of the universe.

Still, there was something to be said for Popper. He *did* bring in thousands of new members, a few of whom turned out to be good Gnomons, and all of whom paid monthly dues and bought books and study materials from the Gnomon Press.

Mr. Jimmerson was of two minds. He wavered. One day he was resolved that Austin must go and the next day he would defend him in a heated session of the Council. More than once he had to raise his little bronze rod, the Rod of Correction, to calm tempers. Mapes and Epps demanded that Popper be silenced. If not, they warned, he would soon be their Master. Already he had changed the Society into an ungainly beast that Pletho Pappus would hardly recognize, to say nothing of Pythagoras and Hermes Triplex, and if they, the Master and Council, stood by and allowed this headstrong young man to further corrupt the brotherhood, then the judgment of history would indeed be hard on them, and rightly so.

The argument was telling and in his heart Mr. Jimmerson knew that something would have to be done. In February

1940 the painful decision was made. Austin Popper was to be formally "humbled," and assigned to a menial administrative job in the Temple. The axe was poised, and then, just before it fell, something happened that changed the picture.

A few months before, in September 1939, with the outbreak of war in Europe, Sir Sydney Hen had fled England with his robes billowing behind him and come to Toronto, Canada. Mr. Jimmerson invited him to make his home in the Temple in Burnette. Hen declined with thanks. Every courtesy was extended to him by the Canadian Gnomons, who found him a suite of rooms in a lakefront residential hotel that was filled with chattering widows.

Fanny Jimmerson went to Toronto for a Christmas reunion with her brother and she was very much upset at what she found. He was bent and had lost his teeth. His neck was prematurely wattled. The elf locks were gone and indeed all his hair except for a semicircular fringe in back that hung straight down, dead and gray like Spanish moss. The poisoning report, the henbane story, which Fanny had dismissed as one of Sydney's hysterical flights, turned out to have been all too true, though the French Rosicrucians had been unjustly blamed. The poisoner was a young man named Evans who had been lightly dusting Sir Sydney's muffins with arsenic on and off over the years. Hen described him as a "paid companion." The boy's motive was not clear, with the police suggesting that Welsh peevishness was somehow behind it all, and in any case there was not enough evidence to prosecute. "All I could do was pull his ears and sack him," said Hen.

Fanny extended her visit so as to nurse Sydney and prepare restorative meals for him. She brightened up the place with bits of song and decorative touches and small pots of vegetation, including some of Sydney's favorite ferns and spiky desert succulents. His appetite gradually returned. She bundled him up and took him for walks along the lake. The icy winds made his cheeks glow. His eyes cleared. She bought him a puppy and Hen taught the little dog to shake hands and how to untie simple knots that had been loosely tied in one of his older sashes.

Some of the ladies in the hotel approached Fanny to ask if it was true that her brother was a baronet. Physical wreck that he was, Sir Sydney still had a certain air, and the ladies were curious about him, this titled mystery figure on the sixth floor. Fanny responded in a friendly way and the ladies proposed a tea party, with Sir Sydney as guest of honor. He agreed to attend, to allow the ladies to honor him and look him over for a half hour or so, if certain conditions were observed. There must be no receiving line, no cameras and, above all, no handshaking. He would not stand or even sit. Arrangements must be made for him to recline. The conditions were met. Hen wore a white cassock and gold chain and embroidered slippers. He thoroughly enjoyed the affair. The cakes were good and the ladies hovered about his recumbent form and listened attentively to his far-ranging opinions.

Toward the end of January, Fanny left him in fairly good health and in the hands of a rich widow named Babette. A few weeks later, in February, a Toronto newspaper published a long letter from Hen that rocked the Gnomon Society.

He began his remarks with an attack on Popper, calling him "Austin Rotter" and "a low American farceur" and "a confidence trickster of the very lowest type," and went on to bring a full and stinging indictment against American Gnomonism. No doubt, he said, the leadership in Indiana, U.S.A., meant well, but it was very weak. Substantial changes could be expected now that he, Hen, was on the scene. As Grand Prior of World Gnomonry he was seriously considering revocation of the charter of the American Temple in Burnette, and would certainly do so if that Temple did not act soon to purge itself of Popper and Popperism.

All this, out of the blue. It was quite a spirited blast from such a frail figure. Mr. Jimmerson's reply was strong stuff too. He gave an interview to a Chicago newspaper, saying it was shameful that a Master, albeit a junior one, of the Gnomon

Society, a secret brotherhood based on principles of Hermetical and Pythagorean harmony, had seen fit not only to make such false and scandalous charges, but to make them publicly. As for any "charter," there was none to be revoked, just as there was no such title in Gnomonry as "Grand Prior," but if there was ever any revoking to be done, then he, Lamar Jimmerson, First Master of the New Cycle, successor to Pletho Pappus and tutor to Sydney Hen, would do it.

Hen came back with another letter to the editor, a short one this time, to the Chicago newspaper. He wrote:

> Please be advised that the Gnomon Society can no longer recognize degrees awarded by the gang of Indiana ruffians led by the impostor Lamar Jimmerson, who styles himself First Master of the New Cycle. Lamar Jimmerson is Master of Nothing. He is a grey nullity whose teaching is worthless and whose conversation is tiresome beyond belief and whose book, *The Jimmerson Spiral*, purporting to contain some later writings of Pletho Pappus, is the most brazen forgery since the Donation of Constantine.

Trailing after Hen's signature there were many titles and capital letters.

So it was that the break came and the Society divided into the Jimmerson school and the Hen school, and thus did Popper escape the axe. To discipline him now, the Council saw, would give the appearance of acknowledging Hen's authority and yielding to it.

The bitter exchanges went on and on. Hen's favorite weapon was the letter of ridicule. Mr. Jimmerson fought back with a barrage of pamphlets that kept the Latvian printers hopping. Then Hen stepped up the campaign, initiating the battle of the books, by having his people remove Mr. Jimmerson's books from libraries and bookstores and destroy them. Popper countered with a program of defacement, ordering the Jimmerson men to fill in all the closed loops of letters in Hen's books with green ink, to underline passages at random in that same green ink and to scrawl such comments in the margins as "Huh??!!" and "Is this guy serious?" and "I don't get it!" in red ink, the aim being to break the reader's concentration and so subvert the message. He also commissioned a drawing of a pop-eyed, moronic human face, that of a collegiate-looking fellow with spiky hair and big bow tie, and had rubber stamps made of it. The face had a strange power to annoy, even to sicken the spirit—one had to turn away from it—and Popper directed that it be stamped on every page of Hen's books, in a different place on each page so that the reader could not prepare himself.

4

The press grew tired of Gnomons and moved on to other things. The public likewise lost interest, almost overnight. War was coming, the country was preparing for a mighty crusade and the Popper rallies suddenly had a shabby, dated air of selfishness about them. The crowds dwindled away to nothing. Popper had run out his string, or so it appeared.

He went back to the Temple to think. Once the life of the luncheon table, he now took a sandwich outside to the fountain and ate alone, or rather with Squanto, the two of them resting on the rim of the circular stone basin. There were goldfish in the pool, and at the center of it, atop a cone of granite, there was fixed the gnomon, or upright part of a sundial, a flat bronze object resembling a carpenter's square. From a window in the Red Room, Mr. Jimmerson could look out on the scene, at the sparkling plumes of water, at the little shifting rainbows, at the simple bronze symbol of his order, at a chastened Austin Popper. He found it pleasing. This was the proper state of things at the Temple, the right pitch, this drowsy afternoon air of not much going on, a state very close to that of sleep.

But with the Japanese attack on Pearl Harbor, Popper was off and running again. Here was an opportunity. Once more he was alive with ideas. First came the Gnomon blood drive, with the brothers laid out in rows, rubber tubes coming out of their left arms and their right arms raised in military salutes for the news photographers. Then on to the army. The Society's first duty in this crisis, Popper said, was to set an example, and how better to do it than for the entire male staff of the Temple—excluding the Master, who, in a manner of speaking, had already borne arms for his country—to enlist in the army as a body. It was their duty and it was just the kind of thing to catch the eye of President Roosevelt and the national press.

The Council agreed and even the cynical Huggins acquiesced. They rallied to the colors *en bloc*. Popper arranged for full press coverage of the swearing-in ceremony at the Federal Building in Chicago. Bates, Mapes and Epps wore their robes. Maceo and Huggins stood slightly to one side with the rest of the staff in fuzzy 1941 business suits. All were solemn and held their right hands up in a rigid way, fingers tightly closed. Popper himself did not take the oath, explaining to the others that the Secretary of the Navy had placed him on "strategic standby." Just what this was and how he came to be placed on it, he was not free to disclose, other than to say that he was working for the Secretary in an undercover capacity. From high official sources, he said, he had learned that he was number eight on Herr Hitler's American execution list, to be shot on sight as a public nuisance.

Whatever Popper's naval duties may have been, they did not require him to range far from Burnette, Indiana. He stayed close to the Temple, where he alone now had the ear of the Master, and where he worked long hours developing new schemes for gaining the patriotic spotlight.

Their next move, he advised Mr. Jimmerson, should be to go to Washington with a carefully prepared plan for winning the war through the use of compressed air and the military application of Gnomonic science. He had already worked out a schedule. First they would pay a courtesy call at the White House and then go to the War Department for a working session with General Marshall. There the full plan would be presented. Afterwards they would hold a press conference and give a report, a kind of broad outline of the plan, cleared of secret matter but including a few tantalizing details. For the newsreel photographers there would be a demonstration of *boktos*, or Pythagorean butting, the old Greek art of self-defense, which was to be incorporated into the army's physical training program. That same night, having arranged for five minutes of radio time on the Blue Network, Mr. Jimmerson would sit before the microphone and again discuss the Gnomon victory plan in a general way, closing with some brief inspirational remarks for the nation.

"Air?" said Mr. Jimmerson.

"*Compressed* air," said Popper. "What you're thinking of, sir, is ordinary air, the air we breathe, which is so soft and gentle we hardly notice it. Compressed air is something else again. It packs a real punch."

He explained, Mr. Jimmerson listened and became thoughtful. He had no qualms over releasing sharp blasts of air against such vicious enemies as the Jap and the Hun and sending them tumbling across the battlefield, but surely it would be wrong to allow the Hermetical Secrets to be used in the bloody business of warfare. He expressed his misgivings.

Popper said, "Remember, sir, we're talking about barbarians here. One of our early Masters wasn't so squeamish in dealing with them. One of the very greatest of Masters."

"Who was that?"

"Archimedes. Don't you recall how he jumped into the battle with all his scientific tricks to help defend Syracuse against, who was it, Tamerlane, I believe, yes, and won the day? Or no, wait, they surrendered, and when it was all over Tamerlane found our man drawing triangles in the dust with his finger."

"Didn't he ask Tamerlane to get out of his light?"

"How right you are, sir. So he could finish working out his geometry problem."

"He couldn't see to work for the shadow."

"No, sir."

"The fellow was blocking off his light."

"Yes, sir."

"Standing in the doorway, don't you see, with the sun behind him so that his shadow made it hard for Archimedes to see what he was doing down there in the dust."

"With his figures, yes, sir."

"Down there on some kind of dusty floor."

"Yes, sir, I understand."

Mr. Jimmerson fell into another thoughtful silence. Presently he said, "We talk of light. Pletho Pappus tells us we must labor in darkness in order to bring light. I'm sure you know the passage, Austin, and yet you seem to think it is our business to attract attention and make a public spectacle of ourselves. How do you reconcile the two positions?"

Popper finessed the question by not answering it. By way of reply he said that a news photograph of Lamar Jimmerson wearing his Poma and his Master's gown and having a chat with President Roosevelt in the White House would cut the ground from under Sydney Hen. Such a picture would be of more value than a million pamphlets in showing to the world just who the true leader of Gnomonry was. Hen would seethe with rage and stamp his little feet like Rumpelstiltskin when he saw that picture in *Life* magazine.

"A wonderful scene, don't you agree, sir? Hen furioso. What I wouldn't give to see that little dance."

Mr. Jimmerson agreed that Sydney's fit would make an amusing show, and he had to agree too that in these dark days the President certainly had a call on his best advice. "I suppose you're right, Austin. We must do what we can."

The ten-point victory plan was prepared and in early June of 1942 the two Gnomons took it to Washington in a locked briefcase. Some thought was given to having Maceo drive them in the black Buick, but then there was the problem with gasoline ration stamps—and Mr. Jimmerson would countenance no dealings with the black market—and so in the end they went by rail. They traveled by day coach, no Pullman space being available, and had to stand part of the way. Fanny had wanted to go but she was five months along in a surprise, mid-life pregnancy and her husband would not allow it. Hotel rooms were all but impossible to get. At the last minute their congressman was able to secure them one small room at an older downtown hotel called the Borger. It was a threadbare place near the bus station. The trip was hot and tiring. At the Borger a midget bellboy called Mr. Jimmerson a "guy."

"Is that guy with you?" he said, in his quacking midget voice, as Mr. Jimmerson, a little dizzy from his long train ride, veered off course in crossing the lobby.

"Yes, he is," said Popper.

"Hey! Hey! Hey! Yeah, you! Where do you think you're going? The elevator's over here!"

Their room was just wide enough for the two single beds and a little leg space between them. Popper sat on one bed and began at once to make telephone calls. He seemed to be trying to make appointments. It struck Mr. Jimmerson that he had left all this until very late. Mr. Jimmerson lay on the other bed and looked over his speaking notes. Tomorrow was the big day.

Popper winked at him and said he had just arranged a double date with two hostesses named Bobbie and Edna who worked at a nearby night spot that had a good rumba band. "I think you'll like Edna, sir. She's a fine, strapping girl. A real armful, Bobbie tells me."

Mr. Jimmerson was astonished. Popper said, "My little joke, sir, nothing more. When people are hot and weary I've often found that a light note is just what the doctor ordered."

That night three Gnomons from the local Pillar came to call on the Master. One was a chubby young man named Pharris White. He was a part-time postal clerk who attended law school at night and who wrote long letters to the Temple on the subject of certain prime numbers and their Pythagorean significance, or lack thereof. Sometimes he sent telegrams. In the hollow place under his lower lip there was a tuft of seven or eight yellow bristles. He carried a satchel. Though he was only a Neophyte, he spoke very freely to the Master, even offensively, demanding to know why he, White, as an ordinary Gnomon, was denied access to the truly secret books by Those Who Know, and kept in dismal ignorance of the truly secret rituals and the truly secret numbers.

Mr. Jimmerson politely told him that he could hardly be expected to discuss such matters on a social occasion like this. White took notes. The other two Gnomons were older men, a municipal judge and a retired streetcar motorman, who simply wanted to meet Mr. Jimmerson and bask in his radiance and have him sign their copies of *Why I Am a Gnomon*.

Popper, still on the telephone, became annoyed with them as they chattered and shuffled about in the tiny room, adding their body heat and cigar smoke to the stifling air, and when he saw Pharris White stealthily rooting around in Mr. Jimmerson's bag he jumped up from the bed and ordered them all to leave. The Master had given them quite enough of his time. He was here on an important government mission and had papers to study.

As they trooped out, Popper caught White by the sleeve. "One moment, White. Let's have a look at your Gnomon card. I want to check the watermark."

"My card is in order."

"Then you won't mind."

White produced his membership card. Popper glanced at it and then whipped out a rubber stamp and stamped VOID across it in purple block letters. "There. You are now a P.S. Get out."

"You can't do this."

"On your way. We don't know you."

"You're making a big mistake."

"And don't write us any more letters. Understand? You savvy?"

"You think you can treat me this way because I'm poor and have to go to night law school."

"All law schools should be conducted at night. Late at

night, in rooms like this. No, I'm turning you out of the Society, White, because there's something wrong with your mind. I can see it in your eyes. They don't look right to me. Your eyes and your pallor tell me all I need to know. Maybe you can get some help elsewhere. We just don't have the time to fool around with people like you. Why aren't you in the army, anyway?"

Pharris White left with his satchel.

Mr. Jimmerson slept badly. He couldn't get his limbs distributed comfortably on the narrow bed. The scene with the young man had been disturbing and he was homesick and concerned about his wife—a middle-aged woman expecting a child—and he had forebodings about what the next day would bring. Popper continued to ring up people far into the night. His telephone manner was unctuous. Mr. Jimmerson turned away from the wheedling voice and the glow of the table lamp and tried to rest. When at last he did sleep his exhalations were moist and troubled.

The next morning, as he inspected himself in a mirror, he told Popper that it had been a mistake to leave Fanny at home. She would have remembered to unpack his gown and hang it up. It was now all wrinkled and puckered. The garment was made of unbleached linen, with a few golden threads interwoven in the cloth to catch the light. Just below the right shoulder, in gold leaf, there was the figure of a gnomon, enclosing a staring all-seeing eyeball.

Popper assured him that the wrinkles would go away after he had walked about some; gravity and the steamy Washington air would do the trick.

"But where is my Rod? My Rod is not here, Austin."

"You can't find your Rod of Correction?"

"I know I packed it. I saw it yesterday."

"That slug Pharris White. He must have taken it."

"Surely not."

"Yes, I saw him pawing over your things with his nimble,

mail-sorting fingers. He probably thought it was gold. I should have searched him."

"Do you know, he pulled my necktie."

"I wish you had spoken up, sir."

A hasty inventory showed that White had made off not only with the Rod, in its rosewood box with silver fittings, but also with Mr. Jimmerson's knotted rope, for escape from burning hotels, and some miscellaneous papers and a complete suit of the Master's cambric underwear. The strange clerk had apparently stuffed away in his satchel whatever fell to hand.

The missing Rod of Correction was a bronze bar about as long as a new pencil and just a bit thicker. Better suited perhaps for poking than for administering any sort of serious beating, it had nonetheless great symbolic power, the power of the Magisterium, and Mr. Jimmerson had only to raise it a fraction of an inch to silence even a roaring speaker like Austin Popper.

"Well, if it's gone, it's gone," said Popper. "Anyway, good riddance to Pharris the white rat and much good may it do him. We need to shake a leg, sir. Here, let me help you with your Poma."

He pulled the cap down snugly against the ears and fastened the chin strap. The strap was a recent innovation, strictly for street wear, a protective measure against the Poma's being blown away or snatched in broad daylight by one of Hen's men. He walked around the listless figure, tugging here and there at the gown, then stepped back to appraise the effect. "Behold! The Master of Gnomons! Ready to go forth! Come on, sir, chin up. Take it from me, things will look much brighter after some coffee and scrambled eggs."

But Mr. Jimmerson did not feel much better after breakfast. The sidewalk was already hot at nine o'clock and the soles of his ceremonial sandals were very thin. People looked at him. Children stopped to stare openly at his feet, great spreading white organs that were coated with hair like the feet of some arctic bird. He danced about on the hot concrete, alternately placing one foot atop the other, as Popper tried to hail a cab.

It was a long day, full of disappointments, and in later years Mr. Jimmerson's memory mercifully failed him as to the sequence of events. His congressman was kind enough to pose with him on the Capitol steps for a photograph but after that he met with nothing but indignities.

For all his telephoning, Popper had come up with nothing more than a brief note from the congressman, which asked in guarded language that courtesy be shown to his two constituents, Mr. Jimmerson and Mr. Popper. There were no appointments. The note availed them nothing at the White House gates. There they were stopped by guards, suspicious of the Master's unusual attire, and were not even permitted to enter the grounds with the tourists, much less see the President. One guard said, "Is the circus in town?" I didn't know the circus was in town." Another kept saying, "So solly, no can do," as Popper protested the treatment.

Next they were turned away from the State Department. Then on to the War Department, where the note did get them past the duty officer in the lobby. They wandered about in that labyrinth for hours. The Battle of Midway was taking place at this time and anxious military men were racing up and down the corridors shouting bulletins at one another. The two Gnomons were bounced from office to office. No one had time to hear them out or look at the victory plan or even allow them to sit down for a moment. Mr. Jimmerson's gown became soaked with sweat. The peak of his Poma wilted and toppled over. Popper finally cornered a young army captain who agreed to give them a few minutes of his time. But he seemed to think they were astrologers and that their plan had to do with the stars and he sent them on to the Naval Observatory.

It was there, on Observatory Hill, that the two became

Oil and Gases and the Institute of Nonferrous Metals in Bucharest, had taught "science" at the Female Normal College in Dobro and had been librarian at the Royal Wallachian Observatory, with its three-inch reflecting telescope, limited mostly to moon studies, atop Mount Grobny. But his abiding interests were alchemy and a lost continent called Mu, a once great land 6,000 miles long and 3,000 miles wide that was now at the bottom of the Pacific Ocean.

The food came, Mr. Jimmerson dug in. Popper and Golescu resumed their discussion of alchemy, with Popper stating forcefully that while the Gnomon Society was in fact privy to this ancient secret (though the practice was under ban in the New Cycle), the Rosicrucians, otherwise very decent fellows, had been running a stupendous bluff in the matter, ever since their first shadowy appearance in Europe some three hundred years ago. They knew nothing. Golescu put questions to him. Popper's answers were ready if equivocal. Mr. Jimmerson ate his supper and said little.

Out of courtesy rather than any real curiosity, he asked the professor how he had happened to leave his homeland— was it not called the breadbasket of Europe?—and come to America.

Golescu considered the question. "Romanian peoples are restless peoples," he said. "Our first thought is to fly, to get away from other Romanians. Here, there, Australia, Washington, Patagonia. Impatient peoples, you see. Always the jumping around. Very nervous. In all Romanian literature there is not a single novel with a coherent plot."

Mr. Jimmerson had difficulty following this kind of thing but Popper encouraged the little man and drew him out.

Golescu became louder and more assertive, revealing himself as an independent thinker. Charles Darwin, he said, had bungled his research and gotten everything wrong. Organisms were changing, it was true enough, but instead of becoming more complex and, as it were, ascending, they were steadily degenerating into lower and lower forms, ultimately back to mud. In support of this he cited the poetic testimony of Hesiod, and gave the example of savages with complex languages, a vestige of better days. He had dubbed the process "bio-entropy" and said that it could clearly be seen at work in everyday life. One's father was invariably a better man than one's self, and one's grandfather better still. And what a falling off there had been since the Golden Days of Mu, when man was indeed a noble creature.

He was an authority on history and literature and boasted of having solved mysteries in these fields that had baffled the greatest scholars of Europe. Through Golescuvian analysis he had been able to make positive identification of the Third Murderer in *Macbeth* and of the Fourth Man in Nebuchadnezzar's fiery furnace. He had found the Lost Word of Freemasonry and had uttered it more than once, into the air, the Incommunicable Word of the Cabalists, the *Verbum Ineffabile*. The enigmatic quatrains of Nostradamus were an open book to him. He had a pretty good idea of what the Oracle of Ammon had told Alexander.

"So, where is your mysteries now?" he said. "Gone. Poof. For me, child's play."

His favorite books, the ones he never tired of dipping into, were Colonel James Churchward's *The Lost Continent of Mu*, *The Children of Mu* and *The Sacred Symbols of Mu*, along with Ignatius Donnelly's *Atlantis: The Antediluvian World*— though he could only agree with Donnelly's theories up to a certain point. He was proud of having introduced these works to southeastern Europe. He had presented many papers on them to learned societies, and had given many popular lectures, illustrated with lantern slides.

"Go to Bucharest or Budapest and say 'Mu' to any educated man and he will reply to you, 'Mu? Ah yes, Golescu.' In Vienna the same. In Zagreb the same. In Sofia you shouldn't waste your valuable time. The stinking Bulgars they don't know nothing about Mu and don't want to know nothing."

With a sudden flourish he brought a small copper cylinder from his vest pocket. "How old do you think this is, my friends? A thousand years? Five thousand? Do you think it came from Egypt? From some filthy mummy? Then I am sorry for your ignorance. This is a royal cylinder seal from Mu, the Empire of the Sun. See? The cross and solar device? It is unmistakable. Golescu can even tell you the name of the artisan who made it. Here, use my glass and be good enough to examine these tiny marks. You see? Those strange characters spell the name Kikku, or perhaps Kakko. I admit to you freely that in the state of our present knowledge Muvian vowels are largely guesswork. But yes, I also tell you that a living, breathing man with the sun shining on his face and with a name something like Kikku fashioned this beautiful object in the land of Mu—hold on to your caps—*fifty thousand years ago!* I would like it back now. And please, no questions about how it came into my hands. Questions about Kikku the coppersmith of Mu? Fine. I am at your service. Only too pleased. Questions about how did Golescu get his hands on this wonderful seal? I am too sorry, no, not at this time. You will only be wasting your valuable breath."

Mr. Jimmerson knew a thing or two about sunken continents himself and he was amazed that a college professor such as Golescu could be taken in by Churchward's nonsense. For he too had read *The Lost Continent of Mu*, a book in which he had found almost every statement to be demonstrably false. No small literary achievement, that, in its way, he supposed, but then there were people like Golescu, and innocent people as well, perhaps even children, who were gulled by Churchward's fantastic theories. Donnelly was sound enough, a genuine scholar, but Churchward would have it that Mu—"the Motherland of Man"—was the original civilization on earth, that it was a going concern 25,000 years before Atlantis crowned its first king! What a hoax! Three hundred pages of sustained lying! How was it that the American government couldn't put a stop to these misrepresentations and this vicious slander of Atlantis? Or at least put a stop to these cocksure foreigners coming into the country with their irresponsible chatter about Mu?

But Mr. Jimmerson, his temples pounding with blood, saw that it would be improper for him to engage in a quarrel with such a man and he said nothing.

It was getting late. Golescu, egged on by Popper, seemed to be just reaching his stride. He called for two pencils and "two shits of pepper." Popper found pencils and sheets of paper. The professor proceeded to give a demonstration of his ambidexterity.

"See, not only is Golescu writing with both hands but he is also looking at you and conversing with you at the same time in a most natural way. Hello, good morning, how are you? Good morning, Captain, how are you today, very fine, thank you. And here is Golescu still writing and at the same time having his joke on the telephone. Hello, yes, good morning, this is the Naval Observatory but no, I am very sorry, I do not know the time. Nine-thirty, ten, who knows? Good morning, that is a beautiful dog, sir, can I know his name, please? Good morning to you, madam, the capital of Delaware is Dover. In America the seat of government is not always the first city. I give you Washington for another. And now if you would like to speak to me a sequence of random numbers, numbers of two digits, I will not only continue to look at you and converse with you in this easy way but I will write the numbers as given with one hand and reversed with the other hand while I am at the same time adding the numbers and giving you running totals of both columns, how do you like that? Faster, please, more numbers, for Golescu this is nothing. . . . "

Popper said, "Oh boy, is he cooking now! How about this fellow?" Mr. Jimmerson tried to cut the performance short by calling room service and asking for another pot of coffee and some more cherry pie. Despite the interruptions, the professor went on and on, and again declined the offer of food, his policy of solitary dining extending to cover even such small fare as this.

His last show of the night had to do with some small pinnate leaves taken from a vine or herb that he refused to identify. "Not at this time, no, I am too sorry. That is for me alone to know." He had taken five or six of the leaves from his coat pocket and was holding them up for examination. They were still faintly green and glossy on the upper side, though dry and curling.

"Isn't he something?" said Popper, pointing with a toothpick. "Look at that, sir, *leaves*. He had *leaves* in his pocket. I wonder what kind of leaves they are. In what way are they special, do you think? Well, you can just bet there's a story behind them, and a good one too. What in the world will this fellow come up with next?"

Mr. Jimmerson didn't care to guess. He was ready for bed.

Popper said, "Wait. I think I've got it. I do believe Cezar is going to brew us a pot of tea. Yes, some sort of Romanian health beverage or Rosicrucian Pluto Water."

"Not tea, no," said Golescu. He had cleared a space on the table, pushing back the crockery and napkins and bones and rinds and crusts and other rejected edges of things, and placed there a candle stub and two glass vials of chemicals and a little hand-cranked grinder, with which he began to macerate the leaves. "A demitasse, eh, ha ha, such a funny joke. Perhaps you like this cyanide in your tea. What, you take one gram or two? For me, no, thank you very much. Ha ha. Tea."

Mr. Jimmerson retired. He slept through the crushed leaves experiment, waking now and then to note with irritation that the lights were still on and that Austin and the professor were still talking. On his next trip, and God grant it would not be soon, he must remember to bring along his plywood board for a bed stiffener. And tomorrow he must not forget to pick up a box of dark chocolates for Fanny. A mingling of darkness and light. He would have used that, Pletho's favorite phrase for the world, to good effect in his radio speech. He had never had much confidence in the victory plan, or even fully understood all its many points, but why had the radio address been canceled? Politics? He had never thought much of Roosevelt anyway, or of his party. Rum, Romanism and Rebellion wasn't the half of it these days.

5

He went back to Indiana and took little further interest in the war. He slept through much of it. Let someone else deal with the Central Powers this time. And the Japs. According to the newspapers, the little monkeys couldn't see very well. They were clever, and quick on their feet too, remarkable jumpers, but their jiujitsu would prove useless against the rapid and sustained fire of our Lewis guns.

Still, as with many others, Mr. Jimmerson was to suffer loss and misfortune. Even the birth of his son turned out to be a mixed blessing. Coming to motherhood so late, Fanny was much taken with the child, and she lavished all her attention on this tardy arrival, baby Jerome, to the neglect of her husband. "Look, Lamar!" she said. "What a little pig he is for his milk!" Sometimes Mr. Jimmerson held Jerome on his knee and patted his back and said jip jip jip in his face in the way he had seen others do, but he really didn't know what to make of the drooling little fellow and his curling pink feet, almost prehensile. And he was at a loss to understand the change that had come over his wife. People seemed to be pulling away from him, receding.

He passed more and more of his time alone, in his wingback chair before the fireplace in the Red Room, a copy of the *Codex Pappus* in his lap. At the age of forty-six he had become chair-bound. Pharris White's remarks had set him wondering if there weren't perhaps some higher secrets he had missed, something implicit, some deeply hidden pattern in the fine tapestry of Pletho's thought that had escaped him,

49

and so he read and pondered and drifted in and out of sleep while the baby crawled about on the Temple carpets and great armies clashed around the world. At the age of forty-six Mr. Jimmerson was already looking forward to his senescence.

Meanwhile, Sir Sydney Hen, Bart., had become mobile. Now radiant with health and joined in a kind of marriage to the rich widow Babette, he began to stir. His new book, *Approach to Knowing*, had just been published, and it was his claim that he had written the entire work, excepting only bits of connective matter, while in a three-day Gnomonic trance, this being an exalted state of consciousness not to be confused with an ordinary hypnotic stupor or any sort of Eastern rapture. It was revealed to him in the trance that he had "completed the triangle" and "scaled the cone" and been granted "the gift of ecstatic utterance," all of which meant that he had gone beyond Mastery and was no longer bound by law or custom.

Deep waters, as Hen himself admitted. There was more. Other men—other Gnomons, that is—could aspire to this singular state, and might even achieve it by undergoing a rigorous program of instruction in Cuernavaca, Mexico. Babette owned a house in Cuernavaca, a sprawling, enclosed place with swimming pool and blazing gardens, and it was here that Hen established his New Croton Institute for Advanced Gnomonic Study.

Candidates for the school were carefully selected. They had to have clear eyes and all their limbs. There was a fee of $1,200, payable in advance, nonrefundable. There was one week of forgetting followed by three weeks of learning. There was a rule of silence. They slept on a cold tile floor and fed on alfalfa sprouts and morning glory seeds. Their reading was restricted to Hen's books. Hen stood behind a screen as he taught them, in the morning and again in the afternoon, to lute music, or rather to lute strumming. Noel Kinlow could not actually play the lute; he simply trailed his fingers across the strings from time to time, on a signal from Hen, to point up some significant recurring word or phrase. The candidates were bled weekly, by Kinlow, and not of the customary pint but of an imperial quart at each draining. On successful completion of the program, with thin new blood coursing through their emaciated bodies, they were at last permitted to look Hen in the face. He embraced them and presented them with signed copies of *Approach to Knowing* and with some black gloves of the kind worn by the Templar Masons, and sent them on their way, staggering across Babette's courtyard. Any lingering, as of graduation day fellowship, was discouraged. Kinlow herded them to the door, saw them clear of it and closed it sharply behind them.

This Noel Kinlow was Hen's current male companion, a young Englishman who had been an elevator boy at the apartment house in Toronto when Hen picked him up. Babette did not approve of the arrangement but was comfortably resigned to it. As a woman of the world she knew this was the price she must pay for being Lady Hen, consort to the Master of Gnomons (Amended Order), and she found the price acceptable.

They made a striking group. Hen, of course, was always distinctive in his black cape and red Poma. Babette, who was buxom to say the least of it, wore bright yellow caftans and other loose garments that trailed the floor, so that one could only guess at the contours of her body, though one could make a pretty good guess. She was also fond of pendulous ear ornaments. The reedy Kinlow, in contrast to Babette, liked tight clothes, the tighter the better, and he usually came forth in a pinch-waist lounge suit made of some mottled, speckled, yellowish-green material. It was a hue not met with in nature and not often seen outside the British Isles, where it has always been a great favorite with tailors. The little yapping terrier, when traveling, sported a starched white ruff.

All through the war years this colorful family—Sir Sydney, Lady Hen, the little dog and the light-stepping Kinlow—could be found bowling up and down the continent between Toronto and Cuernavaca, sometimes in a Pullman compartment and sometimes in a white Bentley sports saloon, chatting merrily, sipping Madeira and snacking on pâté and Stilton cheese, there being no rule of silence or forbidden food at Hen's antinomian level.

Mr. Jimmerson was saddened to see his old friend now so completely estranged and sinking ever deeper into the murk of self.

He said, "I don't understand what he means by going beyond Mastery. What's next, do you think, Austin?"

"It's hard to say with Hen, sir. Nothing would surprise me. Astral traveling. Tarot cards. At this moment he may be prancing through the woods playing a flute. The man's an enigma to me."

They were sitting in the Red Room before a fire. Mr. Jimmerson was turning over the pages of Hen's latest book, *Approach to Growing*, a sequel to *Knowing*. Popper was reading an encyclopedia article about California. On the table between them, under the fruitcake and coffee cups, there was a mud-stained letter from Sergeant Mapes in Italy, which neither of them had gotten around to opening. Above the fireplace there was a color portrait of the Master in full regalia, and from the mantel there hung Jerome's Christmas stocking, lumpy with tangerines and Brazil nuts, though he had no teeth. Jerome was asleep. Fanny was out with church friends distributing Christmas baskets to the poor.

Popper fed a glazed cherry to Squanto. The jaybird was getting old. One wing drooped and he no longer talked much in an outright way. During the night he muttered. Mr. Jimmerson leaned forward and jostled the burning logs about.

"But why should Sydney be so bitter?" he said. "All these ugly personal remarks about you and me."

"Ah now, that's something else. That's quickly explained. First there's his nasty disposition. Then there's his envy of your precedence in the Society. Then there's this. Hen is English. We, happily, are Americans. In the brief space of his lifetime he has seen his country eclipsed by ours as a great power. Hen very naturally resents it."

"I never thought of Sydney in that way, as a patriot."

"Listen to this, sir. The motto of California is 'Eureka!' Isn't that interesting? *Eureka. I have found it.* What is our motto here in Indiana? Do you happen to know?"

"Let's see. No. Our state bird—"

"Surely we have a motto."

"Yes, but I can't remember what it is. I've been doing some thinking, Austin, and I have an idea that Sydney must be under the influence of some malignant magnetic force. This fat lady he has taken up with. I wonder if—"

"Look, sir, a picture of Mount Whitney. Isn't that a magnificent sight? It gladdens the heart."

"Yes. The snow. On top."

"Correct me if I'm wrong but I don't believe we have any eminence in Indiana much higher than a thousand feet."

"Yes, I think you can say that nature presents a more formidable face in California. But you know, Austin, I sometimes think if I could just talk to Sydney man to man for a few—"

Popper took the book from Mr. Jimmerson's hands and flung it into the fire. "Excuse me, sir, that was very rude, I know, but I can't sit here and let you torment yourself with that poison."

"You might at least have—"

"Listen to me, sir. Hen and his ravings and his Mexican concentration camp—this is just a piddling episode in the vast time scale of Gnomonism. The man's a mayfly, the fluttering creature of an hour. Why should we take any notice of him? He works in sun-dried bricks. We are building in marble with Pletho. Now I want you to put Hen out of your mind. Will you do that for me?"

They looked into the blaze and waited silently for the flash point. The book covers writhed and then burst into yellow flames. "There. A fitting end for trash."

It was not Popper's way to interrupt the Master or snatch objects from his hand but on this night he was tense. He was leaving the Temple the next day, leaving Burnette, pulling stakes, in circumstances that did not allow him to say goodbye. Over the past few months he had conferred often with Golescu in Washington via telephone. Their plans had been carefully laid and on this very night the professor was approaching Chicago by rail. Popper was to join him the next morning at Union Station and from there they would travel west together.

The trip had been delayed over and over again because of Golescu's difficulty in settling on an auspicious date for leaving his job and making a journey and undertaking a new enterprise. Popper himself was not so particular as to the alignment of the planets. He had a problem with the U.S. Selective Service, and it was one of growing urgency. He had never registered for the draft and had been lying low, in the Temple, since the Washington trip. Then, an informer, one of Hen's men, turned his name in to the local draft board. A series of notices and summonses were sent to Popper, with little result, and his secretary, a dull girl, unwittingly aggravated the situation.

Popper had instructed her to answer all unknown correspondents with a Gnomon leaflet and a photograph of himself on which he had written: THANKS A MILLION, AUSTIN POPPER. This was faithfully done. The draft board, in response to its letters and telegrams, had received five or six of these autographed pictures before turning the matter over to the G-men.

But when these officers finally arrived at the Temple with a warrant, Popper had been gone for almost a week, leaving behind him an enormous telephone bill and a note to Mr. Jimmerson saying that Laura had taken a turn for the worse and that he was racing to her bedside in San Francisco.

Mr. Jimmerson was bewildered. He read the note several times and turned it over to look for help on the blank side.

Who was Laura? He had never heard Austin speak of a sweetheart or sister or any other dear one of that name, sick or well.

He showed the note to one of the federal agents, a hefty young man who seemed familiar but whom he could not place. He did not recognize Pharris White, still neckless but trimmed down a bit and wearing a tan fedora. White was now in the FBI, which had become something of a haven for lawyers seeking to avoid military service. He shook the warrant in Mr. Jimmerson's face. "I mean to serve this personally," he said. "If you're holding out on me, Jimmerson, I'll put you away in a cell with Popper. Nothing would please me more. This Master of Gnomons business doesn't cut any ice with me. Did you ever hear of misprision of a felony? Accessory after the fact? Here, I want to see that cap." He examined the Poma with rough disdain and even placed it clownishly atop his own head. The agent in charge of the raid spoke sharply to him about these unprofessional antics and made him return it.

Mr. Jimmerson said he was confident that he would hear from Austin in the next few days. The draft evasion matter could only be a misunderstanding. A telephone call to the Navy Department would clear it up at once. From Popper's secretary the agents learned that Popper had been singing and humming snatches of California songs in recent weeks.

Thus there were signs in abundance pointing to the Golden State, Popper believing that one could not lay it on too thickly, and it was there that the search for him was foolishly pressed.

6

Popper and Golescu stepped off the Burlington Zephyr in Denver, well short of San Francisco, and then took a bus to the old mining town of Hogandale, Colorado, high in the mountains, at the headwaters of the Rio Puerco, known locally as the Pig River or Nasty River. Popper carried one suitcase and a perforated box with Squanto in it. Golescu had a good deal of luggage, including two sacks of dried mud. Wasting no time, they rented a derelict house at the foot of the sloping main street of Hogandale and went to work.

It was a hard winter for the two city men, neither of whom had ever handled an axe or shovel. At night they tramped through the snow to the abandoned gold mines and collected buckets of dirt. The frozen ground was utterly lifeless, a mineral waste, but Golescu had the European notion that the back country of America was alive with snakes and scorpions and so took great care where he placed his feet. Popper assured him that these vermin were asleep. The real menace to the hikers of America, he said, was the rusty nail. Boards bearing these upright nails were lying about everywhere. Puncture your foot on one and within an hour your jaw would be locked firmly shut, never again to open, and you would be raving with brain fever. Golescu minced his steps with even greater care. By day the two men chopped wood and stoked the iron stoves and tended their potted plants.

The professor had brought with him a plentiful supply of seeds and cuttings. Soon every windowsill in the old two-story

frame house was crowded with pots and makeshift recepta-
cles, from each of which sprouted a spiky green shaft. The
pots were tagged by number. A log was kept for each one.
There was detailed information as to the different potting soils
—the fertilizer content, the acid-alkali balance and, most important of all, the origin of the soil, the mine it came from,
whether the Perkins Drift, the Old Woman No. 2 or the Black
Dog. In addition, there were control pots, some containing
pure sand and others gold-free mud from the banks of the
Potomac in Washington.

This plant that was the focus of all their attention was
creeping bagweed, or *Blovius reptans*, a mat-forming vine
found growing rank in England and Europe along roadsides
and in ditches and untended lots. The pinnate leaves of bagweed were alternately evergreen and deciduous, so that while
some leaves were shed over the year, the vine was never barren of greenery. In this respect it was like the magnolia tree
and the live oak. Bagweed, which had a way of choking out
other vegetation, was universally despised by gardeners. Live-
stock refused to eat it. Even goats turned away from it. Bugs
and worms gave it a wide berth. Bagweed had little decorative
value, and despite the strong camphor smell given off by the
bags or pods, it had never found a place in folk medicine.
Apparently unremarkable, then, except for its hardiness and
seeming uselessness, creeping bagweed did have one redeem-
ing quality, and this was nothing less than the power to de-
posit gold in its leaf cells. To be sure, the gold appeared in
only microscopic traces, but it was gold nonetheless, and gold
that was easily recovered and of an elemental purity.

Professor Golescu had hit on the bagweed discovery, or
rediscovery, after piecing together clues found here and there
in hundreds of books on alchemy, most notably in the works
of Theophilus the Monk and Dr. John Dee. The revelation
came in stages. For years he had prowled the library stacks
and bookstalls of Bucharest, avid from his youth to lift the veil

and know all. As early as 1934 he had broken through certain allusive writings to learn that gold might be taken from the leaves of a common flowering plant.

Identifying the leaves, however, was another matter, and to this problem he finally had to apply the tedious method of systematic exhaustion. He planted at least one specimen of every genus offered in the colorful seed catalogues of England and Holland. He crushed and processed thousands of leaves, using cyanide and zinc shavings as extractives, and in the end he always came up with the same mess of black sludge, but never any gold.

Then in the summer of 1940, while he was in London waiting for his American visa to be forged, it struck him suddenly that the plant might be one not cultivated by man, some nuisance growth, and he went out into the countryside and gathered seeds from a variety of nettles, thistles, dandelions, nipplewort, chickweed, bagweed and other coarse vegetation. He resumed his experiments at his boardinghouse in Washington, and two years later, in the spring of 1942, he first saw the tiny points of gold precipitating on the zinc flakes. He drew his head back from the spectacle with a start. The jeweler's loupe dropped from his eye. "So. And I am not expecting you from this stinkweed."

Golescu regarded other men with contempt. They were so many dim background figures in the central drama of the world, which was the life of Cezar Golescu, and he took no interest in them except as they might be able to alter the course of the drama, whether to aid him or thwart him. He enjoyed dazzling them with a show of learning now and then, but there were so many things they were unworthy of knowing or incapable of understanding, and these things he kept locked away in his head. Of his gold research he spoke not a word to any person in Europe or America until the chance meeting with Popper.

Popper's presence had something to do with it; men naturally confided in him and sought his approval. Even Golescu was not immune. He found himself boasting to this stranger and blurting out things. But there was more to it than that. He was concerned as to how he might best exploit his discovery and had decided that what he needed was an American business partner who knew the ground. Popper's intelligence was, of course, of a lower order than his own—so much the better for control purposes—but Popper was clearly a man of affairs, with that lupine glint in his eye that suggested he would usually be at the forefront of any scramble for a prize.

The thing that tipped the scales was Gnomonism. One of the few secret orders that Golescu had not been able to penetrate was the Gnomon Society, his difficulty being that he had never found a Gnomon until Popper came along. Did the organization even exist? Was there anything in it? He took pride in his Masonic degree, for he knew that his white linen apron was more ancient than the Golden Fleece or Roman Eagle, and more honorable than the Star or Garter, but so many of these brotherhoods had let him down with their grandiose claims and paltry secrets. Still, one could not give up the quest. Much ancient wisdom lay hidden, even from Golescu—the arts of Mu, the Alkahest formula, the *elixir vitae* —and it was his mission to search it out.

Perhaps the Gnomons did know something. In any case, the hand of fate was evident in that first encounter with Popper at the Observatory. It was a day on which the moon was in crescent, signifying increase. Popper had loomed up before him quite suddenly, like some figure in an oriental tale, identifying himself not only as a Gnomon but as Cupbearer Royal to the Master himself. He had spoken well, saying, "I don't know your name, sir, or what your work is, but I can see that you are a man of exceptional powers. I saw it from thirty yards away."

And Popper had quickly proven himself worthy of the professor's confidence, seizing on the bagweed discovery to show how it might be turned to account. If the weed produced a little gold out of indifferent soil, he reasoned, then why should it not produce a great deal of gold when planted in soil known to be auriferous? The idea had somehow not occurred to Golescu and he was stunned by what he saw as a brilliant leap. Two heads were indeed better than one, if the other one was Popper's.

Their plan took form. Popper called it Banco Plan. They would go to abandoned gold mines in the West and surreptitiously test the soil. When they had located the most productive property they would lease it as cheap grazing land and plant it in bagweed. Entire mountain ranges would be covered with a carpet of creeping bagweed. Nature would do most of their work and no stamping mills or monstrous smelters would be needed—only a leaf chopper, a few vats and some cheap chemicals. Within a year or two they would be sitting atop tons of gold, which they would sell off in measured driblets, in the way of the South African diamond kings, so as not to swamp the market.

By way of a cover story, Popper introduced himself to the citizens of Hogandale as Commander DeWitt Farnsworth of Naval Intelligence, lately wounded in the Philippines. He affected a limp and wore a soft black hat and Lincolnesque shawl. He had come to the mountains to convalesce in the sparkling air, as well as to help his refugee friend, Dr. Omar Baroody, with his sticky experiments in weed saps, from which he hoped to develop a new kind of rubber, so desperately needed in the war effort. Herr Hitler and General Tojo would give a good deal to know Dr. Baroody's location.

As it turned out, no one in Hogandale cared. The fifty or so inhabitants were a dispirited lot of nesters and stragglers who had been beaten down by life. Brooding as they were, constantly, over their own humiliations, defeats, wrecked hopes, withered crops, thoughtless children and lost opportunities, they had no curiosity at all about the two strange men who had rented the old Taggert house at the bottom of the hill.

After a few weeks Popper no longer bothered with the false

names or the limp, though he did continue to use the walking stick. He felt safe. They were not likely to be found out here, marooned in pelagic America, far from any shipping lanes and with no smudge of smoke on the horizon.

For security reasons Golescu would allow no strangers in the house, not even a cleaning lady. Most of the housekeeping chores fell to Popper. He found the work and the reclusive life disagreeable and often had to remind himself of the great reward that lay at the end of the ordeal. Eating as they were on one ration card, Golescu's, they had to stint on coffee, sugar and fresh meat. Their food ran largely to canned soup, potted meat, boiled eggs, crackers, white bread and dark molasses.

The house was cold. The only insulation was newspaper sheets pasted to the rough plank walls, and the paper was now in tatters, with the long black columns of Colorado news crumbling away. The one warm room downstairs was the kitchen, where Popper set up his cot, next to the cast-iron range. There he cooked and washed and read magazines and talked to Squanto. Golescu made his nest in an upstairs room, which he kept locked and where he maintained a potbellied stove and a small brick furnace and a hand-cranked blacksmith's forge. Late into the night he could be heard clumping around up there tending his vessels.

From the very beginning he had pestered Popper about the Gnomon secrets, pressing for admittance into the brotherhood. But Popper, usually so accommodating, made excuses and put him off, until one night he bluntly told him that he must give up all hope of ever becoming a Gnomon.

"No Moslems, I'm sorry," he said. "No Mussulmen. It's a different culture. Alien thought patterns. I don't say it's fair but there it is. Furthermore, I should tell you that all these personal appeals are embarrassing to me and demeaning to you. My hands are tied, you understand. Our laws are written in blood on the dried guts of a serpent. But look here, Cezar, don't take it so hard. You people have your rich oral tradition.

Your songs of the desert. Why can't you be satisfied with that?"

Golescu knew nothing about the desert, and the truth was that Moslems *were* eligible for membership in the Society— the candidate had only to profess belief in the Living God, much as a Mason must acknowledge the Great Architect of the Universe, with no further religious test—and for that matter Golescu was not a Moslem but a communicant of the Romanian Orthodox Church. He could not get this simple fact across to Popper. What was more irritating, Popper affected a solicitous curiosity about the professor's supposed faith. Suddenly and unexpectedly in the middle of a conversation he would raise some Islamic point.

"Are you permitted to eat sardines?" he said. "Please don't hesitate to speak up if I offend." And "Tell me honestly, Cezar, is it true that Mahomet's body is suspended in midair in his tomb? Have you seen that with your own eyes?"

After a while Golescu stopped protesting and made no response of any kind to these queries. He turned sullen and abandoned all efforts to become a Gnomon. Then in an amazing turnabout, Popper announced one morning that the observation period was over and that Cezar must now prepare himself for instruction.

"A time of testing," he said. "Nothing personal, I assure you. Everyone is turned down at first. Those who come to us unbidden must undergo special scrutiny. We like to put them under stress and observe the squirming pattern. Sometimes we slap their faces and see if they cry. Some do. You would think they had been beaten within an inch of their lives. But all that is behind us now. On behalf of the Gnomon Society I bid you welcome. You are that one man in a hundred thousand who is ever chosen."

The professor was so moved as to express gratitude, a rare lapse, and he was further shaken to learn that "the passing over" into Gnomonism was the work of a single afternoon.

The instruction was scanty. Golescu had not seen so short a creed since he had attended that Knights of Corfu school in Vienna. The pledges and oaths were of a familiar kind and gave him no problem, but he was troubled by Popper's warning about the Dark Laws. These were nine arbitrary rules that Neophytes and Initiates were not allowed to know. Should they violate one, however, they would be cast out of the Society. The induction ceremony lasted only about an hour and concluded with Golescu's running around the Taggert house seven times with his mouth open.

Popper stood on the front porch in overcoat and shawl and urged him on. "Pace yourself!" he shouted. When the circuits were completed he went down the steps to congratulate the professor, who was gasping and whose whiskers were coated with frost. He took Golescu's hand in a firm and prolonged Gnomon grasp and formally proclaimed him a Neophyte and Brother in Good Standing.

Brothers or not, the two men were already drifting apart. The hard work, the deadly cold, the dull diet, the isolation—all these things made for short tempers. They began to find fault and snap at one another. The fog was depressing and added to their feeling of confinement. From morning till night the lower end of Hogandale was enveloped in a white mist, and living in this cloud made them irritable and affected their sense of balance and depth perception. They glided into doorframes, as on shipboard, and stubbed their toes on the stairs.

Golescu made the better adjustment, but he had his bagweed. The plants flourished in their pots despite the cold and the weak light. He became attached to them, stopping at each one on his morning round to jot a note or poke about in the dirt or playfully thump the little gray bags that dangled beneath the gray blossoms.

Popper, who had no interest in horticulture as such, drew closer to Squanto. He and the jay took their meals together at the kitchen table while Golescu ate his soup and crackers alone in his upstairs room. It was at this time that Popper began to drink heavily.

Hogandale had two business establishments. At the top of the hill on the highway there was a Sinclair gasoline station, where the bus stopped, and down the way, past a dozen empty store buildings, there was a combination saloon-grocery-post office called Dad's Place. Every afternoon at about four o'clock Popper could be seen emerging from the mist below, a black apparition with a stick, not so much the boulevardier as the hiker with his staff, leaning forward against the slope and marching steadily upward toward the first drink of the day at Dad's Place.

The saloon was dark and drafty and smelled of kerosene. There was no music, not even a radio, and no popcorn or other gratis snacks. Dad and the few customers, grizzled coots to a man, were sunk in a torpor so profound as to choke off all attempts at conversation. Displays of robust ignorance Popper was prepared for, but not this morbid hush. At first he brought Squanto along to perform. He would put seeds, crumbs or bits of cheese in one ear. Squanto would peck at the stuff and all the while Popper would nod and make quiet replies as though the bird were whispering things to him. Squanto delivered cigarettes up and down the bar. He told fortunes from a deck of playing cards, plucking one card from a spread fan. Popper had lately taught him to say "cock-a-doodle-doo," the words, but none of this amused the barflies and so he gave it up and left Squanto at home.

There was a whiskey shortage too and in order to get one shot of bourbon Popper first had to buy three shots of nasty brown rum. Getting drunk at Dad's Place was little better than staying sober at home and so one afternoon he passed it by and went to the top of the hill and caught a bus for Rollo.

Rollo was the county seat and had life more or less as Popper remembered it. There were theaters, churches, banks, bars, streetlights. There was a schoolhouse made of field-

stone, with paper flowers pasted to the windows, and a play-
ground where the children joined hands and danced about in
a circle at recess. There was a courthouse, also of fieldstone,
and Popper used this as a pretext for his frequent trips, telling
Golescu that he was looking up land titles at the clerk's office.

Actually he was scouting out the bars. The best one was in
the Hotel Rollo. The drinks there were good, the toilet was
clean and just off the lobby there was a small writing room,
with desk and free stationery, where Popper sometimes wrote
letters to the editor of the local newspaper, commenting on
current affairs and signing himself "Harmless Elderly Man"
and "Today's Woman." But the hotel drinks were expensive
and Popper finally settled on a place across the street called
the Blue Hole, where they were cheaper. This bar was con-
genial without being boisterous and the management there
insisted on only one shot of rum to one of bourbon.

Popper soon became a favorite with the Blue Hole regulars, he having put it about that he was a wounded airman,
the pilot of a "pursuit ship" who had been obliged on more
than one occasion to "hit the silk." He could not, however,
be drawn much further on the subject of aerial combat. He
waved off questions, shaking his head modestly and offering
to buy a round of drinks.

In a short time he came to like the rum, to prefer it, to
demand it. The cheaper and rawer it was, the better he liked
it. He reflected on this quirk of human nature and told June
Mack, the barmaid, that it was one of God's most merciful
blessings that people grew to love the things that necessity
compelled them to eat and drink. The Hindoos, for example,
ate nothing but rice, and you would have to use bayonets to
make them eat chicken and dumplings. It was the same with
the Eskimos and their blubber. Don't, whatever you do, try to
snatch blubber away from an Eskimo and force on him a
thirty-two-ounce T-bone steak, medium well, with grilled onions and roasted potatoes.

June Mack took a shine to Popper. He was an excellent

tipper and by far the most romantic figure she had ever had the pleasure to serve. She hung on his words and learned that in college he had been a star athlete, captain of both the varsity eleven and the varsity nine. He had gone on to become a New York playboy in top hat, living a life of ease and frivolity, carousing nightly with his lighthearted pals and their madcap sweethearts along "old Broadway." Then with the war came responsibility. He disliked talking about these experiences but she could see that he had suffered and that for all his bright manner there was some secret sorrow in his life.

Popper became fond of June too, and each time she brought his drink, always a generous measure, he would catch her withdrawing hand in flight and give her fingers a little lingering squeeze. One thing led to another. He treated her to dinners and walked her home after work to her wee house on Bantry Street. Their problem, the ancient predicament of lovers, was one of finding a place where they might be alone. Neither of them owned a car and it was much too cold for any sort of outdoor dalliance. June lived with her mother in a house that had only three small rooms, so there was nothing doing at Mack house.

One day Popper proposed a visit to his "ranch" in Hogandale. June was not nearly so coy as he supposed her to be and she accepted at once. Indeed, she could hardly believe her luck, Austin Popper being easily the best catch in the Blue Hole if not in all of Rollo. She was curious about the ranch. Popper was vague as to its size, speaking of it as "my little spread in the clouds," or dismissing it as one of his many hobbies. She knew he had a shadowy partner, a sick old man, and that they grew experimental plants in their house, some kind of high-protein weed that would revolutionize the cattle business, but it was not always easy to follow the things Austin said and she had no very clear picture of the arrangement.

Sunday was June's free day. Popper came to call before noon and made complimentary remarks about her auburn hair, set in rigid waves by some heat process, and her harmonizing green dress. He suggested that they take a turn around the courthouse square, so he could show her off, and then go on to the Hotel Rollo for an elegant Sunday feed before catching the bus to Hogandale.

But June had two surprises for him. It was time to show her stuff in the kitchen and she would treat him for a change. She had collected some things in a sack and would prepare him a home-cooked meal at the ranch. Popper was pleased. He rummaged about in the sack and saw that she had picked up some of his favorite tidbits, including chicken livers, fudge, deviled eggs and a can of sweetened condensed milk, very hard to find these days. With that they would make some snow ice cream.

The second and greater surprise was that Mother Mack was to accompany them. She, a plump squab like her daughter, hastened to say that she hoped Mr. Popper would not take it amiss, as suggesting in any way that June needed a chaperone, or that she, Mrs. Mack, was pushing herself forward. It was just that she had been housebound all winter and would like to join them in their outing, in their excursion through the countryside and a day at the ranch. Would it be inconvenient? She knew that three made a crowd. Would she be excess baggage?

"Certainly not," said Popper. "The more, the merrier. Three, you know, is the perfect number. Unity plus two. It's just the thing. I should have thought of it myself."

He was already a little drunk and on the bus ride to Hogandale he got worse. He drank openly from half-pint bottles of rum that he kept stowed in the major pockets of his overcoat and suit coat. There was a certain amount of gurgling and spillage that June found embarrassing. Here was a loutish side of Austin she had not seen before. At the Blue Hole he was always the gentleman, always removing his hat and never spitting or blowing his nose on the floor or using foul language. She wondered if he might be nervous. Men were so odd in their dealings with women.

What had escaped June's notice in recent weeks was that Popper had become a drunk. The decline had been rapid, and she, blinded by affection, had failed to recognize the signs— the rheumy eye, the splotchy face, the trembling hand, the loss of appetite, the repetitive monologue, the misbuttoned shirt and, perhaps most conclusive, the use of ever smaller bottles, this being the pathetic buying pattern of many alcoholics. She knew nothing of his solitary drinking, at all hours, in bed, on the street, in moving vehicles and public toilets. Huggins at his worst had never been so completely bedeviled.

He became loud and jolly on the bus, talking to the passengers at large about his dream of the night before, in which a rat had raced up his trouser leg. June and her mother looked away. An old woman at the back said, "A rat dream means your enemies are stirring. That's what the dream book says."

On arrival in Hogandale, June was annoyed to find that she and her mom would have to walk down a steep hill. Their short legs and platform shoes were ill suited for such a rough descent.

Popper said, "This tramp in the snow will get our blood going. It will make us crave our dinner all the more."

As they stumbled along, June suddenly remembered Austin's partner. She expressed concern that there might not be enough food for four people, and further, that the food was rich and perhaps unsuitable for an old man in poor health.

"Oh no, he won't be joining us," said Popper. "Cezar is not a sociable man. He lies up all winter and lives off his hump. He'll be upstairs mashing his weeds. I'll leave a little pot of something outside his door that he can eat with his ivory chopsticks. If we're lucky we won't even catch a glimpse of him."

They had reached the desolate edge of town.

"Careful now, ladies, watch your step."

On a rocky lot there loomed up out of the mist an old house made of gray boards. It was frankly a house, angular and upright: There were no cows about and no pens, barns, troughs or other signs of pastoral industry. No collie dog named Shep ran to greet them. The woodpile was just that, a low sprawl of sticks minimally organized, like something beavers might have thrown together. Under a window toward the rear of the house there was a snow-capped mound of cans and garbage. It was a ranch unlike any the two Macks had ever seen before.

"A little haze today," said Popper, assisting the ladies up the icy front steps. "It's nonsense, of course, keeping our doors locked like this, but Cezar insists on it. All these chains. I have to humor him in such things. He was once a very distinguished man in his field but is now just as crazy as a betsy bug."

Inside the house there was a greenish gloom. June was almost overcome by the camphor smell. She was no stranger to the fetid rooms of bachelors but this place had a sharper odor, like that of the sickroom. Bagweed covered the floor. The house was ankle deep in foliage, the thick green mat broken only by narrow trails which Popper and Golescu had beaten down in their passage across the rooms. The runners had ramified and intertwined so that it was no longer possible to identify a particular leaf with a particular plant, except at or near the base of that plant. Chairs and tables were frozen in position by the strangling coils of bagweed. Along the windows some of the sill boards had been split by the driving force of the weed.

June said, "Look, Austin, there's a bird in the house!"

"What, a bird? Impossible."

"There. On the back of that chair. See? I mean, jeepers, a bird in the house!"

"I believe you're right. Yes, it is a bird, June, and it looks to me like a blue jay, a very impudent corvine bird. I wonder how he got in. Don't worry, I'll handle this. Maybe you'd better stand back, Mrs. Mack, until we know where we are with this animal. I mean to get to the bottom of this 'bird in the house' business."

He whacked the cane against his palm and advanced on Squanto. "Well now, what's your game? Speak up, sir, how did you get in? Did you think this was a bird sanctuary? Are you looking for bright objects to steal? Or is it food? Did you think you were going to nip in here and then just nip out again with some of my toasted nuts? Nothing to say? Not talking today, are we? You might at least have the courtesy to greet my guests."

Squanto cocked his head from one side to the other and then gave his speech. "*Welcome June. To Mystery Ranch. Welcome June. To Mystery Ranch.*"

The words were fairly clear and the Macks were delighted. Popper extended his forearm. The bird hopped onto it and sat there with the gravity of a falcon.

"Oh yes, they thought you were a bad boy, Squanto."

"Squatto, is it?" said June.

"Squanto."

"A talking bird," said Mrs. Mack. "I've heard of people keeping canary birds but not jaybirds. I didn't know they could talk."

"He's quite old now and new words are difficult for him. It gets harder and harder to drive anything into his little crested head. Anyway, Squanto and I are glad you enjoyed our little joke. I happen to think a light note is important. It sets a friendly tone. It breaks the ice. Speaking of which, let us move on to the kitchen, ladies. I'll stoke up the fire and we'll be much warmer in there. The vines are not so thick on the floor there and I've moved the cot and the table back against the wall. We may want to dance later. The important thing now, as I see it, is for June to get into her apron toot sweet. We've had our bit of fun, and now, I don't mind telling you, I'm ready to get down to serious business and tackle some of those chicken livers on toast points."

In the kitchen there were black windrows of soot on the floor but little bagweed, except around the base of the walls. The table and chairs were spackled with white-capped bird droppings. Burlap bags were stuffed around the window frames. Overhead there was a long stovepipe and from the rusty elbow joint there came a steady fall of fine soot.

"Here, ladies, drape these towels over your heads, if you will, please. Don we now our gay apparel. That black stuff will get in your hair and it's the very devil to get out, not to mention your nose and ears."

Popper and Mrs. Mack sat at the table while June bustled about. Mrs. Mack would have liked to rest her arms on the table but the oilcloth was sticky with molasses. It pulled fibers from her sweater. The kitchen was poorly furnished. The few cooking vessels had deposits of carbonized grease at their bottoms. There were no measuring, beating or sifting instruments. The only condiments were salt and pepper, all mixed together in a glass jar with ice-pick holes in the lid.

"Saves a step or two," said Popper. "Takes the guesswork out of seasoning."

June and her mother drank hot chocolate topped off with floating marshmallows. Popper stayed with his rum, mixing it with hot water and molasses. He talked on and on in an extravagant way that confused Mrs. Mack. All she could think to say was, "Well, aren't you smart!" to the bird, who had lapsed into muttering and squawking. Popper drank and chattered away and tried to pick out a tune by dinging a spoon against the glassware. June was a plain cook, no bay leaves or underdone chicken breasts for her, but she was a good cook and she became more and more exasperated with Austin. All this loving effort for a babbling drunk.

When at last the dinner was served his head fell. The Macks likewise bowed, and then after a time they saw that he was not, as they had thought, lost in a prayer of thanksgiving, but asleep. They left him to his nap and spoke in whispers as they ate. His head sank in jerks and his face was not far from the livers and congealing gravy on his plate when there came a voice from the doorway.

"What do these women want? Get this gang of women out of here."

It was Professor Golescu. He was wearing bib overalls with a black buzzard feather stuck in the breast pocket. With his worker's cap and pointed beard and glittering eyes he looked like V. I. Lenin. June was astonished. Austin had spoken of his associate as "demented" and "badly stooped" and as having "abnormal brain rhythms," and yet here was no such pitiful figure but rather a well-formed and dynamic little man who set her pulse racing.

The cold draft from the open door brought Popper around. He shuddered and sat up. "Ho. Cezar. Come in and warm yourself. Ladies, my partner, Cezar Golescu. He comes to us from the Caspian Sea and his name means 'not many camels.'"

Golescu said, "Who are these women? Our agreement was no women and no drink."

"Don't mind him, ladies. You must make allowances. He has no manners. I had always thought that the laws of hospitality were universal but it seems Cezar and his people, the Shittite people of central Asia, have their own ideas about these things. Look at those eyes. We are entering a new age of reptiles."

"Where is my soup?"

"He wants his soup. Well, we can't talk soup until you take off your cap. These ladies are my guests."

"You are drunk again, Popper."

"Not at all. We are simply having a civilized evening of good food and good conversation. Where is the harm in that? It makes for a change. This is my good friend from Rollo, Miss June Mack. And over here, though you would never guess it, is her mother, the very charming Mrs. Mack. Now if you think you can be polite, Cezar, you are welcome to join us. Or you can go back to your weeds. Suit yourself but we can't have you standing there in the doorway scowling at us like that."

Golescu was wearing brown knit gloves with the finger ends cut off, gardener style, the better to feel things and take their measure. His exposed fingertips were a larval white. He tapped them together and stared at June. Her pug nose did not come up to his leptorhine ideal of female beauty but in other ways she pleased him. A long woodpecker nose and heavy legs—"the big hocks," as he put it—these were the qualities that Golescu first looked for in a woman. June met his appraising gaze with her own.

"I want these women out of here," he said, and wheeled about and left.

Popper turned up his hands. "My apologies. What more can I say? You see how it is. The man is loco. I know we must appear ridiculous to you, living here like this, like wild beasts in this Mato Grosso, but you get deeper and deeper into a hole and you don't know quite how to get out. Anyway, our party pooper is gone and let's say no more about him."

June said, "What about his soup?"

"Don't worry about him. He keeps coconut cookies in his room. I've seen them. You'll never believe me when I tell you what he has on his wall up there. Diplomas? A favorite poem in a frame? Some bathing beauty? Not on your life. Give up? It's a picture of his king."

"You haven't eaten anything, Austin."

"Nothing? Are you sure?"

"You look gray. I'll heat up those livers. It won't take a minute."

"No, no. To tell you the truth I'm a little queasy. Just a spoon or two of ice cream maybe."

He ate a bowl of snow ice cream and then pulled some blankets about his shoulders and curled up on the cot and fell asleep again, facing the wall.

Twilight came early to Hogandale, when the sun dropped below the peak of Puerco Mountain. June lighted the kerosene lamp. Mrs. Mack announced that she had had quite enough of ranch life and was ready to go. June was about

ready too, but outside it was growing dark and sleet was rattling against the windows. She knew nothing about the bus
schedule and she had no intention of walking back up the hill
unescorted. She tried to rouse Popper. The more she shook
him, the more he contracted into a ball-like form, presenting
a smaller and smaller surface to the attack.

June took the lamp and boldly made her way through the
bagweed and up the stairs. The banister glistened with hoar-
frost. She found Golescu's room and spoke to him through
the locked door. He said nothing. She explained the situation,
that Austin was in a deep sleep, out for the night apparently,
and that she and her mother wished to return home. Could
he not help them? There was a scrabbling movement within
the room but there came no reply. Sobs and hysterics, she
decided, would avail her nothing with this man, a tough for-
eigner of some kind, not likely to be moved by female tears.
She stood there and considered how best to flush him. Cajol-
ery? Money? Warm food?

The door opened and the professor appeared before her
with one hand casually at rest in a coat pocket. The cap was
gone and in its place there sat an alpine hat. He had changed
his work clothes too and was now wearing a belted woolen
suit and dotted bow tie. The buzzard feather was in the
breast pocket. He wore glasses with perfectly round black
frames. General Tojo himself had no glasses that were any
rounder.

"How would you like to go to the pictures with Golescu?"
he said.

Surprisingly enough, he knew when the buses ran, and he
escorted the Macks all the way back to Rollo. They arrived in
time to catch the last show at the Majestic. He knew his way
about town and had in fact been to this theater two or three
times before.

Popper had told June that nothing would get the professor
out of the house, but there was one thing and that was a
Jeanette MacDonald movie. He seldom missed one. Cut off

as he was from the world, he still managed to stay current on the coming attractions in Rollo by way of movie calendars that were delivered by hand each month over the entire county, even to the old Taggert house. When a new calendar came, he circled any notice of a film starring Miss MacDonald and laid his travel plans accordingly.

On this night, of course, any picture would do. He had not had such a soft armful as June Mack at his side in a very long time, and the show itself and its featured players were a matter of indifference to him.

As luck would have it, there was a musical cartoon of the kind he liked, with some toys coming to life in a toy shop after the toy maker had gone to bed. He hummed along with the singing dolls. The feature was good too, a murder mystery with a circus setting, in which an escaped gorilla figured as a red herring. It was not June's kind of picture. She liked the ones with big city nightclub scenes, with perky cigarette girls in their cute outfits, and dark sleek men who whispered orders to henchmen, and pale ladies in white satin gowns who drank highballs and took calls on white telephones. The selected short subject was puzzling to Golescu. It was all about a luxurious rest home in California for retired movie stars, a beautiful estate set in rolling hills, with cottages and swimming pools and all the latest medical equipment. Nothing was too good for the Hollywood old-timers who had worn themselves out with their antics before the camera. When it was over the lights came up and ushers appeared at a quick march to collect money for the home in cardboard buckets. Each of the Macks gave a dime. Golescu dropped in a penny. America, so far from the Danube, was a strange land and he was still not clear as to the nature and extent of his duties here. Among other things, it seemed, he was expected to help Errol Flynn with his retirement plans.

At the close of the program the moviegoers shuffled out and paused in the lobby to put on their heavy coats and think over some of the things they had seen. Golescu looked into their faces. "Where are the Red Indians?" he said. "For months I am living in the West and I am seeing no Amerinds."

June said, "I think they live in Arizona, don't they, Mom?"

"You got me."

"Arizona or New Mexico, one. Wait a minute. I forgot about Thomas. He's some kind of Indian."

"I am anxious to see the solemn old chiefs in their round hats," said Golescu. "Their squaws and papooses. Those noble faces are from Mu. I am most anxious to measure their heads."

At Mack house, after Mrs. Mack had said good night and gone to her room, the professor sat on the sofa with June and showed her his membership cards from various secret brotherhoods. Then some tricks. He wrote with both hands. He balanced a glass of water on his forehead, tossed three nickels into the air and caught them on the back of one hand. He drove two nails with a hammer in each hand. June offered him some squares of fudge. He declined. He brought out his cylinder seal and told her a little about Kikku and the burial customs of Mu. But he went through all this in a mechanical way, with none of the old Golescu brio, and after a time fell silent.

June ventured a thought. "Do you want to know what I think, Cezar? I think you must have some secret sorrow in your life."

He admitted that his work was not going well and that life in the old Taggert house was grim. Hogandale was worse than Mount Grobny. He didn't know how much longer he could tolerate Popper's drinking and his insults. The man was a lunatic. He had once been at the very top of the Gnomon Society, a trusted keeper of the secret knowledge of Atlantis, and was now a raving drunk. You never knew what was going on in his head, what he might say next, or even what his raucous bird might say.

"But you and Austin are alike in some ways," said June. "No, it's true. Do you want to know what I've noticed? I've noticed that neither one of you ever laughs. Austin has a wonderful smile but that's as far as it goes. And you never even smile."

"So, you expect me to cackle, do you? My dear girl, Romanians are known all over the world for their hilarity. I love nothing better than to laugh but my life it is not a joke. Or it is a joke if you like but not a good one. I am engaged in serious work and how can I do it properly when I am living in an icehouse with a crazy man and eating garbage? Such conditions. Yes, and I am half crazy myself from inhaling mercury fumes. How can I laugh? Much better I was living in Mu fifty thousand years ago."

Following these remarks there was a lull, a highly charged calm, and then with no warning the professor sprang. He threw his arms around June and buried his face in her stiff and tawny wavelets and called her his "little mole" and his "tulip."

June was taken by surprise. From cultivated men she expected more chat, a longer stalking period, as with Austin, who had sat on this same sofa and pawed her a little in an absentminded way, and pecked her on the cheek, but never making a decisive move. Perhaps he had held back out of wariness, sensing the steady gaze of Mother Mack on the back of his neck, she with one inflamed eyeball pressed to a door crack and her teeth bared in a rictus from the painful effort to see and hear everything. Or from a failure of nerve, or concern about the difference in their ages. Or from a simple lack of ardor. Whatever his reasons, Popper had been much too slow off the mark to suit June and had thereby forfeited his chance.

7

On Monday morning Popper awoke in a tangle of blankets. He lay there and turned matters over in his head. Why could not their production of gold be further facilitated by nature? Get some bugs to eat the bagweed. Then feed the bugs to frogs and the frogs in turn to snakes. At each step of the pyramid there would be a greater accretion of gold, and at the apex, serpents of gold, their scales glittering with the stuff. He must present the idea to Cezar.

He also resolved to stop drinking and to ask June Mack to marry him.

"Today's the day, Squanto."

He got up and for the first time in months went through his Gnomonic breathing exercises. One could fall off the Jimmerson Spiral but one could also swing back aboard. He boiled some eggs, a long business at this altitude, and made coffee with the same water. He ate two eggs and left two for Cezar. On one he idly scrawled, *Help. Captive. Gypsy caravan.* Cezar wasn't such a bad fellow. A pouting little pedant and much too full of himself but a man of some substance for all that. What was their production of gold anyway? He must ask Cezar.

"Watch this," he said to the bird, and went about collecting bottles and pouring rum down the sink. Renunciation was not only exhilarating, it was easy.

Squanto was resting in the sunken crown of an old felt hat. His head was pulled down into his shoulders and his neck feathers were fluffed out against the cold drafts. He had the crazed look of a setting hen. Popper spoke words of assurance to him. Spring was just around the corner. June would suffuse their dreary lives with sunshine. Her very name gave promise of it.

There was a lot to be said for the ladies, he told the unblinking bird, apart from their physical charms. They were loyal. Hard workers. They were on the whole a civilizing force and had made good fathers and useful citizens out of many a slavering brute. Women were brave too and not the least bit squeamish about the corruptions of the flesh. If anything they were attracted to that muck. All those nurses. At the same time you must keep them in check or they would drive you crazy. They would presume and push. They were contentious, unreasonable, expensive, randomly vicious and would demand far too much of your attention. There was nothing meaner than a mean woman. With their gabble and nagging they could give you a preview of Hell. But that was the worst of it and there was much to be said for them.

As he was leaving, Popper paused in the doorway and said, "Just a little longer, Squanto. Hogandale is not such a bad place. We'll look back on all this later and have a good laugh together."

He took the noon bus to Rollo and went directly to the barbershop in the basement of the Hotel Rollo. There in a back room he had a shower bath, a long steamy pounding, while his suit was being pressed and his shoes shined. Then a shave with hot towels. On the way out, with his burnished cheeks glowing like apples, he stopped in the bar for a short beer, which hardly counted as a drink. The bartender said a man had been looking for him.

"Who was it?"

"I don't know. There was something of the bill collector about him. I told him nothing."

"Good work."

Popper had the bar to himself. He ordered another beer and took it to the table by the big bay window. He looked out on the town of Rollo with goodwill. Seeing the post office, he was tempted again to send a postcard to Mr. Jimmerson. How thrilled the Master would be to get a Poppergram out of the blue. But the time for that had not come. Outside the court-house he saw a deputy sheriff in Sam Browne belt reading something. No doubt a writ of some kind. A short man stood beside him, waiting. He wore a fedora and long brown over-coat that brushed the tops of his shoes. No doubt a lawyer, about to swoop.

It was true, the man was a lawyer, but he was also Special Agent Pharris White, and the deputy was reading, not a writ of attachment, but an FBI sitrep, or situation report, which ran: *Popper, Austin. Age unknown. Origins obscure. Position and momentum uncertain. Disguise impenetrable. Tracks dim. Sightings nil. Early apprehension doubtful.* The reading done, the deputy and the short man got into a green Ford sedan and drove away. Popper did not recognize White and made nothing much of the scene, now so neatly concluded.

He moved on to the Blue Hole, greeting the regulars with his usual "Keep 'em flying!" They cringed on their stools from the sunlight that came streaming through the open doorway, and they too reported that a man had been looking for him. The fellow's manner had put them off. He seemed to think he was the cock of the walk, if not the bull of the woods, and the barflies had told him nothing. "Good work," said Popper, and he bought a round and took a short rum himself so as not to put a damper on the occasion. June Mack had not yet come on duty.

Just as he settled in at the bar, Popper heard a familiar voice. He turned and saw Cezar Golescu, not where he should have been, at the old Taggert house wolfing down eggs, but here in the Blue Hole, back there in a dark booth having a glass of wine against the teachings of the Koran and talking to some crew-cut Indio.

"Cezar!"

"Yes, I saw you come in, Popper, but I can't talk to you now. I am engaged in private business."

"What in the world are you doing here? In your belted suit?"

"A private matter. I will be with you shortly."

Popper went back to the booth. "This won't wait, I have something that will make you sit up. Have you thought of using bugs to help process our stuff?"

"Yes, I have. No bug known to science will eat B.W. Bugs are not on my agenda today. If you don't mind, this is private business."

"Then I will leave you to it."

"Please do."

Popper returned to the bar and Golescu resumed his lecture to Thomas, the Ute Indian. Thomas drove a coal delivery truck. He was a man about sixty years old with close-cropped gray hair. No consumptive oriental type with flat face and thin limbs, he was a big strapping Plains Indian with fierce Armenoid features. He had just finished eating fifteen dollars worth of fried oysters, the house specialty, and was now smoking a cigar and drinking a mixture of beer and tomato juice. Golescu was paying.

On the table between them the professor had spread out his many membership cards for Thomas to see. He had already taken measurements of Thomas's skull and was now going through the epic tale of Mu once again, of how, after the cataclysm, a handful of survivors had been left perched on rocks in the middle of the Pacific Ocean, the water lapping at their feet, and how from that remnant Thomas and all his red brothers had sprung.

Thomas had understood most of this the first time around. He found it only a little less convincing than the story of how his people had hopped from rock to rock across the Bering Strait, at low tide, but he still couldn't see how it affected him personally, or his coal route, and had said little in response.

"Yes, I am sitting here face to face with a living, breathing fossil," said the professor. "I have dreamed of this moment. You, Thomas, are nothing less than a degraded Muvian."

Thomas said nothing. Golescu tried another approach. "Just for the moment let us forget the rest and look at the two languages and how they so nicely correspond." He spread his fingers and pushed them together in an interlocking way to give an example of correspondence. "Like that. See? It is amazing how the language of Mu and your own tongue, the Uto-Aztecan tongue—not your physical tongue, of course—" Here Golescu pointed to his own tongue with jabbing motions, and shook his head no.

"Did I hear you right? Did you call me degraded?"

"Please, no, a scientific term. There is no offense. 'Devolved,' if you like. I myself am a degraded Roman. I boast of it. Does that surprise you? I know you have heard of the great Roman Empire. Those were my people, Thomas. Did you think I was a Slav or a Goth? What a funny joke. My people came to Dacia under Trajan's Roman Eagle. I am more Roman than Mussolini, who pretends he is restoring the Empire. Is my name not Cezar? What the hell kind of name is Benito? Mexican? Names are important. I will tell you that if Remus had killed Romulus then the Roman Empire would have been the Reman Empire and the Catholic peoples would go on their pilgrimages to the eternal city of Reme and I myself would be a degraded Reman. But all that is by the way and my point is simply this, that each of us has a noble heritage. And yet what is mine compared to yours? Nothing. Agriculture, metallurgy, bathrooms, celestial navigation, radios, typewriters—all these things your people of Mu invented many years ago. And your calendar! So accurate! Like a fine watch of seventeen jewels!"

June arrived, wearing loose, pajamalike trousers that were gathered in at the ankles. Popper moved to meet her at the door. He took her hand but before he could speak she said,

"Austin! You look so nice! You've heard the news, then? It sure gets around fast in Rollo these days."

"What news is that?"

"Cezar and I have an understanding."

"A what?"

"We are seeing each other now. You were so silly last night. Cezar took me home and we fell in love right there on Bantry Street."

"Cezar Golescu took you home?"

"Yes, and shame on me, I let him get fresh. It was like lightning hit us, Austin."

Popper dropped her hand and leaned forward on his stick for support. He had a vision of June sitting on Cezar's lap. He saw little beardless Golescus crawling around on the floor of Mack house and peeping out at the guests from behind the furniture. How bold she was. Nothing of the stammering maiden twisting a handkerchief in her hands.

"This is hard to believe, June."

"We can still be friends, can't we?"

"Why yes, certainly."

She turned about in a modeling move to show her red Scheherazade pants. "How do you like my new outfit?"

"Very nice."

"Cezar doesn't want other men looking at my legs."

"I see."

"There was something else I wanted to tell you but I can't remember what it was."

"This will do for now."

Rising voices came from the Golescu booth.

Thomas said, "It sounds to me like you're leaving God out of this."

Golescu said, "I have not mentioned God."

"Wasn't that what I said?"

"But this is about Mu."

"I don't see how you can leave God out of this unless

you're cut off from God yourself. He is right here at this table."

"In a sense, yes. I fully agree."

"God made the sun. I don't worship the sun and never did."

"Not you personally, no, but in Mu they saw the sun as the central manifestation of God's glory, as did so many early peoples. In Colonel Churchward's book you will find it all clearly explained."

"I wouldn't have that book in my house. I wouldn't have it in my truck."

"Please—"

"Where are you from anyway, you Nazi devil? You dog eater. You call me a fossil and you say I'm degraded but I'll tell you something, mister, you're the one who is cut off from God and not me. I have felt His burning breath on my face."

"I am hearing it, the poetry of Mu!"

Thomas left in anger, pausing at the bar to turn and point his finger at Golescu and say, "There's no way in the world I can walk with that man and walk with God at the same time."

Popper went to the booth and slid into Thomas's seat. "Who's your pal?"

"His name is Thomas. A private matter."

"He left his cap."

"He will come back for it."

It was a railroad man's cap, made of some striped material like mattress ticking. The high bloused crown was blackened with coal dust and hardened from repeated soakings of sweat.

"I'm not so sure," said Popper. "This cap has seen plenty of hard service. He may well write it off and buy a new one. Something with earflaps this time."

"Thomas will come back and apologize to me. I know these people better than they know themselves."

"No, Thomas can't walk with you and neither can I. We're finished, Cezar. Where are you keeping our stuff? I want an accounting. I want my gold and I want it now."

"Very well."

Golescu took the buzzard feather from his coat pocket and removed a tiny plug from the end of the shaft. He tapped out a little powdery heap of gold on the table. "There. Banco. Half is yours. Take it and go."

"There's not enough gold there to crown a tooth."

"About six dollars' worth."

"Where's the rest of it? This is one of your desert tricks."

"There is no more. That is our winter's work. That is our golden harvest from eleven hundred pounds of leaves."

"You've gone wrong somewhere in your recovery methods."

"No, I have not gone wrong. I have tried everything— zinc, cyanide, caustic soda, chlorine, distillation, sublimation, calcination, fulmination. Let us not forget high-temperature incineration. Always the result is the same. This dirt, that dirt, always the same result. The production of gold is constant but small. It is not a function of the soil. Your idea was no good. Very stupid. Gold from the earth, you said, and you bring us out here to the headwaters of the Puerco River to get rich. I listen to a foolish American who never in his life taught science. Bagweed does not take up bits of gold from the earth, you stupid man. No, it *makes* gold. It *synthesizes* gold. All you have done is waste my valuable time."

"What you're saying is that creeping bagweed is a hoax. In Washington you told me you could work wonders. You had me worrying about swamping the market with gold. Now you tell me we have broken our backs for six dollars."

"Bagweed is bagweed. You cannot question the integrity of the plant."

"My big mistake was to trust you."

"I snap my fingers at you."

"You were never a team player, Cezar."

"May I say you look like an eel, Popper?"

"You and your planet of Mu. I should have known better."

"Mu is not a planet, you ignorant man. Please, take your

gold and go. It is good that we go our different ways. I am on the way up and you are on the way down. Me to big things, you to the gutter."

"I won't soon forget your slights and snubs of Squanto. Not once have you ever spoken to him, or even nodded to him in passing."

"It is true what you say there. I don't talk to birds."

"I was right to keep you out of the Society. Oh, yes, you're still a P.S. and don't you forget it. Did you think a Neophyte was a true Gnomon? You made a fool of yourself, Cezar, running around the house out there with those two wind-blown runnels of frozen snot curling across your cheeks."

Golescu was shaken. He sipped at the red wine to cover his confusion, then tossed his head and said, "Ha. I laugh at your Cone of Fate. To me it was all such a funny joke."

"I'll tell you something else. I have watched you eating."

"What?"

"Through my spyhole. I watched you in your room."

"You spy on my privacy?"

"A bit of quiet fun."

"This is a shameful thing you confess to."

"I watched you eating your macaroons. Not the straight-forward bites of an honest man, just ratlike nibbling around the edges. A kind of savoring, I suppose. Making it last too. I watched you leaning over your table lost in thought. The Führer at his map table. I saw you writing drivel in your diary. The bagweed of journals—one part gold per trillion. And late at night—often I waited up for this show—I watched you punching up your pillow for minutes on end, and then lining up your little shoes beside the bed, always in the same place, ready to be jumped into like firemen's boots. I've seen that picture of your king on the wall too."

"My king?"

"Over your bed. King Zog."

"Zog? Are you mad? What do I care for Zog of Albania? That picture is a hand-tinted photograph of my mother."

"Yes, no doubt that's what you told our immigration people. You had your story ready. You knew you were on thin ice, bringing a picture of your king into our republic, where we bend the knee to no man. When they found it and confronted you with it, you went into a Babylonian flutter and said, "No, no, it's just Mom Golescu!"

June brought a bowl of peanuts to the table. "My two handsome beaus," she said. "Listen, Austin, I remembered what it was I wanted to tell you. A man came by the house this morning looking for you. It was an FBI man named Pharris White in a real long overcoat. He said he knew you."

"FBI" registered clearly enough but for a moment Popper could not place the name. Then he remembered. But Pharris White a federal dick? Could it be the same person? P. White of the long telegrams? What next? The winter was frittered away, his sweetheart beguiled by a Turk and now jail.

"Yes, an old lodge brother. Overcoat White. Thank you, June."

Golescu caught her hand and kissed her fingers as she was leaving. He smirked at Popper.

But Popper was thinking about Letter Plan. This was an escape maneuver prepared in anticipation of such news. He would thread his way west on a series of local buses to San Francisco and there take refuge in Chinatown with an old Gnomon friend, James Wing. The plan was named for Poe's tale "The Purloined Letter," whose point Popper had misunderstood to be this, that the best hiding place is that place where a search has already been made. Poe was only one of many well-known authors with whom Popper professed familiarity, and of whose works he had read not a single word. He came by his information on such matters indirectly, through magazines, radio programs and hearsay.

For an instant, in his panic, he thought of leaving Squanto behind.

"What are you doing?" said Golescu.

Popper was pushing the table away from him. He pushed

it against Golescu's midriff and pinned him to the back of the booth. With a puff of breath he blew away the heap of gold. Golescu struggled but could not raise his arms. Popper took a rubber stamp from an inside pocket and stamped VOID across each of the professor's membership cards, still spread on the table, eight or nine of them, Rosicrucian, Brothers of Luxor, every last one of them. Golescu kicked and threw his head about and squealed and snarled but there was nothing he could do. Popper tipped the table over and left the Blue Hole at a run.

He circled about through alleys for a time and then ducked into a pool hall with painted windows. He drank bottled beer and waited there in the smoky room. When night came he hired a taxicab to take him to Hogandale. It was an old car, high and square, with oval rear window, just an evolutionary step or two beyond the kind with bicycle wheels and tiller. The going was slow. The driver was an old man who said he hoped to keep the car running until 1950. By that time, according to the newspapers, the war would be over and everyone would be flying around in autogyros.

He was a sporting old man and gave no difficulty when Popper asked him to stop at the top of the hill in Hogandale and turn off his lights. Popper went forward on foot to see how things lay. He saw a Ford sedan parked in front of Dad's Place. He made the connection. Yes, it was the one with the twin spotlights he had seen in front of the courthouse. The man with the deputy must have been Pharris White. They were in Dad's Place now, trying to get some sense out of Dad and the coots, a hopeless business.

Popper thought at first to wait them out, then wondered if audacity might not be the better card. A lightning sortie. Quickly in and out to get Squanto.

He went back to the cab and asked the old man to coast down the hill with no lights and glide to a stop at the old Taggert house. "A child custody case," he explained. "I'm picking up Baby Bill for his mother." Even so, the descent was noisy. The unpowered car made more racket than Popper would have believed possible. The old man stood on the brakes, worn-out mechanical brakes, and the car slewed about in a great screech of metal on metal. But no one emerged from the saloon.

The ground fog had lifted from lower Hogandale. The old Taggert house stood clearly revealed in the moonlight. Popper wondered if the time would ever come when he would miss the place and its white vapors, as he missed the Temple. Probably not, he decided.

"Honk your horn if anyone comes along."

"It don't work."

"I won't be a minute."

He was a little drunk. He fumbled with the keys and the ice-cold locks and chains. His feet became tangled in the bagweed and he kicked at the stuff. He had trouble finding a lamp and getting it lighted. "I'm back," he called out to Squanto. "It's me. We're going bye-bye. We're off again but not on the choo-choo this time. It's Letter Plan and James Wing. We'll have our own little upstairs room on Grant Avenue."

When he entered the kitchen he found Squanto dead in the crown of the old hat. His toes were curled and his beak agape. Popper dropped the lamp. The burning kerosene spread across the floor. He reached for the stiff little body, the plumage all purple, blue, black, gray and white. Would it never end, this evil day that had begun with such promise? Now here was Squanto dead and the house afire. He wrapped the bird in a handkerchief. "You were a good friend, Squanto," he said. "You couldn't sing and you weren't much of a flier but I know in your heart you soared." He put the shrouded body in a coat pocket and stamped ineffectually at the fire.

Headlights raked across the window. There came the sound of car doors slamming. Popper went to the window and wiped at the frost with his coat sleeve.

There in the yard was the Ford, lights ablaze, and Pharris

White standing beside the taxicab. He was holding a flashlight on the old man. But could that be White? The fellow must have shed a hundred pounds. The Justice Department had certainly trimmed him down. At his former weight he would not have had the agility expected of a special agent, and there would be the risk too of his getting stuck in doorways and bathtubs, further cramping his efficiency, not to mention Mr. Hoover's chagrin at having to call out the fire department repeatedly to dislodge one of his men with hacksaws, wrecking bars, acetylene torches and grease.

Would the old man talk? He could hardly be expected to perjure himself for a stranger. Did it matter? It would be no feat for a man like Pharris White, with his legal training, to see a taxicab parked at a house and from it deduce or infer a passenger. Now the deputy sheriff was moving away from the Ford. No doubt he had been chosen for his knowledge of the terrain and for the blinding speed with which he could pinion a man's arms behind him. He was pointing and shouting. He had seen the fire, and Popper's face in the window. More shouts. White sprinted for the front porch, moving well, Popper noted, at the new weight. The deputy was circling around to the back.

The fire, still more or less local, was gathering itself for a general eruption. When the officers opened the two doors, front and rear, a draft of air swept through the house and the flames swirled up as in a turbine. Popper protected his face with the crook of one arm while using the other to flail away at the crumbling floor with his stick. He cleared a sizable hole, grabbed his bag and dropped through to the ground. In the ensuing confusion he crawled away from Hogandale, frantically brushing coals off his high-pile overcoat.

He made his way across the frozen surface of the Nasty River, here little more than a creek, its corruption locked up for the winter, and then up the slope of Puerco Mountain, the talus giving way under his feet. When he rested he lay spread-eagled on the earth like a man holding on for dear life to a flying ball. He could feel no Telluric Currents flowing into his body. The mountain was dead. Near the peak was the main shaft of the mine called Old Woman No. 2. Inside he found a cranny he liked. He scooped out a little grave for Squanto with a sharp rock. One day they would put him away like this, with dirt in his mouth. He ended the day on his knees, gasping for breath and smelling of burnt wool.

8

uggins and Epps did not return from the war. Bates, Mapes and Maceo came back to the Temple to find the Master in his chair in the Red Room, much as they had left him. He looked much the same, except for his Poma. Corrosive fumes from the steel mills had eaten small holes in it and left it all but hairless.

Mr. Jimmerson had settled deeper into a life of contemplation. In the morning he read a page or two of Pletho and attended to the administrative duties of the Gnomon Society, a half hour's work at most, there being only four active Pillars left in the country. During the afternoon he dozed and dipped into old books. At night he revised his list of pallbearers again and again, and, with his love for fine print, reviewed his many insurance policies with the aid of a magnifying glass.

The Temple itself was in disarray. Maceo was shocked by the mess. The problem was that Mr. Jimmerson was now living alone in the big stone house.

Fanny had left him and taken little Jerome with her to Chicago. She was now following a career of her own in door-to-door sales of cosmetics. That is, she had started at that level, but in just two years had risen to become an executive vice-president of the company, and as such, commander of all the salesladies in the Great Lakes District. There was no divorce. Indeed, she was still fond of Lamar and she paid his property taxes and his utility bills, but she had her own work now and no longer wished to share his sessile life by the fireside.

Mr. Jimmerson looked on the separation as a temporary one, he having read in a newspaper article that women in mid-life often pulled such stunts as this. They became unbalanced from some female condition called "menopause" and took up such things as painting, spelling reform and politics. The condition soon passed and they came around. But Fanny didn't come around and she didn't come back, except for brief visits. In a short time the household staff was gone too. Mr. Jimmerson couldn't remember to pay them and they drifted off one by one.

Mapes and Maceo set about to put things right again. Mr. Bates, who was ailing, was not of much help. Maceo cleaned up the Temple and the grounds. He soon had the house back in efficient working order, with regular changes of towels and bed linen, and regular meals. His specialty was gravy. The four bachelors grew fat on it. They ate gravy on potatoes, gravy on rice, gravy on toast, gravy on biscuits, until their foreheads shone with grease. The big biscuits were broken into steaming halves with the fingers, then laid flat and slathered with gravy, then further divided into quadrants with a furious clacking of cutlery on the Temple china. And there was always plenty of dessert, for Maceo had been a cook on a submarine, where the men were plied with pies and ice cream as a bit of extra compensation for their hazardous duty.

Mapes had the harder task of reviving the Society. It seemed shameful that he and the Master should be as fat as pigs while the brotherhood languished. But what to do? Some strong restorative was needed. Was he the man for the job? He had doubts. Wasn't he more the faithful custodian of the flame than the great captain? Much as he disliked Popper, he knew that Popper would not hesitate to act—no, he would be pounding on the victim's chest with his fists and shouting to the nurses for more voltage and ever more powerful injections.

But that was Popper's way. His, Mapes's, way would be more in keeping with the dignity of the order. Slow, perhaps, and not very dramatic, but leading in the end to a healthy growth, as opposed to the pathological growth of the Popper years.

After long consultations with the Master, and by telephone with the remaining Pillars, Mapes prepared a recovery plan. There were two major recommendations.

The first was that an effort be made to attract young men to the Society—specifically young war veterans. Along with them, perhaps, would come some federal money. That was what everyone looked to now. It would be no easy job. Today's young men were dazzled by the claims and presumptions of science. They had been taught to jeer at other systems of thought. Yes, the scientists were riding high these days, preening themselves over their latest triumph, the A-bomb. They were boastful men of insufferable pride, these materialists in white smocks who held the preposterous belief that nothing could be known but through the five senses. But the great wheel was turning and Mapes suspected that these fellows had had their day.

The second recommendation was that peace be made between the Gnomon Society and the Gnomon Society (Amended Order). A reconciliation would have to be worked out at the very top, between Mr. Jimmerson and Sydney Hen, and then in orderly stages the divided brotherhood could come together in Pythagorean harmony. Here again there would be difficulty—a fine touch would be needed in any approach to the prickly Hen. All the same, Popper would not be around to interfere and to antagonize Hen, and what better time than now for a truce, with the entire world turning to peaceful pursuits?

9

en had also been lying fallow in recent years. Since the battle of the books there had been hardly a peep out of him. Rumors floated up from Cuernavaca but nothing in the way of direct and reliable reports.

Some of the rumors were scandalous, such as the one that he was keeping two Mexican women on the side, in addition to his lawful wife, Babette. A diet of pine nuts and tiny yellow peppers was said to have made a new man of him, and a wild man at that. There was a story that he was dosing himself daily with enough laudanum to stupefy three strong men. Another one had him dead, stabbed by Mexican monks, or drowned in his onyx bathtub by Babette and Kinlow, who had grabbed his ankles and held them high while he glubbed in the soapy water. There were whispers that he was making pots, ashtrays, wallets and sandals, and composing discordant music in a peculiar scale and notation of his own devising.

All lies. The truth was that Sir Sydney, except for an unwonted silence, was pretty much the same old Hen. He had closed his advanced study program—the cow-eyed acolytes got on his nerves—and what with the disruptions of war and his own negligence his Amended Order of Gnomons had collapsed. At this time he had fewer than a dozen active followers left, among them Mr. Morehead Moaler of La Coma, Texas, who also belonged to Mr. Jimmerson's order. Mr. Moaler somehow managed to keep a foot in both camps. Hen had heard nothing from his London Temple in almost two years. But then neither had the world heard anything from Hen. He published nothing and said nothing ex officio. Even within the walls of the New Croton Institute his speech was less a matter of words than of long, plaintive sighs.

TO HEAR MUCH AND SPEAK LITTLE

These words of Pletho Pappus he had carved across the archway at the entrance of the Institute.

The silence was a calculated one and came about in the following way. Hen fell sick. After a day or two in bed he had Kinlow hire some public mourners. Kinlow rounded up some old women in shawls and had them stand outside the villa and wail, their arms raised in quivering supplication. He then hired some newspaper editors to publish accounts and photographs of the demonstration, all going to show what a beloved figure the Master of Gnomons (Amended Order) had become in Mexico. A news service picked up the story and spread it about. The response was good. There came letters and telegrams expressing sympathy, a few visitors and even some applications for membership in the Society.

Hen's illness was not serious, no arsenical muffins this time, but it did keep him laid up for a while and he put off answering the mail and receiving visitors until he should feel a bit stronger. Kinlow noticed that the volume of mail grew. More visitors came. Some stood outside on tiptoe and tried to catch a glimpse of the Master through the barred windows. Kinlow pointed out to Hen that his retreat from view had enhanced his stature. There were benefits to be gained from preserving a grand silence. Myths grew in the dark. Hen was thus persuaded to adopt his new role of "the Sphinx of Cuernavaca."

He was not to emerge from his shell, or what Kinlow called "the Pyramid of Silence," until the summer of 1945, when the All Clear was sounded across Europe. In July of that year Hen announced that he was returning home to England. The joys of quiescence, while real enough, were pale indeed when compared to those of center stage.

He chose New York for his first public appearance. There in a dockside press conference he said that he felt called upon to help rebuild his country, from which he had been away far too long. The cloistered life was important, and not to be despised, but the great dreamers and thinkers must never forget that they were also citizens, or in his case a subject, but in any case, members of the larger community with certain obligations.

He had prepared a White Paper for the government, having to do with the restructuring of English society along Gnomonic lines. He saw a special counseling role for Gnomons in the postwar world, particularly in London, "the epicenter of Gnomonism," and could only hope that His Majesty's ministers would prove receptive to his scheme for "a new order of reality and England happy again." These ministers must, however, get it through their heads that under no circumstances would he, Sir Sydney Hen, be available as a candidate for public office. Likewise, whilst he could hardly disobey a direct command from his king, he believed the House of Lords to be altogether too puny an arena for a man of spirit.

"And now, goodbye and God bless you," he said in closing. "We'll see you again in about three years. There is much work to be done."

The New York reporters took all this down and put it in their papers in strings of stiff little paragraphs of equal size and diminishing importance.

But in Southampton, England, the ship reporters were not so kind to him. They came aboard in a pack with photographers and were turned loose on the celebrity passengers, who had been assembled in the first-class dining saloon. The journalists looked over the field, then moved in quickly on a tennis star in white, a surly poet in rags, assumed for the occasion, and a movie actress of the second or third rank. Hen was ignored, written off as a bishop in some church or other.

He, Babette and Kinlow were in full feather too, a photographer's delight if nothing else, but Hen could get no attention. One reporter, an older man, vaguely remembered him and paused for a moment to listen. Hen launched into his prepared remarks, then stopped to ask the man why he wasn't taking notes.

"Rubbish" was the reporter's brutal reply. "You flatter yourself. This is not an interview. You're a back number, Hen. I should have bet you were long dead, mortally beaned by a falling coconut in some brown place like Morocco. Or from squatting out in the sun too long and eating too many dates. You'll be lucky to get a bare mention in the arrivals column."

It was a bitter homecoming. In London he found that his Temple had been seized in default of taxes and turned into a government home for unwed mothers. The big bronze doors had been taken away to be melted down for munitions. There was no room to be had at the Savoy, where he had once kept a suite, or at any other hotel. His club, the November Club, grudgingly agreed to put him up for a night or two on a camp bed, but refused to accept Babette or Kinlow, or even let them through the door. They were left to spend their first night in London walking the streets and resting in a Leicester Square movie theater. Hen's old friends were not forthcoming. His few remaining Gnomon brothers were dead or widely dispersed. His female cousin at Little-Fen-on-Sea would not return his calls. People on the street looked straight through him, as though they could not see his aura, or the odic fire streaming from his fingertips.

He appealed to the Botanical Roundtable and the Association of Distressed Gentlemen, and through these groups was at last able to get a room. It was an attic bedroom across the river in a Lambeth rooming house, which seemed to be filled with Egyptians. The room was small, with scarcely enough space for the three travelers and their nine trunks. All three had to sleep in one bed, Hen, his wife and male secretary, with Babette placed in the sunken middle for balance. Lying there against her broad back, listening to the whining of Kinlow on the other side of the mound, Sir Sydney could not believe that things had come to such a pass. Could this be England, treating her distinguished men so?

It was certain that some monstrous campaign had been mounted to humiliate him, or worse still, to efface his name. He wondered if the French Rosicrucians might not be behind it. Or Madame Blavatsky's people. Or some of Aleister Crowley's grisly gang. Or the Druids. Or the crafty Popper, who very likely had some of his agents here among all these Yank soldiers. Or the Freemasons, whom he had once suspected of setting up an X-ray machine in the house across from the Temple, and directing the beams into his bathroom at head level. It was never proven but how else explain the bathroom buzz in his ears? They had covered their tracks well, these sons of Hiram, and had squared the police with a Masonic wink. They were all in the Craft together.

Some sinister body was at work to bring him down, of that there could be no doubt. The method employed was obvious. It was the old story—these people were deflecting his Gnomonic waves and scattering them so that they were lost into the air, adding somewhat to the reddish glow of London. But wasn't there something wrong here too on a different scale? With the war over, he had expected to come home to a jubilee, and yet everything was so dreadful. The place was in tatters. Where was the festival? The emanations were all wrong and there was no energy release. There was no egg for his breakfast either, no butter for his toast, no melon slice, no hot water for his bath. Even clothing was rationed, though Kinlow did manage, through the black market, to lay in a supply of the peculiar green suiting material he so loved.

Their stay was cut short, from three years to four days. Babette, fingering the golden topaz that lay on her bosom, complained that she had not yet seen any shows, heard any concerts, attended any parties or met any important people.

She had so hoped to be presented at court. What about Strat-ford? What about their tour of Kew Gardens? What did it mean, all this marching and countermarching?

Hen did not often cross Babette—*La Mujerona*, the Big Woman, as she was known to the servants in Mexico—but this time he took a firm stand, so angered and shaken was he.

"Enough," he said to her. "Have done, woman. We're leaving. It is my will."

The timing was all wrong, he explained. It was a terrible mistake, this journey, and they were returning at once to the flowers, the sunshine and the fresh tomatoes of Cuernavaca. The Hen convoy, borne here on a wicked tide, was wheeling about.

He ordered Babette to pack and he sent Kinlow along to the British Museum with the white marble bust, warning him to take care with it, not to dally, to stay out of the pubs and leave the soldiers alone. Hen had commissioned a Mexican artist to fashion this heroic bust of himself, a startling object, a sort of Aztec Hen, with jade eyeballs and coral teeth. He had intended to make a ceremonial presentation of it to the nation, but now, fearful of another rebuff, thought it best to handle the matter quietly.

Kinlow grumbled about having to lug the statuary across town.

"The thing must weigh fifty pounds, sir."

"Not another word. Go."

Kinlow could not find a taxi. He set out walking. In the middle of Lambeth Bridge he stopped to rest and watch the boats. Then, in a swelling fit of anger, he lifted the bust over the railing and dropped it into the river. On his return he was still pouting.

"Do you mind?" he said, in his sharp way, to an old man who was blocking the doorway of the rooming house. The man had a bulging forehead. He wore thick glasses and a black bowler hat with curling brim, a size nine at the very least, and a black suit with trouser legs that were too short. At his heels there were arching holes in his socks, providing a glimpse of ankle flesh that was none too clean. His rattail mustaches were so void of color as to be barely visible. He made no apology and did not give way.

"One minute, please, of your time, sir. Is this number 23 Grimalkin Crescent?"

"It is."

"Sir Sydney Hen is putting up here?"

"Yes, if it's any of your business."

"Ah. Then there's no mistake. I'm sure the Master must have his reasons for dossing down here with all these Gyppos. Do you have a cigarette?"

"I don't smoke."

"And quite right too. What so many people fail to consider is the damned insidious expense of tobacco. You are not by any chance Sir Sydney yourself?"

"Of course not."

"You would be a younger man?"

"Much younger."

"I don't see well at close range, no matter what you may have heard about my extraordinary spectacles, but I should have known from your step that you were a younger man. Yes, from an older man you expect a stumbling, festinating gait like mine. You do know Sir Sydney, I take it."

"I am his private secretary."

"What luck. I saw his name in the arrivals columns and they sent me along here from his club. I thought there must be some mistake with the address. Too bad about the Temple, eh? Hard lines. All those stinking nappies in the hallways. But we mustn't weep over a pile of bricks. When can you arrange an appointment for me?"

"What do you want? Who are you?"

"My name is Pletho Pappus. I come to speak of clotted bulls' blood and of a white heifer that has never known the yoke."

"How very interesting."

"My card."

"Pletho Pappus is long dead."

"Presumed dead. It suited me to lie low for a season."

"How very interesting."

"It is near the time when I shall make many things clear. Would you like to know why our Gnomon Society is not prospering? Let me tell you, sir. It's because there are too many backbiters, cankerworms and cheesehoppers in positions of authority. These people must go."

"I think you're talking absolute bloody nonsense."

"My card."

Kinlow took the card and read it. There was an address in a lower corner, and in the center these words:

T. Pappas
Eastern Knick Knacks
Honourable Dealing

"This says T. Pappas. It's not even spelled the same way."

"A ruse. Theodore."

"So? A printed card. Your name is Pappas. London is full of Greeks and I daresay many of them are named Pappas. If you truly are from Greece. I rather suspect Dublin. By way of Hyde Park."

"Will you be good enough to present my card to Sir Sydney?"

"Sir Sydney is out. He's engaged elsewhere. He's not buying any rugs just now."

"When will he be free?"

"I don't know. His calendar is quite full."

"Do you have a cigarette?"

"No."

"Perhaps I should wait here."

"No, that won't do."

"No trouble at all, I assure you."

"It's not on, my friend."

"Quite all right, I don't mind waiting."

"Very well. Look here. Sir Sydney is lunching at his club tomorrow. Be there on the pavement at one sharp and he will give you three minutes to state your business."

"Wonderful. One, you say? That will suit my convenience too. Now as to the etiquette. Even as a child I was a stickler for form. What's the drill? Are there some things I should know? May one, for example, contradict Sir Sydney on small matters?"

"No, one may not. You may not dispute his lightest remark. Remove your hat as you approach him and keep your eyes well cast down. No handshaking and no sudden movements in his presence. Speak only when spoken to and then briefly and to the point. And no need to bring along any of your Eastern titbits. Now off you go, chop-chop, there's a good fellow."

But the old man stood his ground and placed his hand over the doorknob when Kinlow reached for it. His mustaches began to undulate with what seemed to be a life of their own. Neither dark nor bushy, there was nothing of the Aegean about them. The two growths were set far apart and twisted into thin strands, so that the effect was of insect feelers or catfish barbels. He took off his glasses and wiped his eyes with his woolen necktie. "Here, would you care to look through my spectacles while I do out my eyes? Would you like to see how the world appears to Pletho Pappus?"

"No."

"It's not the phantasmagoria you might expect. It's not at all what you might expect. Won't you have a go?"

"No."

"The offer is not an idle one. I think you will be pleased."

"Get out of my way, you brute."

"Well, I mustn't keep you. Until tomorrow then, at one. Yes, the November Club, an excellent idea." He rubbed his belly with the flat of his hand and rotated his jaw about in ponderous chewing movements. "A bite of lunch and then some talk. Nothing fancy for me, thanks, a cold bird will do, with a bit of cabbage and some green onions. I can't remember when I last had green onions. With a drop of something along the way." He threw his head back and raised his fist to his mouth in a drinking arc, with thumb and little finger extended. "Then some serious talk. Blazing words, in such combinations as Sydney Hen has not heard before. Until tomorrow, then. A very good day to you, sir."

The next day at one Sir Sydney was a long way from his club. He was at sea having his lunch on board a Mexican sugar boat called *La Gitana*, the only transatlantic vessel on which passage for three could be found at such short notice. It was a comfortable ship. The weather was good. Babette, like most wives, handled adversity better than her husband, and she was determined to make a pleasant voyage of it, despite the lack of such amenities as a swimming pool, deck chairs and midmorning bouillon. The *Gitana* had a jolly master, Captain Goma y Goma, and a jolly crew. Each night after supper the off-watch gathered in the lounge under the bridge to hear Babette perform at the upright piano. Her milk-white fingers flashed over the yellow keys, true ivory, and she sang famous arias, after which there was a less formal session, a sing-along, with free beer, courtesy of the Señora. The party went on far into the night, with the men singing the ballads and dancing the dances of their native lands.

Hen took no part in it. He sulked and took to sighing again. He kept mostly to his cabin, but now and again appeared on deck, making his way forward to the prow, where he would strike a pose with his cape streaming behind him. He stood there at the very apex with his hands braced against the converging sides and his head thrust forward and cleaving the wind like a figurehead. He mused on the throne of Atlantis, and the crowned skulls of the ten princes, utterly lost in the mud many fathoms beneath his feet. He felt his isolation. He felt the great weight of being a living monument of Atlantis, indeed its only monument. Jimmerson and his crowd hardly counted.

The ship was three or four days out when Kinlow remembered to tell Hen about the old man with thick glasses. Hen, who was not very attentive to the spoken word, didn't take in the account the first time around. Listening closely to other people, he found, and particularly to Kinlow, hardly ever repaid the effort. The name Pletho did, however, register with him at some level, and later in the day he asked to hear again about the old man.

Kinlow made an amusing anecdote of it, only slightly distorting the facts. He told how he had been accosted by this false Pletho with a dwarf's wedgelike head and holes in his socks, and of how the man had been impertinent in seeking an audience. The old fellow made outrageous claims and obscure remarks, whereupon Kinlow cut short the blather and sent him packing, end of story.

Hen thought it over. He had a sleepless night. At breakfast in the morning he demanded a more detailed report. He wanted a full description of the man and he wanted to know his exact words. After this was given, he questioned Kinlow closely.

"I want to see that man's business card. Where is it?"

"I threw it away."

"What was the address on it?"

"I don't remember."

"What amulet or ring did he wear?"

"None, that I could see."

"Did he have—great personal charm?"

"He had no charm."

"What did you make of his eyes? What impression did you get from his eyes?"

"An impression of pinkness and of welling moisture."

"What evidence did he give in support of his charge that the Gnomon Society was infested with cheesehoppers?"

"He gave no evidence at all."

"Just the bald accusation?"

"Nothing more."

"Did you inspect his boots?"

"I inspected his socks."

"Was he wearing a surgical boot on one foot? A heavily built-up shoe on either of his feet?"

"I didn't inspect his boots. I can only say that they must have been dark and shabby, in keeping with the rest of his togs."

"It did not occur to you that the man may very well have been who he said he was? Pletho, in his sly mode?"

"Frankly it did not, no, sir."

"Or very possibly the Lame One?"

"No, sir."

"He may well have a younger brother, Teddy Pappus, for all we know."

"Yes, sir."

"And you refused, repeatedly, to look through his glasses?"

"Yes, sir."

Hen dismissed Kinlow. All day long he paced the forward deck in thought. He walked back and forth in the rain, with a point of light, a bit of St. Elmo's fire, playing about on the brass button atop his Poma. That night he summoned Kinlow to his cabin and had him relate yet again the account of the old man in the doorway. Kinlow appeared in his dancing pumps. He had grown tired of this grilling and was annoyed at being called away from the party in the lounge. Babette's opera selections were so much yowling to him, but that business was over now and the real fun had started. He put his hands on his hips and rolled his eyes in exasperation and rattled off the story again in a singsong manner. Then he whirled about to go.

Hen stopped him with a clap of his hands. "None of your pirouettes in here, sir! Don't turn your back on me! Be seated! This instant!"

Kinlow did as he was told.

Hen said, "You take far too much on yourself, Noel. Do you have any idea of what you've done to me? No, of course not. Thanks to you, I am a forgotten man. I am all but ruined, thanks to your Pyramid of Silence. And now in your brash ignorance you have turned away from my door the one man who—"

"Really, sir."

"Don't interrupt me. The one out of all others—"

"That sod? You can't be serious. I mean to say, really now."

"Not another word. Listen to me. Did the bulls' blood mean nothing to you? Think, man. The burnt bullocks of Poseidon. That was the sign. A child would have seen it. Pletho Pappus, I tell you, was at my very doorstep and you send him away like a beggar."

"You didn't see this man, sir. You didn't see his ears. You didn't smell him."

"What then, do you expect Pletho to appear before us in a cloud of fragrance? We know nothing of his current situation, what access he may have, if any, to a lavatory. His standards of personal hygiene may not be ours. He's an extraordinary man, I grant you, but he's only a man and this is just the sort of playful approach he would take. His little effects. The genuine Pletho touch. His pungent mode. He would hardly feel obliged to sponge down for the likes of you. I should have known him at once, fresh or foul. Oh, you make me sick. I can't bear the sight of you. Get out. Go to your cabin and remain there. No more fandangos for you, sir. Hand over those castanets!"

Kinlow brazenly defied the order and continued to move freely about the ship and to carouse nightly in the lounge. Hen went to Captain Goma y Goma and demanded that Kinlow be shut away under guard for the rest of the voyage. The captain temporized, not being clear on just what the offense was, and in the end he had Kinlow take his meals in the galley with the cook so that Hen would not have to look at him across the table.

Hen set off another stir late one night. He woke suddenly from a vivid dream and sounded the fire alarm, turning out the crew. It had come to him in the dream that Pletho, who could lower his respiration rate to that of a toad, had stowed away in the baggage. Nothing would do but an immediate search. All nine trunks had to be brought to his room and emptied, the clothing heaped on the floor. When this was done, with no result, Hen went about rapping on the panels, in the way of a conscientious volunteer examining a magician's trunk. But no hidden compartment was found and no dormant Pletho.

By the time the *Gitana* docked at Veracruz neither Kinlow nor Babette was speaking to Hen. Babette had made the mistake of trying to cheer up her husband. She went to him one afternoon, at the bow, with a surprise gift she had been holding back until the proper moment. It was an English rose cutting in a can of English earth—just the thing, she thought, to lift his spirits. But he saw the gesture as a taunt and he took the can and flung it into the ocean. Babette slapped his face and got rouge on her hand. He pushed her away.

Such bitter feeling led to a separation, with Babette stopping over in Veracruz for an indefinite stay. The accommodating Captain Goma y Goma made the necessary arrangements and personally saw to her comfort. Kinlow stayed too, in a small room adjoining Babette's refrigerated suite atop the Hotel Fénix. In the early morning he could hear the scrape of her coat hangers on a pipe as she selected her outfit for the day. They shared a balcony, where they took their breakfast together, with the harbor panorama all before them, and the marching naval cadets, and from which height Kinlow dropped orange peelings and worthless coins onto the heads of the sidewalk people some eighty feet below.

"Please yourself," said Hen to his two bedfellows, and he traveled on by train and bus to Cuernavaca, alone with his thoughts. He wondered if the gardener had cut back the oleander and the bougainvillea. He wondered if the maids had strangled his little dog. Of all the mysteries of Gnomonism, and there were many, none was so baffling to him as the mystery of how Pletho Pappus had gone about choosing Lamar Jimmerson and Noel Kinlow as the two men on the planet to whom he would show himself.

10

apes had made no measurable gains for the Society. The Veterans Administration, having looked over his prospectus and the *Codex Pappus* and the various works of Mr. Jimmerson, rejected without comment the Society's application to have Gnomonism accredited as a course of study for veterans—which meant no government money by way of the GI Bill. Diplomacy too proved to be a blind alley. Mapes's delicately composed letters to Sir Sydney Hen went unanswered, thereby stalling the Jimmerson-Hen understanding.

It all came to nothing, then, three years of hard work, or rather less than nothing, as the Society in Mapes's hands had actually lost ground. At the close of his stewardship there remained only two dues-paying Pillars left in the country, outside Burnette. One was in Naples, Florida, under the direction of a baker named Scales, and the other was Mr. Morehead Moaler's group in La Coma, Texas, just outside Brownsville.

Six big reclining chairs stood empty in the Red Room as a daily reminder to Mapes of his failure. He had bought these matching leather recliners and arranged them before the fireplace in a semicircle for the summit meeting that, it appeared, would not now take place. Mr. Jimmerson and Sir Sydney, with their aides, all of flag rank, were to have sat in them at varying angles, the ones they found most comfortable, feet well forward, this pride of recumbent lions hammering out the truce terms, popping up and falling back as the moment demanded, in the give-and-take of negotiation.

Mr. Jimmerson kept to his old wingback chair. Nearby was Austin Popper's chair, in which no one else was permitted to sit, not even Mapes, who had to provide his own, a stool, drawn up close to the Master, the better to get and hold his attention. This made for a clutter of chairs and tables in a fairly small area, seven of the chairs never used.

Mapes often felt that his words were lost in all the furniture. He could keep the Master's attention for no longer than two or three minutes at a time. There was no one else in the big stone house he could talk to. Mr. Bates was in and out of the hospital and Maceo never had much to say.

Mr. Jimmerson had lately taken to walking about in the Temple with his face in a big book of one kind or another. He moved at a slow glide through the rooms, reading silently. Now and then he stopped and broke into a low, appreciative murmur over some happy turn of phrase or some interesting fact come to light. "Just looking something up," he would say, with an apologetic grin, when encountered on one of these strolls.

Mapes came to the unhappy conclusion that the Master had lost his sense of mission and had abandoned himself to the study of antiquarian lore for its own sake. The old man simply would not bestir himself. He was content to pad around the Temple in his molting Poma, looking things up in books. He offered no guidance, no word of praise or blame. Mapes felt unappreciated and just barely visible in the long shadow cast by Austin Popper. He decided there was nothing more he could do. It was time to begin his new life in radio.

He remained at the Temple until the following spring, when he applied for admission to a school for radio announcers in Greenville, South Carolina. The school was owned and operated by an old army friend. A prompt reply came, offering him the position of dean of the school. He accepted, but put off telling the Master of his decision for a day or two, shrinking from what he believed would be a painful scene.

But the Master took the news in stride. He said, "You're much too hard on yourself, Mapes. We'll talk about that another time. Here, I want to show you something."

They were in the Red Room. Mr. Jimmerson held a world atlas on his knees opened to a map of North America. He had been tracing straight lines on it with pencil and ruler. The lines joined Burnette, Indiana, with Naples, Florida, and La Coma, Texas. "Take a look at this."

Mapes looked and said nothing.

"Well? Don't you see? How our Temple and the two Pillars form the points of an equilateral triangle?"

"Yes, I see that."

"It could hardly be chance."

"No, I suppose not."

"I was just looking something up in the atlas when it jumped out at me."

"Yes. I wonder, though."

"What?"

"This Burnette–La Coma line seems to be a little longer than the other two."

"A bit perhaps."

Mr. Jimmerson was peeved with Mapes, who, for all his dedication, had never shown warm feeling for the symbolic forms. He had a good mechanical understanding of them but the music escaped him. Neither was he quick, like Austin, to grasp the significance of a thing.

"Perhaps just a bit. Or a simple illusion. There is a certain distortion, as you well know, in all map projections."

"That's true."

"Doesn't this suggest something to you?"

"I'm not sure I see what you're getting at, sir."

"Gnomon solutions for Gnomon problems. No shadow without light. Pletho's Twenty-seventh Proposition."

"The Twenty-seventh?"

" 'Look not to the meridian of the land of the seven rivers but look rather to the delta and know that the way in is likewise the way out.' "

"You see some application?"

"Certainly I do. What are we looking at here if not the Greek letter delta? You worry too much, Mapes, about trivial things, and you miss the important event right under your nose."

"I do worry about our slippage in membership. You don't think that's an important problem, sir?"

Mr. Jimmerson didn't think so. His reading of the situation was that no such problem existed. Gnomonism was self-correcting. The brotherhood had contracted, true enough, in terms of crude numbers, but that need not be regarded as a real decline. It might even be argued that the Society was now standing at flood tide, what with the perfect triangular balance of Burnette, Naples and La Coma. What they must do now was clear enough. This particular triangle with one side perhaps a bit forced, must be enclosed in a circle, a curving line that would ever so gently touch the vertices and then continue on its endless flight. Within that figure would be allegorical values to be carefully worked out, using Pletho's sliding segmentation scale and the compass of Hermes. Then, and not before then, the Jimmerson Spiral might be introduced into the calculations, with what amazing results time would show. The way in was the way out.

Mapes took his leave for South Carolina. Mr. Jimmerson and Mr. Bates and Maceo wished him well in his radio career. They said they would miss him but did not go so far as to ask him to stay on.

11

It was another spring four years later when Popper turned up at the Temple. Rumors about him had drifted in to Burnette but nothing in the way of direct and reliable reports. There was one story that he had been found dead of multiple gunshot wounds in a Joplin tourist court. Another one had him walking the streets of Los Angeles in an alcoholic daze, wearing brick-red rayon trousers, feigning deafness and living on charity. In yet another one he was said to be locked away in a state institution, where he was hopping, barking, twitching and kept under close restraint.

Mr. Jimmerson dismissed these rumors as nothing more than Sydney Hen's poisonous gossip. Austin had his own good Gnomonic reasons for whatever it was he was doing. He would return to the Temple in his own good time.

A light drizzle was falling on the day he came back. Maceo was outside, standing in the shelter of the gazebo. He was watching the big cement trucks with their tilted ovoid vats turning slowly about. Popper appeared on foot, picking his way through the construction litter. Maceo followed his approach but didn't recognize him in his horn-rimmed glasses, tan raincoat, black wig and soft plaid hat. There was nothing deceptive about the wig. It was ill-fitting and too black, and the hair was matted in ropes and whipped up into whorls and peaks and frozen in place with wax.

"Here, have a pen on me," he said to Maceo. "One of the new ballpoints. Say, what's going on here, my man? New highway? Elevated expressway?"

Maceo looked away and fell into the minstrel-show performance that he used with white strangers. "Sho is," he said.

"Right over the old stables. And look, the big oaks are gone too, and the rose arbor and the garage. There's the old Buick exposed to the weather. I don't like this. I call this a dirty shame. This was once such a showplace. That house was the architectural glory of Burnette."

"Sho was."

"I used to live here, you know."

"Sho nuff?"

"Is the Master in?"

"He at his books. Busy with his thoughts."

"I tried to call. What happened to the phone?"

"Mr. J. taken it out. He say nobody ever call 'less they want something."

"That's the Master for you. But what's going on? All the curtains drawn. The place is like a tomb."

"Mr. J. say some things easier to see in the dark."

"What a brain. That's the Master all over. You still don't know me, Maceo?"

Maceo raised his eyes and looked him over. "Well, I declare. Mr. Austin Popper."

"Sho is. Put 'er there, compadre. I'm back."

They went inside to the Red Room. Mr. Jimmerson was in his chair with a book. "Yes?" he said, peering up at the stranger with the grotesque hair. "Can I do something for you?"

Popper took up a position before the fireplace. He crossed his arms and arranged his feet in a Gnomonic stance and uttered the first words of the ancient Atlantean exchange.

"Tell me, my friend, how is bread made?"

"From wheat," said Mr. Jimmerson, now roused.

"And wine?"

"From the grape."

"But gold?"

"You come to inquire of me?"

"I come in all humility."

"It is well that you do so."

"What is it then that you propose?"

"Whatever it is, you may be sure I shall perform. Austin? Is that you?"

"It's me, all right. How in the world are you, sir? What are you doing here in this red twilight? You've put on some weight, I see. You and Maceo both. Here, sir, I brought you a little necktie organizer. I don't know what I would do without mine."

Popper gave no very good reasons for his long absence or for his failure to communicate with the Temple. He waved off questions about the recent past, explaining that he was still not free to discuss his intelligence work for the government. "It'll all come out in thirty years, that secret stuff," he said. He went on to say that he was now living in "a western city," where he was happily married to an attractive older woman named Meg. Meg not only had money of her own but was a trained dietician into the bargain. All their meals were scientifically planned and prepared. She bought him a new red Oldsmobile every year. They had a town house, a cabin on the lake, and kept registered spaniels. For two years running they had been voted the cutest couple at their country club. On alternate weekends, when they were not entertaining guests at home, they distributed baskets of food, representing a nice balance of the four food groups, to poor people.

"You'd love Meg, sir. She's just a great gal. But hey, I'm talking too much about Meg and myself. I want to get filled in on you. How I've missed the old gang. You and me and Mr. Bates. Huggins, Maceo, Mapes, Epps. What would be the odds on putting together another team like that? You couldn't do it these days. Tell me, sir, what's new with you? Can you put me current? Who's cutting your hair, by the way?"

"Maceo."

"I know you used to like your temples left full but they do

say the close crop is more sanitary. Tell me, how is Mr. Bates?"

"He's in a nursing home."

"You're not serious."

"His back was hurting and so they pulled all his teeth."

"Doing fairly well now?"

"His back still hurts. He can't eat anything."

"But coming around nicely? Getting proper care?"

"They don't turn him over often enough."

"He's bedfast?"

"Not exactly."

"Gets up every day and puts on his clothes?"

"Not altogether, no. Not every day."

"Off his feed, you say."

"No, he stays hungry. He just can't chew anything."

"But his color's good?"

"Not real good."

"But otherwise fit? Has all his faculties? Takes an interest in community affairs?"

"Not much, no."

"How I've missed the old Red Room. But you know, I don't remember these recliners at all. What are all these big chairs for?"

"They've been here for years, Austin. Mapes brought them in here and lined them all up for some kind of meeting."

"Good old Mapes. Such a useful fellow to have around. I hear he's more or less running the show these days."

"Oh no, he's gone. Mapes left us some time ago. He went off somewhere to go into radio work."

"Radio repair?"

"I don't think so."

"Not commentary."

"Yes, I believe it was his plan to talk on the radio. I can't say I've ever heard him talking on the radio."

"What, Mapes at the mike? The big broadcast of 1952? I'm

sorry, sir, I don't see it. I see Mapes at middle-level retail management. I don't see Mapes at the console with a bright line of patter."

"I may have it wrong. Do you still have your cockatoo, Austin?"

"Blue jay. No, sir, he caught the flu and died, poor little fellow. Back during the war."

"You didn't get another one."

"No, sir, I couldn't very well get another Squanto. Besides, Meg won't have anything around but blooded dogs."

"Look, Austin, your chair. I saved it for you. It hasn't been moved. Your room is waiting for you too."

It soon came out that Popper's visit was more than a social call. He had a plan. Life had been good to him, he said. His country had been good to him and Indiana had been good to him. Any number of people had been kind to him along the way, most memorably Mr. Jimmerson, who had taken him in when jobs were hard to come by, and who had launched him on the Jimmerson Spiral. Lately, in his prosperity, he had been reflecting on all this, and considering various ways of repaying the debt of honor. Direct handouts of money were not the answer. A shower of rupees in the street was always good fun but the gesture had no lasting effect. The solution he had hit on was political. Public service was the answer. His contribution would be to the cause of better government, whereby all would benefit. What he wanted to do was to help Mr. Jimmerson become governor of Indiana.

It was a breathtaking proposal. "Governor?" said Mr. Jimmerson.

"Yes, and I've already done a little spadework in preparation. You know Dub Polton, don't you, sir?"

Mr. Jimmerson made an effort of memory. "No, I don't think so."

"The writer? Surely you've heard me speak of him. My old friend Dub? W.W. Polton, our Indiana author?"

"No, I can't place him."

"I'm surprised. Well, you can take it from me, we're lucky to get him."

"Get him for what?"

"You've probably read his Western novels without making the connection. *Abilene Showdown?* *'Neath Pecos Skies?* Dub wrote those under the name of Jack Fargo."

"I don't read many new books."

"Dub goes way back. He's an old newspaper reporter. His first book was a WPA project called *The Story of the Fort Wayne Post Office, 1840–1940.* It seems to me there used to be a copy of that lying around here in the Temple."

"I don't remember it."

"His first and, some people say, his best. My personal favorite is *Here Comes Gramps!* A humorous family memoir. You know how I like a light touch. Dub's a real pro, and not a bad egg once you get to know him. He's done it all. Humor, suspense, poetry, romance, history, travel—there's nothing he can't handle. He wrote *So This Is Omaha!* in a single afternoon. Did you ever read a detective story called *Too Many Gats* by a man named Vince Beaudine?"

"No."

"That was Dub. Does Dr. Klaus Ehrhart ring a bell? *Slimming Secrets of the Stars?*

"No."

"Dub puts that name on all his health books. How about Ethel Decatur Cathcart? I know you must have heard about her very popular juvenile series. All those Billy books—*Billy on the Farm, Billy and His Magic Socks.* The kids are crazy about them. Well, Ethel is Dub."

"I don't know any of these people and I don't understand what you're talking about, Austin."

"I'm sorry, sir. I can see now that I've only confused you by throwing all these names at you. I just wanted to give you some idea of Dub's background to show how fortunate we were in signing him up. He's a very busy man and he doesn't come cheap."

"Signing him up for what?"

"For your biography. The campaign biography."

"Oh come now, Austin, I can't run for governor."

"Why not?"

"You know very well that as the Master of Gnomons I can in no way involve myself in politics. Pletho strictly forbids it."

"*Partisan* politics. Surely that's the meaning of the rule. And a darn good rule too, if you ask me. But don't you see, that's what we're out to change. The demagoguery and deal-cutting. People are tired of these professional politicians who hog all the elective offices. Everyone trying to get his snout in the trough. I believe the people are ready for a scholar, who, at the same time, has proven executive ability. A man who won't be in there just to feather his own nest. The administrator of a great if little known empire. Why not Lamar Jimmerson for a change?"

"No, no, it's out of the question."

"Our problem is that you've been submerged here in the Red Room for so long. Our first job will be to put you on view in some way. Get you talked about. That's where the biography comes in. Then we'll line up some speaking engagements for you up and down the state. I'm telling you, sir, it can work. There's a time to lie back and a time to strike. I know how these things are done. Our time to strike is now. What is it they say? The man and the hour are met."

Mr. Jimmerson became agitated. It was such an incredible business and yet he had to admit that he liked the idea of the biography, and, come to that, of being governor. Why not indeed? Governors had to come from somewhere and it was his impression that more of them were elected by default, grudgingly, as the best of a poor lot, than by any roar of general approval. Who was the current one? Biggs? Baggs? Boggs? Bugg? Megg? No, Meg was Austin's wife and a fine woman too from all accounts. But *were* the people ready for a scholar? He thought not. They certainly weren't ready for Gnomonism. But then it was not as though you had to meet some absolute standard of fitness; you just had to get a few more votes than the fellows who happened to be running against you at the time, each one defective in his own way. The country had been off the gold standard for years. You wouldn't be running against George Washington, but only Baggs or Bugg. And Austin knew something about these matters. The swearing-in—that would be a grand moment. One hand on the Bible, the other raised, Fanny at his side. A solemn moment. Altogether a serious undertaking. Would he be a good and wise ruler?

He said, "I just don't know about all this, Austin. It's all so sudden and new to me. I have so much unfinished work to do here in the Temple."

"You bet your boots you do and I'm not going to take up any more of your time today. May I offer a thought? Sometimes it helps to put our ideas down on paper. Why don't you prepare a list of questions and we'll get together on it soon. I want you to meet Dub and we'll have to get the phone put back in. A candidate for governor will need a telephone."

12

Later in the week Fanny Jimmerson came to call. She too had a plan.

"Where's the boy?" said Mr. Jimmerson, who always put this question. It was not his practice to say the boy's name.

"He has his archery lesson on Friday," she said.

This was true enough, though any excuse would serve—a flute lesson, a head cold, his tummy hurt or he was having a tea party for his dolls and his baby owl. Jerome usually managed to beg off from these little day trips to Burnette. The gloom of the Temple frightened him. Maceo the black man frightened him. The fountain no longer gushed, no wading to be done there, and there were no children to play with, and no kittens, puppies or piglets to pet. His father, who, unaccountably, gave off wafts of a sweetish, tropical odor, something like that of a cantaloupe, frightened him too. When Mr. Jimmerson made an awkward attempt to embrace Jerome, the boy went stiff and arched his body so as to avoid touching the human tooth that hung from a chain across his father's belly. A gift from Sydney Hen in happier days, this relic was a huge yellow molar that was said to have been extracted posthumously from the jaw of Robert Fludd, the great Rosicrucian.

Fanny limped about the Red Room spraying disinfectant into the air. She spoke to her husband about his weight and about the dilapidated state of the Temple. There were stagnant pools of water in the yard, she said, and clumps of weeds that looked like cabbages. Things were falling into decay all around. Property values were plummeting in the shadow of the big elevated expressway that was cutting across the heart of Burnette.

She complained about the rats, who could be heard pattering and scuffling in the walls, and about Maceo, who continued to turn her friends away from the Temple. She had sent some people along—an Episcopal bishop, some bridge players, a Miss Hine, a retired physician, a troop of Brownies —to look in on Mr. Jimmerson and Maceo had turned them away at the door one and all.

"I don't understand it. I should think you would enjoy a bit of company now and then. It's not healthy, locking yourself away in here so you can eat pies and read all these monstrous books with *f*'s for *s*'s. Not a wholesome life, Lamar. I want to talk to you about Miss Hine and a new arrangement."

She took him out for a drive, then treated him to supper at a downtown cafeteria. He told her about Austin's return.

"Austin Popper? I thought he was killed in the war."

"He's been living out West with his wife, Meg. She buys him a new car every year."

"Austin Popper! With that purplish bird on his shoulder! I haven't thought of him in years!"

"The bird passed away."

He explained about the biography and the race for governor.

"Yes, that sounds like something Austin would cook up," she said. "I must say I always rather liked him, but you couldn't believe a word he said. Of course you're not going to do it."

"I haven't decided."

"You know your own business best, Lamar, but I believe you will be making a great mistake if you go ahead with this."

"Nothing is settled. I do want to talk to that Polton fellow about the book. Austin is meeting with him now. He's a well-known writer."

"Don't misunderstand me. I think you would make an excellent governor. President, even. Well, perhaps not President. I'm just saying that grubbing for votes is not your work. The hurly-burly of it all. Indiana is not Atlantis."

Shinn's cafeteria, their favorite eating place for years, offered good plain food and organ music. Quite a few unshaven bums were here tonight, Fanny noticed, more than last time, lingering over coffee and cigarettes and putting off the next move. Attracted, no doubt, by the blood plasma center next door, where they could always pick up a few dollars. The town was changing.

The dessert trolley creaked to a stop at the Jimmerson table. Mr. Jimmerson looked over the colorful display. He reached for a cup of yellow custard and Fanny gently slapped his hand away. "No, Lamar, you're quite mistaken if you think you're going to have a sweet."

The elderly lady at the organ finished her recital. She rose from her bench, acknowledged the thin applause with a smile that was greatly out of proportion to it, then made her way across the room to the Jimmerson table. Fanny greeted her warmly.

"Do sit down, Naomi, and have some coffee with us. How well you play. And look at you, always so well turned out. It's not fair, you with your musical gift and your eye for clothes too. You make the rest of us look like frumps. Lamar, you remember Miss Naomi Hine, don't you? She worked for me selling door to door until her legs gave way. Isn't she the daintiest thing you ever saw? A perfect Dresden doll. But don't be deceived, Naomi could put her little foot in the door with the best of them."

Mr. Jimmerson had seen this woman's pale head smiling and dipping and swaying above the elevated bulk of Shinn's organ but he did not remember having met her. "How do you do," he said.

"I've heard so much about you, Lamar," said Miss Hine.

Then Fanny got down to business and talked about the new arrangement.

13

For all his jaunty prose, W.W. Polton was a glum little man. Everything he saw seemed to let him down in some way. He was so small that he wore boys' clothes, little suits of a skimpy juvenile cut, the coats chopped off very short. He had the wizened walnut face of a jockey. He was rude. Time after time he cut Mr. Jimmerson short in his reminiscence. He had bad table manners and he scratched the parquet floors with the metal taps on his zippered, high-heel ankle bootlets. He drank one Pepsi-Cola after another, leaving behind him a trail of wet bottles atop fine pieces of furniture.

Mr. Jimmerson, informed by Popper that the artist could not be held to ordinary standards of civility, tried to make every allowance for the fellow. He talked openly to Polton about the Gnomon Society, revealing all that he could reveal to a Perfect Stranger, except on the subject of membership figures. In that area he was evasive. He described the workings of the Jimmerson Spiral and he talked of the high points in his life, of his dramatic meeting with Pletho Pappus in France, of the winning of Fanny Hen, of the flowering of the Society in the 1930s, of the Sydney Hen scandal and subsequent schism.

Polton, however, had his own ideas about the shape and content of the book. He had his own vision to impose and he arrived at the Temple with his own title for the biography—*His Word Is Law!*—before he had even met Mr. Jimmerson. He proceeded to fashion the work accordingly.

His methods of inquiry were odd, or so they seemed to

Mr. Jimmerson. He rejected all suggestions from the subject of the biography and he refused to read any of the Gnomonic texts. Whenever Mr. Jimmerson ventured onto that ground, Polton cut him short. "Nobody wants to hear about those triangles, Jimmerson. Do I have to keep saying it?" Such structural matter as he needed in the way of names, dates and places, he gleaned from old scrapbooks and from direct interrogation of the Master.

Mr. Jimmerson felt that the questions were all wrong. For one thing, Polton seemed to have the idea that Gnomonism had come out of the Andes. He kept asking about "your curious beacons and landing strips in Peru" and "the pre-Incan race of giants" and "the sacred plaza of Cuzco." He pressed the Master about his "prophecies" and his "harsh discipline" and his "uncanny power to pick up signals from outer space," a power which Mr. Jimmerson had never claimed to possess. At the same time Mr. Jimmerson had to admire the man's virtuosity as a reporter, for in all these hours of grilling Polton took not a single note.

Popper, meanwhile, as chairman of the Citizens Committee to Elect Mr. Jimmerson, had prepared a long statement for the press, announcing the candidacy. The statement ran to six sheets. WHY NOT MR. JIMMERSON FOR A CHANGE? was the heading. Directly beneath, in slightly smaller type, were two more questions: WHO IS MR. JIMMERSON? and WHERE DOES MR. JIMMERSON STAND? Below that there came thirty-six thick paragraphs of very fine type, with a check mark by each one, introducing Mr. Jimmerson to the public and purporting to give his position on this and that. It appeared to be the usual campaign stuff—leadership, the future, education, highways, no new taxes at this time—nothing that anyone could be expected to quarrel with or read through to the end. Not even Mr. Jimmerson, with his hearty appetite for black lumps of print, could finish it.

Nor could the Indiana editors, who gave the announcement only a brief mention in their newspapers, those who gave it a mention at all.

"Don't worry," said Popper. "They'll have to take notice when the book comes out. They'll have to provide full coverage when you start making your speeches around the state."

Within a week the writing of the book was done, Polton's manuscript delivered. Popper changed the title to *Hoosier Wizard*, with the subtitle of *Conversations with Mr. Jimmerson*, and whisked the pages away to a job printer before the Master could look them over. His work finished and the balance of his $1,200 fee in hand—paid by Fanny Jimmerson—W.W. Polton moved on, this elfin artist in elevated bootees, anxious to begin work on a new Vince Beaudine thriller he had sketched out in his head while listening to Mr. Jimmerson, or pretending to do so.

"It was all so fast," said Mr. Jimmerson.

"Time is short," said Popper.

He spoke of "seeing the book through the press," and with the Gnomon Press no longer in existence, the Letts scattered, he had the printing and binding contracted out on a low-bid basis.

He did not speak of paying for it. Popper claimed to have a rich wife and, as Mr. Jimmerson remembered it, had suggested that he would underwrite both the book and the campaign, and yet now when the matter of financing came up, he went vague, saying only that his affairs out West were "unsettled." He seemed to be short even of pocket money. Again Fanny Jimmerson had to foot the bill—$7,000 for 21,000 copies of *Hoosier Wizard*. But that was the end of it, she said. They could expect nothing more from her in the way of subsidies for these Gnomon projects.

Popper told Mr. Jimmerson not to worry. "Funds will be rolling in soon from book sales and campaign contributions. You're going to love this biography, sir. I read it at a sitting.

Dub has done a beautiful job. When you consider how little time he had."

They were in the Red Room. Mr. Jimmerson received his freshly minted copy of the book with trembling eagerness. His life in print for all the world to study! He turned through the pages, stopping here and there to read a bit. His conversation, he saw, had been rendered very freely. He could not, in fact, recall having made any of these preposterous statements, nor could he recognize himself in Polton's portrait of the Master of Gnomons.

"Corpulent genius" was fair enough. "Viselike grip" was good. It was pleasing to see his oyster eyes described as "two live coals." The fellow had a touch, all right, but how had he come up with such things as "the absolute powers of a Sultan" and "the sacred macaws of Tamputocco" and "Peruvian metals unknown to science" and "the Master awash in his oversize bathtub" and "likes to work with young people" and "a spray of spittle"? Why was he, Lamar Jimmerson, who never raised his voice, shown to be expressing opinions he had never held in such an exclamatory way that droplets of saliva flew from his lips?

And why was there no mention, that he could find, of Hermes Trismegistus or the Jimmerson Spiral? Why was his name repeatedly misspelled? What was all this about the big bathtubs? Why was so little space devoted to the exposition of his thought and so much space given over to Maceo—"the brooding darky"—who was presented falsely as that popular figure of melodrama, the sinister servant? Where did Polton get the idea that there was a gong in the Temple?

Popper said, "Why don't you read it later, sir? It's probably not fair to the book, just dipping into it at random like that."

"He keeps going on about Peru, Austin. I know nothing whatever about Peru, its major cities, its principal exports, let alone its secrets. I was expecting something—"

"Something quite different, I know. Don't worry, sir, yours is a perfectly normal reaction. The blanching, the starting eyes, the rapid breathing, the hand groping about for support. You should see your face. It's alarming, I know, like hearing your voice on a machine for the first time, but you'll get used to it. This is the way these things are done now. Some of that stuff you mustn't take too much to heart. We have to allow the writer his little fillips. He has to keep the readers moving along. Lazy bums, most of them, as you well know, and fainthearted to boot. A little diversion before nodding off is all those bozos are looking for. You must try to see it as a whole."

"Then you think it's a good book?"

"I'm not going to sit here and tell you that I approve of every single word. Frankly speaking, and just between us, there is more than one passage in there that I don't understand. I know for a fact that Dub has worked in some odds and ends he had left over from a book he did on South America, but that's a common practice now, I'm told, widely accepted, and really, when you get right down to it, where's the harm? I will say this. That work has its own Polton integrity. Give it some time. Believe me, *Hoosier Wizard* will grow on you. I'll tell you something else. It's going to make some people sit up."

But the thing that made them sit up was not *Hoosier Wizard*; it was a paragraph toward the end of the campaign statement that had gone unread until now. This was the dread Paragraph 34, which declared that Governor Jimmerson, upon taking office, would move quickly to sponsor legislation that would close all the nursing homes and old folks homes in the state, and further, would force all householders in Indiana, rich and poor alike, to take in their aged parents and care for them at home "until death should supervene and they be carried away in the course of nature."

The first person to see the threat, and perhaps the only one ever to read the entire document, was the editor of a labor union bulletin in nearby Gary, a man with a keen eye for the sleeper clause in a contract. He sounded the alert by way of a front-page editorial in his paper, with the headline A NUT FOR GOVERNOR? The editorial began with these words: "Who does this guy Jimmerson think he is anyway?" and closed with these: "Let's show this bum where he gets off!"

Others took up the cry. A tide of fear rolled across the state. The householders had visions of their old mothers and fathers suddenly appearing on their doorsteps in cracked shoes, sheaves of medical prescriptions in hand, their goods tied up in bulging pasteboard boxes at their feet.

The daily newspapers were unanimous in denouncing the proposal, calling it "hasty" and "zany" and "ultimately, when all is said and done, not in the best interests of our elder citizens." The chairmen of the Republican and Democratic parties called it "a gross imposition" and "just a terrible idea." In Indianapolis the Kleagle of the Wabash Klavern of the Ku Klux Klan told reporters he was looking over bus schedules in preparation for dispatching a small flogging squad to Burnette "to give this Mr. Jimmerson the whipping of his life." *The Thunderbolt*, monthly organ of the Communist Party, said, "L. Jimmerson is perhaps the least progressive of all the candidates and there is really nothing to be done with such a hyena except string him up by the heels like B. Mussolini." In country club bars there was angry murmuring and threats of taking to the streets in gangs to protest the Jimmerson family relocation scheme.

Popper said nothing. He was in and out of the Temple. Inside, Mr. Jimmerson glided about as usual with a big book in his hand, looking things up. He seldom read the political news in his paper and so was unaware of the furor, until the afternoon the man came to put in the new telephone. The first call to come through to the Temple was a death threat, taken by the telephone installer, who passed on the gist of the message. Wrong number, Mr. Jimmerson assumed, for why should anyone want to "rip his belly open." But then there were more calls, all from strangers and all abusive, and at the end of the day he knew he had done something to annoy a good many people out there.

But what? What were they talking about? Was this another of Sydney Hen's terror campaigns? Had Sydney broken out of Mexico? Perhaps these people were just disappointed buyers of *Hoosier Wizard*. If so, sales must have been brisk indeed, to judge from the number of infuriated callers.

"It'll blow over in a few days," said Popper. "A tempest in a teapot. I wouldn't worry about it. I've already sent out corrections to the papers."

"Some of those people sounded serious."

"All bluster. People who make threats never actually do anything."

They were in the Red Room. Mr. Jimmerson was looking over some of his old lecture material. He got a whiff of something off Popper's breath that he couldn't identify. It was rum. Popper's face was flushed. He hurriedly explained about the offending paragraph in the position paper.

"Then it's not *Hoosier Wizard*?"

"Not at all. It hasn't really taken off yet. I doubt if we have sold four copies. This is something else altogether. But it's old news and fading fast. Let me tell you what I have lined up for us."

"Fanny didn't think it was a very good book."

"Did she just skim through it?"

"I don't know. She said she couldn't see where all the money went."

"*Hoosier Wizard* is not a woman's book, sir. But that's not what this fuss is all about. It's about this Paragraph 34 that would close all the nursing homes. You told me how slack they were in rotating Mr. Bates on his bed. I simply expressed your concern and suggested a remedy. No real harm done. I've already repudiated it. I explained that it was just a trial balloon. That's yesterday's news and we must put it behind us. Here, let me tell you about my coup. I've lined up a major speaking engagement for us. On the twenty-fourth—mark your calendar—we kick off the campaign with a speech at Rainbow Falls State Park. You'll be addressing the Busy Bees."

"Is that the lawyers' club?"

"The very exclusive lawyers' club. Their annual retreat. It wasn't an easy booking, I can tell you, and we must make the best of it."

"I've never been to Rainbow Falls. They say you have to watch your step down there on those slick rocks."

"Right here, see, two-thirty p.m., which was to have been free time, they've penciled you in on their program, between these seminars on 'Making the Worse Cause Appear the Better' and 'Systematic Estate Looting and No One the Wiser.' This is the break I've been looking for. It's a wonderful opportunity."

"Will it be safe? Fanny thinks I should stay in the Temple for a while."

"Perfectly safe. A woodland setting, a secluded lodge, a select audience. Oh, they may be put off a bit at losing their free time. I suppose some of them would prefer to be out on the links knocking a ball around and telling off-color stories, but remember, these men are senior attorneys and distinguished members of the bench. We don't have to fear catcalls or gunplay. They won't be hurling buns at you. They won't try to hoot you down and drive you from the podium. These Busy Bees have clout and money and we're going to need some of those people in our camp."

"All the newspaper articles about Rainbow Falls mention that slippery footing. It seems there's some kind of green stuff growing on those wet rocks down there."

"Yes, but you understand, sir, we're not going down there for a dip. We won't have time to wade the shallows with our trousers rolled up and our shoes in our hands. We're going down there to cultivate some of the most important men in the state. We need to stake out some key ground early. Wasn't it Bismarck who said, 'He who holds the—something or other —controls the—something else'? Controls the whole thing, you see. It was Bismarck or one of those boys with a spike on his hat."

"Kaiser Bill had a spike on his helmet. One of his arms was withered, you know, but I forget which one."

"We'll need a good strong speech. But not too strong. We don't want to overwhelm our audience the first shake out of the box. A light note won't be amiss, not in your opening remarks. An open, friendly tone. There's no telling what weird notions they have about us out there."

"Did you say two-thirty?"

"At two-thirty on the twenty-fourth, yes, sir. But I think we should leave early and allow some time for a little 'Let's get acquainted' session when we get there."

"That's when I have my nap. What about my nap?"

"You can sleep in the car. Maceo will drive us down in the Buick. Will it run, by the way? I've noticed weeds and flowers growing around the tires."

"We don't use it much."

Mr. Jimmerson had begun to move his papers about and hold them up to his eyes. "I've been looking over some of my old talks here, Austin. It's surprising how well they have stood the test of time, if I do say so myself. What do you think about giving them 'Gold, the Celestial Fire Congealed'? That was always well received."

"It would go right over their heads, sir. Something with broad appeal is what we want for the Busy Bees. Not too much about Atlantis. These men are clever but they are not attuned to higher thought."

"How about 'A Stroll Through History'?"

"Your survey of eleven civilizations? There won't be enough time. They're only giving us about twenty-three minutes and we'll want to leave a little cushion at the end for a question period. But not too much of a cushion."

" 'Gnomonism Today'?"

"I don't think so. *Hoosier Wizard* gives us Mr. Jimmerson the Master of Gnomons. Out there on the stump we want to present Mr. Jimmerson the man. Our theme is change. 'Why not Mr. Jimmerson for a change?' That's our pitch. Let's try to work up something along those lines."

14

Over the following weekend Miss Naomi Hine made five trips across town in her little green Crosley car. She was moving her things into the Gnomon Temple. This was the beginning of the new arrangement, whereby the Temple, or part of it, was to become a rooming house, or "guest lodge," as Fanny Jimmerson put it. With some paying guests, she had determined, the big place could pay its own way and thus relieve her of a financial burden. The Gnomon Society, now little more than a corporate ghost, remained the nominal owner, but Fanny felt free to make these dispositions since it was she who had paid the bills for so many years.

Miss Hine, in exchange for a suite of rooms and a small salary, would act as manager. The guests were to be chosen with care. They were to be clean, quiet, nonsmoking, non-drinking Christian gentlemen of the kind that downtown land-ladies are forever seeking through the classified ads, and perhaps sometimes even finding.

Mr. Jimmerson was to be inconvenienced no more than was necessary. He, Popper and Maceo would keep their bed-rooms and bathrooms, along with the Red Room, the screened porch and the inviolable Inner Hall. They would share the kitchen with Miss Hine. The roomers would room upstairs and enter through a back door so that Mr. Jimmerson would not have to see them and nod to them in their comings and goings.

No one had advised Maceo of the new arrangement and at first he refused to let Miss Hine into the Temple. His door-keeping duties had become confusing. Mapes had instructed him to keep everyone out, by way of protecting the Master from insurance salesmen. Then Fanny Jimmerson had sent word down to let everyone in. Then Popper had come along and countermanded that order, ending the open-door policy. With all these threats in the air, Maceo was to screen out obvious thugs and yeggs, all newspaper reporters, which was to say all prowlers wearing shabby suits, and anyone else who looked the least bit odd. For Maceo this would be most white people. The Temple callers all looked more or less moon-struck to him and he could not be bothered trying to sort them out. A little wren like Miss Hine or a maniac with a machete, it was all the same to him.

But Miss Hine's entry was not delayed long and she was soon moving freely about inside the Temple, opening windows, pulling down old calendars and offering decorator tips. She even talked of "knocking out" interior walls.

Mr. Jimmerson had reservations about the new arrangement. He was concerned about careless roomers who might let bathtubs overflow above his head or doze off with burning cigarettes in their yellow fingers. He was suspicious of Miss Hine, the organ player, and her background in public entertainment. The woman was getting on in years but she was clearly a coquette, a flapper, with those scarlet fingernails and blue eyelids. Such women were blazing inside and he feared that at the earliest opportunity she would try to back him up against the kitchen table and press her paps against him and try to nuzzle him and kiss him, married man or not. Would she be parading around the house in her step-ins? Hardly a fit sight for Maceo to see. What could Fanny be thinking of, to put him in such an awkward position? It could only lead to the tawdry spectacle of two women, and old friends at that, fighting over him.

Several days passed and Miss Hine made no improper advances. At no time did she attempt to pin Mr. Jimmerson's ample hams against a tabletop, or touch him in a suggestive manner. But he remained wary and took care to stay just beyond her grasp, sometimes moving crabwise in a quick little shuffle that startled her.

Miss Hine had her own fears, and of course her own little ways. She wrote her name on bits of paper and strips of adhesive tape and tagged all her food. This, from long experience with female roommates, who, without permission, had guzzled her milk and gobbled her cherry tomatoes and pineapple rings and cottage cheese. Here in the Temple it was a needless precaution. Just as she had no designs on Mr. Jimmerson's person, neither did he have designs on her food, all very light fare.

Largely a leaf eater, she could make a meal out of a salad of sickly white shoots. She ate her supper at the cafeteria and such cooking as she did at home ran to cold soup, jellied soup, underdone fish and canned vegetables warmed up in a pan of tap water. Her bread was dry toast. Nothing there to tempt Mr. Jimmerson, no likely medium into which a love potion might be introduced.

On the morning of the twenty-fourth he was ready with his speech, despite the domestic upheaval. He was waiting on the screened porch. He looked at his watch. Austin was sleeping late again. He looked out over the grounds. Maceo was tinkering with the Buick. "The Burick," he called it. The builders of the elevated highway were standing about chatting and smoking. It was hard to catch them in the act of working, of actually joining one structural member to another, but somehow their work got done. The big concrete pilings had now risen to such a height as to block out the Chicago skyline, the higher crags of which had once been just visible through the industrial haze. The loss of the vista meant nothing to Mr. Jimmerson. The soaring handiwork of Chicago Man was less substantial to him than the orichalcum spires of Atlantis.

His glance fell on Miss Hine's sewing machine. She had established a sewing nook at one end of the long porch, and her stuff was there to stay from the settled looks of it. Natural light, she said, was just the thing for fine sewing, and she had proceeded to set up her tailor shop here, where, strictly speaking, she had no right to be. "The solarium," she called it.

The woman was popping up everywhere. Only last night she had proposed a game of cards in the Red Room, another area where she had no business. "How about a hand of canasta, Lamar?" she had said. "You're not doing anything, are you?" Not doing anything! Couldn't the woman see all those books and papers in his lap? Did she think he had time to waste on parlor games? She had her own sitting room, why couldn't she sit in it? She had also presumed on a very brief acquaintance to call him Lamar. There were just three people left on earth who addressed him so—his wife, Sydney Hen and Mr. Bates—and he saw no reason why this little woman should be the fourth. Not even W. W. Polton had taken such a liberty.

All this, with the best yet to come, the roomers. Soon there would be a pack of coughing drifters bumping around upstairs, alcoholic house painters and clarinet players, tramping to the bathroom at all hours of the night. Still, to give the woman her due, she had been very decent in offering to mend his clothes and in putting her tiny car at his disposal. She had brought no cats along with her and no miniature dogs. She did not whinny or titter and had not, so far, tried to embrace him. And, in any case, someone would have to stay behind as caretaker of the Temple when he went to Indianapolis. He would need Maceo at his side in the governor's mansion.

One term, at his age, would probably suffice. Was it two years or four? He read through the closing words of his speech and shook his fingers outward in a remembered gesture from the lectern. It was good to be active again. It was all coming back to him now and he was eager to face his old adversaries, the ignorance and indifference of men, row upon row of blank faces and fallen jaws. It was a good speech with an interesting theme, change, although, to be honest, he had never really seen himself as an agent of political change.

What could he, Governor Lamar Jimmerson, Master of Gnomons, do for his fellow citizens? One service came immediately to mind. As his first official act he would order the Parks Department to install a guardrail all around the base of Rainbow Falls, with plenty of warning signs. Such an inviting place and yet so treacherous. At this very moment white-haired judges and rumpled old family attorneys were down there losing their footing and crying out as they fell and bruised their buttocks on those cruel green rocks, first slick and now hard. But then downstream a bit, below the cascade, all violence spent, wouldn't there be a limpid pool where older men in prickly blue wool bathing briefs could paddle about unobserved with swim bladders under their arms?

Outside there was a roar and an expanding plume of white smoke. The construction workers had pushed the Buick off to get it started. It was a 1940 Buick Century, black, with four doors, a straight-eight engine, the starter button under the accelerator pedal. Maceo, behind the wheel, waved off the pushers with thanks, then turned to look at Mr. Jimmerson on the porch. Mr. Jimmerson nodded once in response, to acknowledge that the Buick was living and breathing again. They looked at each other across the way for quite some time.

It was almost ten o'clock when Popper emerged from his room, smelling of rum. He was nervous. His smile was tight. The black wig was riding low on his forehead. He made no apology for being late.

"Are we ready? Is everything in hand? Pawing the dirt, are you, sir? We need to shake a leg. Has Maceo loaded the books? Here, sir, let me help you with your Poma. There we go, snug does it. Say, what happened to the hair on this thing?"

"It's been falling out for years."

"The dapple effect is lost."

"Yes."

"It needs something to set it off."

"No, it's all right."

"But your Poma no longer has focus, sir. It needs something—right here at the peak, some culminating event. A big yellow jewel would do it, or no, a blue Christmas tree bulb powered by a hidden battery. A soft blue radiance atop the Cone of Fate."

"No, it's all right the way it is, Austin. I don't want my cap wired up. It's Sydney who likes trinkets. He has a brass ball or a marble on top of his Poma. That's not for me. You know how I feel about trinkets."

"Your scorn for ornament. I did know but had completely forgotten."

They joined Maceo beside the rumbling, smoking Buick and there engaged in a discussion over which car to take. Mr. Jimmerson was for the Crosley, he having no confidence in the rotted tires on the Buick. Popper argued that the Crosley was too small for three men and several hundred pounds of books. Maceo agreed, and said that he did not care to wear his chauffeur's cap if they took the Crosley. Mr. Jimmerson pointed out that the Crosley was a later model than the Buick, with sound little tires, offering less risk of breakdown.

"But the Crosley is not a touring car, sir," said Popper. "What about your rest? Have you thought of that? I know a little something about sleeping in cars and, believe me, no one has ever taken a nap in a moving Crosley. And what will those lawyers think when we come driving up in such a clownish little car, with the back bumper dragging from all the weight? 'Look, here are three fellows coming up in a pale green Crosley. I wonder who they are. I wonder what their visit means. Pranksters, you think?' Now is that the kind of reception we want? No, sir, the Crosley won't do."

Mr. Jimmerson tapped a sandal against one of the Buick tires. He now wore thin white socks to protect his feet against the chafing straps. "But look at those cracks," he said. "You can see the cords. We could have a blowout and turn over. We might find ourselves stumbling around in a pasture holding our bloody heads."

"They'll hold up if Maceo takes it slow. Heat is the great enemy of tires."

Maceo loaded the Buick trunk with boxes of *Hoosier Wizards*. Popper and Mr. Jimmerson sat in the back on seats of dirty brown plush.

They were off. Out on the highway the white exhaust smoke increased in volume. The cars behind them had to drop back from a normal interval or be caught in a choking, blinding whiteout. The drivers of these cars were hesitant to pass, to move into the dense cloud, the unknown, and, with Maceo taking it slow, there soon developed a long, creeping, serpentine motorcade behind the black Buick.

"Let them honk," said Popper. "A very low form of expression. If they knew who they were honking at they would blush."

Inside the car the sweet smell of rum was strong. Mr. Jimmerson rolled down a window to get relief and asked Popper if he had taken to drinking in the morning now. Popper did not answer the question. Instead, he reached over to Mr. Jimmerson's wattles and took a fold of flesh between thumb and finger. "Patches of gray bristles," he said. "Here and here. You missed a spot or two with your razor. It doesn't look good at all."

Mr. Jimmerson recoiled, and said, "I don't believe I would talk about anyone's looks, Austin, if I was wearing a Halloween wig like you."

Popper raked the clotted black locks out of his eyes. "I'm sorry, sir, I don't know what got into me. I'm on edge, I'm not myself today. Don't pay any attention to me. It's not a pleasant subject, which of us looks the worse, and I should never have introduced it. I doubt if the point could ever really be settled. The truth is that all three of us, Maceo not excepted, could do with a facial tone-up. What am I talking about? I'm sorry, sir, it's my nerves. I had a bad dream last night. I was out in a desert and a rat crossed my path. He was not scurrying, with abrupt starts and stops, none of your rat sprints, but loping like a cheetah. His ears were laid back. This rat had no local business to see to. He was on a cross-country mission. A rat of doom. When I woke I was soaked in sweat and my heart was thumping, and so I had a couple of rum-and-tonics on an empty stomach. I'll be all right when I get a bite to eat. Once we get this maiden speech out of the way everything will come right. Did you have a good breakfast, by the way?"

"Yes."

"Meg calls it the most important meal of the day."

"I had a good enough breakfast but what are we going to do about my lunch?"

"No need to worry on that score, sir. They'll have a lavish buffet down there if I know my lawyers. Great red haunches of meat and crystal tureens piled high with chilled shrimp. Expense no object. These are not abstemious men. It won't be a soup kitchen."

The tires held all the way to Rainbow Falls State Park. The streamer of smoke gave an illusion of speed and as the Buick rolled down the woodland lane it was like the passing of a comet. But the arrival caused no stir. There was no one on the veranda to greet the Master, no receiving line, no photographers, no reception of any kind. Rain was pattering on the leaves. Maceo began unloading the books. Popper led Mr. Jimmerson up the steps and into the great timbered hall.

The lawyers were drowsy. They had been feeding and drinking for more than an hour and many of them were sunk in leather chairs and couches, dozing, the older ones blowing like seals. A few were still on their feet, standing about in pairs, at the bar, around the snooker table, before the cold fireplace, laughing quietly as they exchanged stories of daring raids on public funds, strife fomented, judgments consumed, snares successfully laid.

At the rear of the big room a boy in a short red jacket was sliding a wooden beam across the doors to the dining room. He was locking up. Luncheon was done.

"This is the limit!"

"This takes the ever-loving cake!"

They began to close in on Mr. Jimmerson and put questions to him in a legal tautolog that he could not follow. The questions became accusations and before long the courtroom gobblers were baiting him from all sides, with no one to gavel them down. The Busy Bees were swarming. Young ones darted in to poke the Master's belly and tug at his gown. Popper tried to answer them and fend them off. Mr. Jimmerson's head swam. He stood there scratching the backs of his hands and saying nothing.

The cross-flow of words became a torrent. It was a talking frenzy. The lawyers were seized, possessed, with a kind of glossolalia. Their speech was no longer voluntary or even addressed to anyone. They jabbered mindlessly into the air, their eyes half closed in a transport, and one man was so driven that he had stopped uttering words altogether and had taken to mooing and lowing and moving his feet up and down in the slow clog dance of a zombie.

Then there came the peal of a little silver bell from above and the hubbub subsided, trailing off through a low ululation to, finally, silence. The strange delirium was broken. A man in a dark suit and with receding waves of gray hair was standing at the rail of the mezzanine gallery. He struck his little bell again with a silver mallet. The lawyers looked up at him, their chief.

"Order," he said. "Pray silence. Busy Bees, your attention, please. Thank you. Tipstaff? Will you wake those delegates on the couches? Will you clear the couches and make a thorough room check? Thank you. A clean sweep-down fore and aft, if you please. Turn them out, Tipstaff, prod their bottoms with your staff, and don't forget to check the canteen and the steam room for skulkers. While you're at it you might check the windows for peepers and sneaks who would learn our tricks. I hate to break up your naps, gentlemen, and your romp, but we have a full docket this afternoon and we really must turn to. It's time to put our brandies and panatelas aside and proceed to business. First, an announcement. A little surprise, or rather a big one. An unexpected guest. I have here at my side a distinguished U.S. Attorney. It is my privilege to know him personally. All of you know him by reputation. So, without further cackle, I give you, gentlemen, the prosecutor's prosecutor, that celebrated pit bull of the Justice Department—"

A pudgy little man stepped forward to the rail. He wore a seersucker suit. His hair was cut in a flat brush.

The lawyers gasped.

"White!"

"Those full cheeks! It's Bulldog White!"

"He's got White!"

"Order," said the chief. "Yes, I have indeed got Pharris 'Bulldog' White, and what is more, my brave advocates, I have persuaded him to read us his full trial notes and citations from *United States* v. *Omega Gypsum Co.*"

White held a fat book aloft and the lawyers cheered.

"And that's not all," said the chief. "Bulldog has also very kindly consented to give us a report on loophole closing. Every year we are closing more and more, but, as we all know, there are still far too many human activities that can be carried on without the intercession of lawyers. Bulldog will give us the current rundown on that from Washington. Ludlow? Is Ludlow on the floor? Ah, Ludlow. It's short notice, I know, Ludlow, but I wonder if you would form up our glee club and give Bulldog a proper welcome."

The man called Ludlow began to shout commands. Thirty or so of the lawyers scrambled about and arranged themselves into three curving ranks. Ludlow stood before them. He rotated a fist high above his head and the men burst forth with a greeting. "Glad to have you, Bulldog! So pleased that you could come!" Then Ludlow sounded a note on his pitchpipe and the men hummed, some of them leaning well into the note. Ludlow raised his arms and the men sang.

Go, go, go, go,
Go where e'er you please,
We're the bow'tied boys of the bar O!
And aren't we busy bees!

Hail then the

On they sang. Mr. Jimmerson was hungry, not to say weary, and things were moving too fast for him. His strength was failing. Where was the roast beef? Since breakfast at the break of day he had not seen so much as a celery stick. And how explain the behavior of these men? First they rail at him and now they seemed to be serenading him. This was what it was to leave home. These were the shocks to be met with outside the Temple. Would this music never cease?

The song had a good many stanzas. Pharris White stood at the rail, taking the tribute with a frozen smile. His gaze ranged over the scene below, then stopped and lingered on the fat man in the gown. *The Master of Gnomons!* That black man carrying boxes was his servant! And that fellow going for the door was—*Popper!*

"You there! Popper!"

Popper glanced back over his shoulder in the way of one who has heard a great rushing of wings, and for an instant the two men looked each other in the face. Even across that gulf and through the hairy clutter of disguise Pharris White knew his man.

"Stop him!"

"My file is no longer active, White!" shouted Popper.

"Your file will be active as long as I can draw a breath! Stop that man! That's not his natural hair! That's Austin Popper! I have a warrant for his arrest!"

But Popper was already through the doorway before anyone responded. He made for the woods and was crashing through the wet underbrush when the lawyers came storming out onto the veranda. There they stopped short, drawing back from the rain, and milled about, uncertain, awaiting guidance, while precious seconds were lost.

Pharris White appeared and they gathered about him expectantly, with most of them giving ready assent to the authority of this cherubic figure in seersucker.

The fleeing man, White explained to them, was one Austin Popper, a federal fugitive of many years' standing, once thought to be dead. He was an elusive fellow. He was not believed to be armed nor was he considered dangerous in the usual sense of that word. At the same time he was desperate and might well resist arrest with his fists, or, if one lay handy, a stick, or even by butting with his head. But they could be assured he was no bruiser. He was out there somewhere in a crouch but they need not fear his spring. As a runner he was probably no better than average for his age and weight. There was nothing in his record to suggest that either his speed or his endurance was in any way remarkable, and yet here again as a desperate man he might draw on hitherto untapped reserves. This man, the aforesaid Popper, affected an air of boldness. He was clever, though not a man of genuine learning. He lived by his wits. He sometimes traveled with a bird. For many years now he had been using writing paper taken from the Hotel Rollo in Rollo, Colorado. No one could say how much of that paper he had carried off. Of his women and his hobbies nothing was known. He held, or did hold at one time, a high position in the Gnomon Society, an ancient and secret order of global reach, with all that that implied, namely, unstinting aid from his brothers, curious winks and hand signs, a code of blood vengeance, access to great wealth, access to dark knowledge, knowledge that was not always fairly shared with deserving Neophytes of the order. These were a few things to keep in mind.

So much for the man himself. Now to the pursuit plan. It seemed to him, Pharris White, that a long line of beaters sweeping across the park would best meet the situation. They would drive Popper. Feints and stalking maneuvers and circling ploys all had their place, of course, but there came a time when you must engage your enemy directly and whip him in the field, and this, or so it seemed to him, was just such a time. He only regretted that they could not hunt him down with torches and dogs. Their sweep would converge on the rock dome known as the Devil's Pincushion, and there Popper would be taken. Then at last this man could be put away and given plenty of time in solitary confinement to gnaw on his knuckles, to think over his crimes and expiate them in cold darkness. Were there any questions? Suggestions? Had they understood his presentation and could he take it that they were in substantial agreement on all the main points?

It was a fairly long speech, given the urgent nature of the occasion, and there was further delay as the lawyers bustled about looking for sticks. Some of the men, a sizable minority, refused to take part in the manhunt, giving as their reasons advanced age, bad weather, compromised dignity, allergies, dependent children, obesity, fear of biting insects, potential mental anguish, pain and suffering and loss of consortium, unsuitable shoes, low-back pain, weak eyes, hammer toes and religious scruples, but there remained many willing hands and Pharris White soon had them deployed in a long skirmish line.

He stood at the center and a bit forward, facing them, the captain of a kickoff team. "Guide on me!" he shouted, to the left and then to the right. "Guide on my baton! Keep your dress and watch your interval! Now! Let's beat! Let's drive!"

He lowered his stick and the men moved out, flailing away at the spring greenery. Their blood was up again.

But there are many holes in the earth, not all of them scrabbled out with claws or tools of iron, and Popper had found himself a burrow long before that drive began. He sat dripping and panting in the dark hollow place behind Rainbow Falls. Far into the night he sat there in that spherical chamber behind a curtain of falling water. He considered leaving his hat floating suggestively in the pool below, then decided that Pharris White would not be so easily taken in. From time to time he dabbed at his hands with a handkerchief. Wet mud wasn't so bad, but dried mud, cracking with the flex of his hand, and tiny clods dangling from his finger hairs, that was not to be endured.

15

There followed another long Gnomonic stasis. Twelve years passed before Mr. Jimmerson made another excursion. He was a pallbearer at the graveside service for Mr. Bates and he went to the doctor now and then but it was a rare day when he set foot outside his limestone sanctuary on Bulmer Avenue. He shunned the light of day and did not leave town again for some twelve years.

No other private residence was left on the street, now cast in cold shadow by the expressway that ran overhead. Standing forsaken, the Gnomon Temple rose up between two parts of the divided highway, within the acute angle of an important interchange, and it sometimes happened that a startled motorist made eye contact with Maceo as he stood before one of the broken windows upstairs, just a few feet away from the streaming traffic.

Directly behind the Temple there was now located a maintenance yard for the city's dump trucks and garbage trucks. This was not the nuisance it might have been because the hammering and clanging that went on inside the yard could not be heard over the traffic roar on the freeway, which was constant, except during the period between 3 and 4 a.m., when there was a slight falling off. Still, in the summer, there was a problem with dust from the yard.

Things had changed out front too. Bulmer Avenue lay in eternal gloom amid a colonnade of pilings, and had become a loitering place for vagrants, petty criminals and youth gangs. When the boys burned tires in the street, the smoke rolled down the corridors of the Temple and stung Mr. Jimmerson's eyes and blackened his nostrils. Tramps came to the door and asked about supper, taking the big house for a rescue mission. There were younger, daring tramps who in winter would lay a plank from one of the freeway pillars to an upstairs dormer window of the Temple, then crawl across it and bed down inside with the pigeons. They left behind them their names written on the walls, their poems, curses and drawings. On the floor they left a mess of wine bottles and newspaper bedding and foul droppings for Maceo and Ed to clean up.

At that, they were less trouble than the paying guests, now long gone, to Mr. Jimmerson's great delight, along with Miss Hine, her innovations and her endless complaints about the sour air in the house. What a time that had been. The vexations! The interruptions! The questions! His answers! *Yes. Yes. What? No.* What a trial for a man engaged in the fine labor of speculative thought. Ed was still here but all the others were gone now, and, with two or three haunting exceptions, their faces forgotten.

The upper part of the Temple had been practically abandoned. Everything upstairs was either broken or stopped up and that area was no longer in use. Winds played about freely through the rooms. There were leaks in the roof. Outside, the old Buick sat earthbound, a rusty black hulk with no wheels. Down in the basement rats nested in the cold boiler.

There was no heat in the house except for that given off by the fireplace in the Red Room, and it was here in the reclining chairs that Mr. Jimmerson, Maceo, Babcock and Ed slept through the long winter nights, the four of them laid out in a row with their hats and coats on, and their blankets tucked up under their arms, like so many first-class passengers on the Promenade deck of a Cunard liner.

Only here and there had the decay been held back. The kitchen still functioned, as did one bathroom. The purple curtains in the Inner Hall had faded and there were bits of plaster on the floor but on the whole this room had retained its static purity, similar to that of the innermost vault of a pyramid.

When the weather was pleasant, Mr. Jimmerson shuffled about from room to room with a big book in his hand, much as ever. "Just looking something up," he would say, in the same apologetic way, but with a grin grown dreadful over the years, so that the person encountered quickly turned away.

Fanny Jimmerson was no longer nearby to keep an eye on things, she having been promoted yet again and rewarded with an assignment to New Jersey, where she now sat on the board of directors of the cosmetics company and lived in semi-retirement. She lived alone in a modest white house about an hour's drive from the scene of her honeymoon, though she did not often make that drive. The boy, Jerome Jimmerson, who was trying to make his way on the New York stage, sometimes came down to spend a weekend with her, but he had his own life now in Japanese puppet theater, and of course his own chums in the close-knit puppeteer community in Greenwich Village, and he did not come down as often as she would have liked. At the beginning of each month, Fanny wrote three letters and mailed them out with checks attached; one went to brother Sydney in Mexico, one to her husband Lamar and one to her son Jerome. Such response as she got was spotty.

As for Miss Hine, she had been called away suddenly to assume another housekeeping burden. One day she packed a few things and drove down to Lafayette to care for her older but smaller brother, Arnold "Tiny" Hine, recently widowed and ailing. It was to be a temporary leave. She was to see Tiny through his convalescence, then return to the Temple. But Tiny's recovery was slow, much slower than the doctor had predicted, and then just when it was thought to be complete he was stricken anew with something the doctor could not quite put his finger on, for all his testing of Tiny's fluids. Tiny complained of a fire in his groin and of a kink in his neck. At times he was in pain—"Don't touch the bed!"—and at other times he was able to go out at night and attend the wrestling matches with his pals. Miss Hine was obliged to extend her stay indefinitely and see to her brother's needs. She fetched things for him, handled his extensive correspondence with coin clubs and coin magazines, served him three meals a day on a tray and turned his television antenna on demand.

This left the Bulmer Avenue rooming house in Burnette without a manager. Neither Mr. Jimmerson nor Maceo was willing to take on the job and attrition soon set in. The roomers got a free ride for a while, as Mr. Jimmerson did not bother to collect the rent, but in the course of things they moved on, fell dead or were arrested, one by one, and no new roomers were taken in to replace them.

The last one was Ed, a young sandy-haired army veteran who wore cowboy clothes and Wellington boots. Ed found a home in the Temple and refused to leave. The food, the pace, the air, the company—everything suited him. He stayed on and was given his meals and a little pocket money in return for helping Maceo around the house. Not that he was of much real help. There was hardly anything Ed could do, even under the strictest supervision. He carried a note in his wallet from a doctor, often brandished, saying that he did not have to work. Neither he nor Mr. Jimmerson could cook and they had a hard time of it, feeding mostly on day-old doughnuts, during that period when Maceo got mixed up with the Black Muslims. This was at about the same time that Popper got mixed up with the left-wing women far away, in an eastern city.

The Black Muslim episode was a curious one. Maceo left in the night and came back in the night without a word. He went to Chicago and stood on a street corner for a month or so wearing a fez, calling himself Fahad Murad, selling Muslim newspapers and trying to scowl at the passing white devils. But it didn't work out, he was no good as a public menace and he didn't find street life in the city fulfilling. He was perhaps too old to become a burning sword of Black Islam and late one night he came back to the Temple wearing his old hat with the Christian brim. He resumed his duties and his old name with no word of explanation.

Then there came bad news from Florida. Scales, the Gnomon baker in Naples, on the Gulf coast, had died, blown up in his garage during the course of an alchemical experiment. There would be no more newspaper clippings from Scales, with photographs showing big sinkholes in Alabama and Florida, giving support to his theory of continental subsidence. What had happened to Atlantis, Scales believed, was now happening to America, though at a less dramatic rate of collapse. Scales, as Scales, was not much missed, even by his family, but with his passing the Gnomon Pillar in Naples was lost, another one down with all hands, and with that loss went the southeastern anchor of the Continental Gnomonic Triangle. So it was that Mr. Jimmerson no longer had an enormous, skewed triangle to work with, but only a bare line from the Temple in Burnette to the last remaining Pillar in the country, that of Mr. Morehead Moaler in La Coma, Texas.

In many ways this simplified his calculations. Working out Gnomonic readings from a line, long or short, vertical or canted, was child's play. But a line had extension only and no depth to speak of. Was this fit work for the Master of Gnomons? Weren't these line readings with their tiresome recurring decimals very feeble stuff? The garage blast in Florida had, overnight, left the Continental Triangle a vast dead zone, and Mr. Jimmerson became despondent when he thought of spending the rest of his life at this paltry business of line analysis.

For a time he all but abandoned his studies, as he had once done years ago. Then one night when he was stretched out on his recliner, with snores and visible puffs of breath all about him, there came a flash of understanding, accompanied by a bodily spasm. The apparent impasse was, he saw, a new opening. A leap at his age! Who would have thought it? For all his accomplishments of the past, he was truly just now hitting his stride. How foolish he had been to think that his best work was behind him.

The leap resolved itself into something called the Jimmerson Lag, which was to complement and shore up the Jimmerson Spiral. The Lag would account for all those troublesome loose ends and recalcitrant phenomena left unaddressed or evaded by the Spiral, or nearly all of them. That which was confused was now made clear, or fairly clear. Briefly put, the Jimmerson Lag postulated a certain amount of slack in the universe. The numerical value of that slippage or lag came to .6002, as best Mr. Jimmerson could reckon it, taking into account the ragged value of pi, the odd tilt of the earth, the lopsided nature of the Continental Triangle and many other such anomalies. How Sydney Hen would fume when he learned of this advance! He had been so maliciously eager to belittle the Spiral, only to come around later in his grudging way, first calling it a lucky hit, then trying to claim it as his own idea! So it would be with the Lag. But how to reach Sydney? Was he still alive? He had been silent for a very long time.

With the principle of the Jimmerson Lag conceived and stated, there now remained the elucidation, or rather the obfuscation. The idea had now to be properly clothed in Gnomonic riddles and allegories at generous Gnomonic length. It was no easy task, forming these long sentences in one's head and dictating them against the roar of the freeway traffic, and Mr. Jimmerson knew that he could never have done the job alone. Maurice was a godsend.

Maurice Babcock came late to the Temple. He was a darkish man about fifty years old, of retiring disposition, a court stenographer from Chicago, a Rosicrucian, not fat but with the soft look of a middle-aged bachelor who has a good job, money in the bank, no debts and no family responsibilities. Babcock did his job well. He minded his own business. He did not speak of his aspirations. He ordered his shoes from England, his shirts from Baltimore and his small hats from a hat shop in Salt Lake City that catered to the needs of young Mormon missionaries. He wore these hats in a seasonal color sequence, from opalescent gray through black, high on his head and dead level with the horizon. He took pills and time-release capsules throughout the day, avoided all foods prepared in aluminum cookware and ate a bowl of bran at bedtime to scour the pipes. His fellow workers regarded him as a hypochondriac but then it was not they who suffered from those dull headaches induced by chronic constipation. He remained a bachelor because there was no woman in all Chicago refined enough for him—Dolores herself did not really measure up—and out of a fear of female extravagance, and an even deeper one of getting tangled up in someone else's family. When he found himself alone in an elevator with a pretty girl he would smile at her with the heavy-lidded smile of an Argentine playboy, but saying nothing and meaning no harm. The girls turned away. In his spare time he read. He kept up with medical developments and indulged a taste for esoteric lore.

His introduction to Gnomonism came one Saturday morning when he was poking about in an old bookstore and ran across a cast-off trove of Gnomon pamphlets and books, including a copy of 101 *Gnomon Facts*, one of the rare, unsigned copies. He bought the lot for a five-dollar bill, took it home and read it through with wonder, lost in triangles for the weekend. *This is the stuff for me.* He knew it at once. *This is what I've been looking for. My search for certitudes is over.* He hastened to Burnette and called on Mr. Jimmerson, hopeful of getting an autograph, a word or two from the Master's lips, more and thicker books, with footnotes longer than the text proper, perhaps even a signed photograph.

The shabbiness of the Temple put him off. The odor reminded him of the holding cells at the courthouse. He was a little disappointed in Mr. Jimmerson's conversation and badly shaken by his grin. The Master was not the white-maned old gentleman with gaunt face and long fingers he had visualized. The big tuber nose came as a surprise.

But for all that, Babcock came back again and again. He knew he was on to something this time. The Rosicrucians had finer robes and the Brothers of Luxor had eerier ceremonies, but in the way of ideas that could not quite be grasped, neither of them had anything to touch the Cone of Fate or the Jimmerson Spiral. Gnomonism was the first really sound synthesis he had found of Atlantean, Hermetic and Pythagorean knowledge. The only one he had found, come to that. In his head he could feel magnetic forces gathering. He knew of some people who would be surprised when the discharge came. And all for a five-dollar bill! What did the bookseller buy with it one-half so precious?

He was initiated into the Society on a day which he had reckoned to be the cusp of a new Gnomonic cycle. The Master had wanted him to revive the Pillar in Chicago but Babcock begged off, saying he preferred to work here at the Temple, at the heart of things, the big things soon to come. Here under the Master's gaze he could hone himself to a fine edge. The wheel was turning, a time of increase was near and Maurice Babcock's proper place was right here at the center of it all. He saw a map take fire and blaze up, as in the movies when they wish to show the spread of something, usually pernicious.

The workload was overwhelming, for Babcock tried at first to keep his court dates and see Dolores and his doctors now and again, as well as take down Mr. Jimmerson's halting words on his stenotype machine. On the commuter train he studied for his advanced degrees. Back and forth he went between Chicago and Burnette, at all hours. Some nights he slept over in the Temple, collapsing on the reclining chair that had been assigned to him. It was not next to the Master, or at the other end, but, to his annoyance, between Maceo and Ed. Ed said he had "dubs" on the end chair.

Babcock's health, never good, declined. His head throbbed under the overload. His ears rang. Once he lay on his recliner for two days without moving or speaking. He lay there with his mouth open and his hands clenched at his sides, unable to speak or raise his head. Birds might have lighted on his face and walked around. No one disturbed him, a long lie-in was hardly an occasion for comment in the Red Room, but when he came around and regained muscular control he was frightened. Then and there he decided to quit his stenography job, at least until such time as he could come to grips with the situation here at the Temple. First things first. He gave up his Chicago apartment, cut his professional moorings and came to live in the Temple.

Three major projects were in hand. In the morning Babcock worked with the Master for an hour or so on the Jimmerson Lag, and then, for a brief period before lunch, on reconstructing the original text of *Gnomonism Today*. Through some mishap at the Latvian printshop, every other page had been left out. Many years had passed since publication but no one had noticed the error until Babcock caught it with his eagle eye. It was not so much that the flow of the work was disturbed or that the broken sentences from one page to the next did not connect—Gnomon literature was not, after all, that tired old business of a thread to be followed, but more a bubbling spring of words—it was the page numbers. What caught Babcock's eye and escaped all others was that the page numbers were not consecutive.

The third project was the new autobiography. After the long midday rest, Babcock took notes for the new version of Mr. Jimmerson's memoirs, for he, the Master, was still not satisfied with *Hoosier Wizard*. There were good things in it, the book had grown on him, as Austin had predicted, and yet at the same time there was something—*wrong* with it. W. W. Polton had gone wrong somewhere. The book had made little impact on the world. There had been only one review and that a very brief one by some ignorant woman on the local newspaper. "Of limited interest," she had written, and "Pays no compliment to the reader's intelligence." These phrases had stuck in Mr. Jimmerson's head, as two of the more favorable ones, such as might have been extracted for use in promotion of the book. But it was not the words themselves that stung—how could a woman, and a journalist at that, ever hope to understand Gnomonism? No, the insult lay in the notion that the life and work of Lamar Jimmerson could be dismissed in a single paragraph no longer than a weather bulletin. But the way in was the way out. This new, genuine memoir would put things right. It would be a true autobiography, every word his own, as taken down by the scrupulous Maurice, and this time the world would be forced to take notice. Sydney Hen would have to take notice. A treat for Gnomons and the lay public alike.

Babcock, unlike Polton, did not try to impose his own ideas on the work. He said nothing but he did think the Master dwelled too much on this man Popper, last seen years ago, in flight at Rainbow Falls State Park. It was Austin this and Austin that and please don't sit in Austin's chair. Popper was none too honest, from what Babcock could piece together, a shady customer who had taken to his heels at least twice, just a step or two ahead of the police. Hardly the stuff of high Gnomonism. But the Master would hear nothing against him. He said that Austin was currently moving in some orbit known only to himself, and that he would return to the Temple in his own good Gnomonic time, to take his place in his chair again, to make known the true reasons for his disappearance, together with all the facts about the woman Meg.

Babcock resented Popper, or his shadow, and he was uneasy around Ed, who was all too palpable. He took Ed for a Southerner and tried to stay clear of him. He seldom spoke to him and then only in the imperative mood, master to servant. Babcock knew no Southerners personally but he had seen them in court often enough—Boyce and Broadus and Buford and Othal, and queried the spelling of their names—and Ed's manner and appearance said Dixie to him. He imagined Ed at home with his family, a big one, from old geezers through toddlers. He saw them eating their yams and pralines and playing their fiddles and dancing their jigs and guffawing over coarse jokes and beating one another to death with agricultural implements. Later, through a quiet investigation, using his court connections, Babcock found that Ed was actually from Nebraska, so it wasn't as bad as it might have been, though Nebraska was bad enough.

The confidential records showed that Ed had been discharged from the army for attempting to chloroform women on a government reservation. The police in several cities suspected him of stealing car batteries and of vinyl slitting. His mother kept a costume jewelry stall at a flea market in Omaha and Ed had once tried to run her down with her own car, while she was in the stall. He had destroyed the fixtures in a North Platte bus station after losing some money in a vending machine, and had twice set fire to his hospital ward. The medical report stated that the mahogany tint of Ed's skin was the result of excessive use of coffee and tobacco, and that while working as a hospital orderly he had a recurring daydream in which he was a green-smocked physician with flashing scalpel. It went on to speak of his "rabbit dentition," to describe him simply as "odd," and to say that he was "disgusted by people crazier than he is." Ed's trade was vinyl repair, learned in a government hospital, though it was indicated in the records that Ed had opened many more breaches with his razor blade than he had ever closed with his invisible patches, so called, which leaped to the eye and never held for long anyway.

Babcock went to Mr. Jimmerson with the reports. He said he didn't mind so much an occasional outbreak of upholstery slitting, but were they wise to sleep in the same room with a pyromaniac who had surgical fantasies? Would they not be wiser to ease Ed out of the Temple, to find him a room and a

job in Chicago or, better yet, Omaha? It was either that or
chain him to a bed in the attic.

But Mr. Jimmerson wouldn't hear of it. "No no," he said,
"Ed's a good boy. You'll see. He gives no trouble and he's a
big help to Maceo in opening jar lids and keeping the tramps
shooed away. Have you ever looked closely into Ed's eyes,
Maurice?"

"No, sir, I have not."

"The whites have a yellowish cast. But it's more than just
his eyes. There are certain other things too that I can't discuss. You don't think Ed came here and took a room by
chance, do you?"

"I'm not sure I see what you're getting at, sir."

"It's an idea of mine. You see, I believe that Ed may be
Nandor."

"Ed? One of the Three Secret Teachers?" He smiled at
Mr. Jimmerson with his Latin gigolo smile.

Mr. Jimmerson turned away from it. "I can't say for sure
but there are many little things that point that way. There's
something in the wind. I can sense it. Something coming to
fruition. It may or may not have anything to do with Ed. Time
will tell. Besides, we need Ed. Ed's a good soldier. I'm an old
soldier myself, you know."

He grinned. Babcock turned away. So that was that. The
Master had spoken.

Nor did Babcock have much success in persuading Dolores that this great change in his life was for the best. He
went over it again and again, telling her what he could, trying
to make her understand the significance of the move.

Dolores was a little younger than Babcock. She was a
druggist who lived over a drugstore in the Edison Park section
of Chicago with her elderly father, who was also a druggist.
She was devoted to her father and to the red-brick drugstore
building, valuable corner property, to which one day she
would fall heir. Her father's name and the date of construc-

tion were spelled out in little hexagonal tiles in the foyer. Dolores was no longer devoted to pharmacy; it was no longer a calling. The great days of pharmacy were over and she had seen the tail end of them, when one weighed powders on delicate balance scales, pounded crystalline substances in a mortar, bound wounds, gave injections and freely prescribed for the neighborhood. Now it was only a matter of counting out pills and typing up labels for the little bottles. Babcock, whom she kept well supplied with samples of all the latest potions from the drug companies, came a distant third in her affections, but still she liked to have him around. She too was reluctant to marry, lest she jeopardize her clear claim to the drugstore, and put her married brothers back in the running for it, but there would come a time, she thought, when she and Maurice would make their home together over that same drugstore.

She said, "You know what I'd like to do, Maurice? I'd like to go over there and look at their towels. Check out the bathroom and the refrigerator. I'd like to size these people up."

"Not today, Dolores. Don't start in again."

"But a tower in Burnette, Indiana. At your age. A professional man like you. I just don't get it, Maurice. I just can't believe there's much to it. You tell me you're sleeping in a chair. You admit you can't get your apricots stewed the way you like them and you say you can't get your brown eggs or your three-bean salad at all. Can't you see you're living in a house of—cards? I almost said a house of pancakes."

"You keep calling it a tower, as though that made it ridiculous. You know very well that it's a Temple and I don't know why you pretend to misunderstand these things. It's not very becoming to you."

"But I never see you anymore, honey. Who's cutting your hair, by the way? It's so short and ragged."

"A man named Maceo. He works at the Temple."

"Your Temple has a barbershop?"

"No, of course not."

"Is that part of it? Short hair?"

"Part of what?"

"Your ritual."

"No, it's just that I'm very busy these days and Maceo is something of an amateur barber. He has these squeeze clippers. He cuts the Master's hair too."

"It makes your head look so small."

Babcock had not thought of his haircut in that way but now he wondered. This pinhead effect—would it slow his advancement? Ruffled, but feigning an icy calm, he said, "My hairstyle and my apricots are not of the slightest importance. What is important is my work. All I ask, Dolores, is that you make an honest effort to understand this decision I have made. So far you have made no effort at all."

Dolores said she would try. But what she continued to see in her head was an old man cackling in a tower.

16

Far from keeping the tramps shooed away, Ed visited with them every afternoon at the dry fountain. There they napped against the retaining wall and there they perched on the rim of the dry basin, undisturbed, except now and then when the street boys, a shrieking mouse pack, attacked and scattered them with volleys of rocks and chicken bones. Ed went out daily to chat with the tramps and to collect his cigarettes, two or three from each man, filtered or unfiltered, ready-rolls only, no butts or "snipes" accepted, and no menthols. The tramps came to understand that this was the price of resting at the Gnomon fountain, and of Ed's company.

Ed was there on that afternoon in early winter when the blue van pulled up before the Temple. It was a camper van with a roof extension, a white plastic carapace. A constellation of seven white stars was painted on the side of the van and under the stars there were white words.

BIGG DIPPER ENERGY SYSTEMS
CORPUS CHRISTI, TEXAS

This was an event, a vehicle stopping at the Temple, and Ed watched closely. The tramps were burning a sofa in the fountain. Ed was standing there with them in their hand-warming circle. A passenger got down from the van, an older man, and Ed broke for the front steps to intercept him.

"Hold it! You can't go in there!"

"Oh no?"

Two cowboys in a standoff. The older man was wearing a cowboy hat and eyeglasses—not a good combination—and a pale blue suit of western cut with bolo tie. His cowboy boots were made of the pebbly hide of some caramel-colored reptile. He carried a briefcase. On a little finger, deeply embedded in the flesh, there was the plain gold ring of a nightclub singer.

"Who says?"

"No visitors without an appointment. Mr. Babcock's orders."

"Look at this place. It's the House of Usher. Is the Master in?"

"He's always in."

"Who are you?"

"Ed. I'm security."

"Head? Your name is Head?"

"Ed!"

"Well, speak up, Ed. Speak from the chest. Say it with confidence. 'My name is Ed, sir, and how may I be of service to you?' You'll never get anywhere in life mumbling your name like that. Here's a dollar for you and a little perpetual calendar. That's the last calendar you'll ever need. I want you to help Esteban with my bags and then you can get back to your campfire and keep an eye on my motor home."

Ed was dazzled by the stranger's boots. He took the dollar and the little plastic calendar and gave way.

It was an older and thicker Austin Popper, never doubtful of his welcome, come home again to the Gnomon Temple. He started for the door, then had a further thought. "No, the bags can wait." He called out to Esteban, his driver, and told him to collect the tramps at the fountain and take them downtown to Shinn's cafeteria and stand them to a good meal, then to a matinee if there was a picture playing that he and all the tramps could agree on. "But no beer and no cash handouts. You too, Ed. Go on, round up your pals. It's a treat on Esteban and me."

Popper seemed to be puzzled by the objection. He said, "Hot? Brownsville?"

Mr. Jimmerson said, "Well, as you know, Austin, I've never been there. I've just always thought of Texas as a burning land. With scorpions and those desert frogs that spit blood from their eyes. I associate that country with citrus fruit. Don't they call that part of Texas the Panhandle?"

"No, sir, they call it the Valley, but you're right about the fruit. Everywhere you turn in Brownsville and La Coma there are Ruby Reds for the plucking. The sweetest grapefruit in the world. Did I not mention Mr. Morehead Moaler's grove? As for the heat, well, yes, there are some sultry days in July and August, but nothing we can't handle with loose clothing and plenty of liquids. Mr. Moaler's place is, of course, fully air-conditioned. On those hot days we can estivate."

It was late at night and once again Popper was sitting before the fireplace in the Red Room with a proposal for Mr. Jimmerson. Three fifty-pound bags of grapefruit, a gift, lay at his feet. He showed photographs of La Coma with its palm trees and little oxbow ponds. There was a dim picture of Mr. Morehead Moaler in his wheelchair, holding what appeared to be a basketball in his lap. Babcock was tending the fire and listening intently, as in court, without looking at either party, his face impassive. So this was Popper. These were his words. Trucks were blatting on the freeway and at intervals Ed could be heard laughing in the kitchen. He, Maceo and Esteban were back there watching television.

Mr. Jimmerson said, "Pletho tells us we should all sleep in our own beds."

"Beds, yes," said Popper. "He says nothing about reclino chairs."

"I just don't see how it can be done, Austin. I don't see how the Master can leave the Temple."

"By simple decree."

"But isn't travel largely nonsense?"

"Travel is total nonsense. It's a great fraud. Our old friend Zeno tells us that motion is impossible—and proves it, the Greek scoundrel! Well, I can't go that far. I can't go along with Zeno all the way on that, but I do know that travel is one of the greatest hoaxes of our time. But look here, sir, what I'm talking about is not travel as such. We're not going on a sightseeing tour. What I'm talking about is a new life in the sun."

"No, I'm afraid it's too late for me, Austin. I don't see how I could ever leave the Temple. There's too much work left here to do."

"Excuse me, but I don't see a Temple. I see a shell. I see red silk peeling from the walls. You're buried alive here, sir, in the world's noisiest tomb. How can you talk of work with those trucks out there going like the hammers of Hell? Look, our eyes are watering from the fumes. The very air is evil. I don't think you realize what's happened. The Telluric Currents have shifted away from Burnette and nothing can prosper here. Look at Bulmer Avenue. Do you remember how it used to be? Now it's a street of bums and juvenile bullies. On every block you can see a twelve-year-old boy holding a six-year-old boy in a headlock. No, sir, I respectfully beg to differ. I can't see a Gnomon Temple."

Popper's homecoming celebration had been subdued, at his own request. He told Mr. Jimmerson and Maceo that he would take it as a favor if they would not press him closely with questions about the recent past, his memory being faulty and a source of continuing embarrassment. But Mr. Jimmerson did ask him about Meg. Popper said he had never known a woman of that name and was pretty sure he had not been married. Would he not recall such an experience? Nor could he remember any trip to Rainbow Falls. Had he actually been here in the Temple since the war, the big war? Incredible! Not just some astral projection? Amazing! He couldn't recall any such visit.

Mr. Jimmerson brought him up to date on *Hoosier Wizard* and the Jimmerson Lag. Popper made a great fuss over the Lag, praising the grandeur of it, and at the same time expressing surprise that the numerical value of this cosmic slack should be so small—only six-tenths of one percent, and a little more.

They talked of bygone days. Popper fell into a confessional mood. "I haven't had a drink in five years," he said. He spoke of his shame and his wasted years as a drunken bum. Since the war he had drifted aimlessly about the country, a burden on society, guzzling rum when he could get it. He had been in and out of jails and hospitals. He had been on the road living a life of stupor, filth, irregular meals and no certainty of shelter from one night to the next. Pedestrians in many cities had been obliged to step over him as he lay curled up on the sidewalk wearing four shirts, three sweaters and multiple layers of verminous trousers, the cuffs bound tight at the ankles with rubber bands, so that he was sometimes taken for a downed cyclist. Five years ago he had found himself in a charity hospital in Corpus Christi, Texas. The doctors told him he had collapsed in a city park with a heart attack and had been brought gasping to the emergency room by a kind policeman.

"I think it was really more of a head attack," he said. "I wasn't exactly off my rocker, but my memory, feeble enough before, was now shattered altogether. They said I wasn't getting enough oxygen to my brain. Just the odd bubble now and then, as I understand it. Well, not shattered altogether, because I knew my name and there were certain dim but familiar figures that kept appearing in my dreams—not least yours, sir, though I couldn't place you nor understand the significance of your conical cap. But on the whole all was a merciful blank. They were very good to me there in that hospital, pauper that I was. The doctors got me back on my feet with blood-thinner pills. My blood was like tar and I thought I was down for the count. They told me to lay off the Crisco and stay away from salt. Did you ever try to eat mashed potatoes and gravy with no salt? A mule wouldn't eat it. But those doctors got me on my feet, God bless them, and then the nurses put me on to a group of recovered alcoholics. More good people. They took me in and introduced me to their methods. The doctors grudgingly admit that those methods work, where their medico methods fail, but the spiritual aspect bothers them. They don't like any system that doesn't involve pills and injections. But credit where credit's due. First the doctors saved my life and then those people saved it again. I haven't had a drink in five years. They restored my self-esteem. In six months I was a new man, wearing a clean shirt and holding down a good job selling bonds over the telephone from a boiler room. I discovered I had a knack for selling things, a gift for hopeful statement combined with short-term tenacity of purpose. But I wouldn't stay hitched. I had a comfortable life and yet something was lacking. I jumped around a good deal. I tried my hand at real estate, selling beachfront lots out of an A-frame office in a patch of weeds. I sold used cars. 'Strong motor.' 'Cold air.' 'Good rubber.' Those were some of the claims I made for my cars, or 'units,' as we call them in the business. I bought fifty-weight motor oil by the case. Then for a time there I had a costume shop downtown. It was seven feet wide and a hundred and twenty feet deep and poorly lighted. My stock was army surplus stuff and little bellboy suits and Santa Claus suits and animal heads and rubber ears and such. I had more uniforms than Hermann Göring and sometimes for a bit of fun I would wear one myself out on the sidewalk to attract attention. Go through a few drill steps. 'Jackets, bells and Luftwaffe shells!' I cried. 'While they last!' Then I saw another opportunity and sold out to an Assyrian. They like to be on Main Street. The lighting is not a big thing with them. He beat me down on the price but I left a few surprises for Hassan in the inventory. That's when I set up Bigg Dipper, a little operation dealing in oil and gas leases. Small potatoes, you understand, but my own show.

That's when I bought my motor home, which is not a luxury but an important business tool. All this time things were coming back to me. No flood of light now, don't get me wrong. I couldn't arrange these events in a consecutive way, and still can't, but I was getting back bits of my past. Little vignettes. Here's an example. The worst block was the 1950s. I had lost that entire decade. Ten years of murk. President Eisenhower? You might as well ask me about John Quincy Adams. Then one morning there at sunrise in Corpus I had a vivid 1950s memory. It was another ocean sunrise in Miami. It was the summer of 1956 and I was in a car with another bum named Dorsey LaRue. Some bums have cars. We had nothing better to do and we were on our way to Detroit to see about getting an advance peek at the 1957 De Sotos but we never made it. We never got out of Miami. Dorsey took his eyes off the road to get a better station on the radio, or maybe to tune in the one he had more clearly, or even to shut it off altogether, I don't know, but he lost control of the car and we smashed into a twenty-four-hour laundromat, scattering night workers and early risers. I remembered that brief motor trip and I remembered James Wing in San Francisco and how kind he was to me. What a gentleman! A hard worker too but he was never really able to get oriental Gnomonism off the ground. I remembered playing fan-tan with James Wing and Dan Soo and Ernie Zworkin. Ernie was the last man in the phone book until Victor Zym hit town out of the blue and nudged him back a space. I remembered riding across the desert stretched out on that long seat at the back of a bus. That was before they put a toilet back there in the corner. There was a newspaper over my face with a headline—I can still see it—that said PREGNANT MOM WITH BAT SENDS 4 PUNKS PACKING. I remembered stealing a banana and getting mixed up with some left-wing women, and then later with a three-hundred-pound doctor named Symes who was trying to put a book together called *Slimming Secrets of the Stars* with a writer named Polton and two promoters named Constantine Anos, unfortunate name, though apt enough, and Dean Ray Stuart. Dean, I should say, was his given name, and he was never, to the best of my knowledge, the chief officer of a college or cathedral, and neither was he connected, as far as I know, to the royal house of Scotland. I doubt if Dean Ray got through the sixth grade. With that bony ridge over his eyes and his mouth ajar he looked like Java Man. He was a publisher but he confided to me once that the only book he had ever read through to the end was Polton's *Billy on the Farm*, as a special favor to Dub, and even there he skipped around some. And his breath. How could I forget that? It would have killed a small bird, I give you my word of honor. You had to fall back a step or two when Dean Ray was confiding. The usual rotten air but with a fishlike tang I've never run into before. What a crew! And the Ivy twins, Floyd and Lloyd, with their matching outfits, always laughing, at the least little thing, and breaking into laughter at the same instant, a dead heat. They looked at each other when they laughed and they opened so wide you could see those little pink flappers at the back of their throats. They were inseparable, I'm telling you, Chang and Eng, and great laughers. Those simultaneous peals haunt my dreams. What a gang! The past, you see, was coming back to me. Now this brings us up to last September when the brain circuits really began to crackle. I was at my luncheon club in Corpus. We meet on Thursdays at the Barling Hotel. Before we sat down to eat I was introduced to the speaker for that day, a state legislator. It was Senator Morehead Moaler, Jr., or 'Junior' Moaler or 'Big Boy' Moaler. Some call him one thing and some the other. Buys all his clothes at the big man's shop. Well, that name rang a bell, or no, it was more like a detonator went off in my head. Suddenly I remembered you, sir, and Maceo. I saw you here in the Red Room. Squanto was up there on the mantel listening to us in his customary attitude, one of perplexity. Bits of my Gnomon past came to me and I saw Gnomon words swarming visibly before my eyes like bees. I remembered that Morehead Moaler had led our strongest

Pillar in Texas and I said to myself, Texas is a big state but how many Morehead Moalers can there be here? Well, at least two as it turned out, for Big Boy was the son of our own Morehead Moaler of La Coma, Texas. I was in contact again! I saw what was lacking in my life. I had been cut off all those years from Gnomonism and the Jimmerson Spiral. I sounded Big Boy out and found he didn't know the first thing about the Gnomon Society, and had no wish to know. He was not a friendly man. When I told him I was in oil he said his first guess would have been grease. But he did arrange for me to meet with his father and I went down to La Coma to pay my respects. What a grand old man! Such pep! So full of fun! He was in his wheelchair and he was wearing his Gnomon sash when he received me there at his beautiful estate. It's right next to the La Coma Country Club, just off the eighth green. Oh, he spoke highly of you, sir, and he was kind enough to remember my work for the Society in the 1930s, which was more than I could do. Do you know what he said to me? He said, 'My life is an open book, Popper,' which was more than I could say. So many chapters better left sealed. We recited the Gnomon Preamble together. I faltered badly but that wonderful old fellow was letter perfect. Do you know what Mr. Moaler thought, sir? He thought he was the last Gnomon. Can you believe it? He thought we were extinct fauna, you and I. His own Pillar had dwindled down to just himself and he feared that you had either passed on or become unhinged. He said he had heard nothing from the Temple in recent years. None of his letters had been answered."

Mr. Jimmerson said, "Well, I don't know what to say to that, Austin. Maceo tells me that the boys sometimes steal mail from our box. But I can't say. I may have his letters back there somewhere. Maurice is helping me catch up on my correspondence. I always wanted to meet Morehead. If only we had had a hundred Morehead Moalers."

"You can and will meet him, sir. Wait till you spring the Lag on him. I want to be ringside for that. Let me tell you about him. So gracious! His gentle humor! His keen glance! We had lunch on the patio, just the two of us, outside the big house. There's a big house and then all around in back there are guest houses. We ate our shrimp salad and strawberry shortcake and listened to sweet little voices raised in song. There were small children out on the grounds having a picnic and when they saw Mr. Moaler they came to their feet and sang to him. After lunch I rolled him around over the estate. It's like a resort, with palm trees and tropical flowers. Did I tell you he made his fortune in sand and gravel? We fed his ducks. I've never seen happier fowls. We had a long talk. We began to confide in one another. He asked me if his son, Senator Junior Moaler, had not struck me as a swaggering moron. Well, what was I to say? After some hesitation I agreed that he had struck me so. A test, you see. Mr. Moaler was testing my honesty. My answer pleased him and he chuckled there in his delicate way beneath the rustling fronds. It was a light note, but not, to my way of thinking, out of place. You see what terms we were on."

Mr. Jimmerson said, "Yes, but you say you don't remember anything about Meg and the registered dogs?"

"No, sir."

"Then tell me this, Austin. Here's something I'm curious about. In all your travels did you never run across Sydney? Did you ever hear anything from him?"

"Who?"

"Sydney Hen."

"Hear from him! I haven't thought of him in ten years! Sir Sydney! Don't tell me he's still creeping around somewhere!"

"Well, I don't know."

"Still clucking, you say?"

"Well, I'm not sure."

"The little prince? Still at large? You're not serious!"

"Well, I don't know for sure."

"But say, we can catch up on Hen later. Plenty of time for that. Make a note, will you, Babcock? Just jot down 'Catch up on Hen' so we don't forget. We were talking about Mr. Moaler. More Moalers and fewer Hens. Let that be our new goal. Right now, sir, I want you to get the picture at La Coma. What we have there is a soft climate, a beautiful estate and a generous patron. We have a rich man who shares our interest in reviving the Society. Listen to this. I sounded Mr. Moaler out about the idea of establishing a Gnomon retreat there and he went me one better. Do you know what he said? He said, 'Why not a new Temple, Popper, right here in the Moaler latitudes?' Now what do you think of that? But wait."

Popper took a small memorandum book from a coat pocket and flipped through the pages in search of something, suggesting that the next point to be made would require precise language. Mr. Jimmerson and Babcock waited in silence and speculated, each in his own way, on what was to come. An important date? Certain dimensions? An extended quotation from Mr. Moaler? A list of names? A poem?

Popper found the page he wanted and jabbed at it with a finger. "There. 'The Great Moaler *Hall* of Gnomons.' That's the name he would like to give to the new Temple. For some reason I keep wanting to call it the Great Moaler *Dome* of Gnomons. I don't know why. That's what comes of not getting enough air to your brain, or the wrong kind of air. A new Temple in Texas, you see, with a library, a laboratory, an observatory, a computer room with humming machines, a carillon, a reflecting pool, a curving palisade of flagpoles to indicate our international character and some shady walkways on which our Adepts can stroll in pairs with their hands clasped behind them, while chatting of philosophical matters and kicking idly at coconut husks. Those are just a few of the things we came up with. The computer room was Mr. Moaler's idea. I would never have thought of it and yet what is Gnomonism if not harmony of numbers? It's amazing what those machines can do. They can reduce everything you know, sir, to a dot. But let's hear what you think of all this,

this Great Moaler Dome, or rather Hall. Here I am rattling on and nobody else gets a chance to say anything."

"Well, Austin, it's interesting that you should mention the shifting of the Telluric Currents."

"Wait, I forgot something. I haven't explained the conditions. Let's get that out of the way first, sir, if you don't mind. Plenty of time later for the Telluric Currents. The last thing I want to do is misrepresent Mr. Moaler's position. He is well known for his good works and he is also known for the conditions he lays down. Here's one example. The small children of La Coma are welcome to frolic on his grounds, but whenever they see him they must stop in their tracks and sing to him or dance for him until he gives a 'Cease singing' signal, which is a sharp clap of those cymbals he has welded to his wheelchair. That's his policy. A little song or some little improvised dance. Quid pro quo. It's the same with the Temple. Mr. Moaler thought at one time of bequeathing his estate to his son, Big Boy, and then later to the Sholto Business College of San Antonio, of which he is a graduate. Then still later he thought he might divide it between the two of them. But where did his real interests lie? More important, where did his duty lie? Men of great wealth have great responsibilities. Had Big Boy or the Sholto people been as attentive to him as they might have been, seeing what was at stake? We went into those questions and others that came up along the way, and I pointed out to him that there were any number of business colleges in this country, probably two or three in San Antonio alone, and all doing a wonderful job too, but that this Great Hall would be a unique institution that would bear his name down through the ages. Mr. Moaler is just as quick as a cat. He saw the cogency of the argument and he is nothing if not decisive. You can't be a quibbler and make that kind of money. He decided right there on the spot to cut Big Boy off and to endow Sholto with a bookkeeping chair, and let it go at that, and to dedicate the remainder of his sand and gravel fortune to this Great Moaler Hall plan—*if*—certain conditions were met. Now we come to his terms and I think you'll agree they're very generous. Here they are in a nutshell. The Master of Gnomons, Mr. Lamar Jimmerson, must go to La Coma and make his home there in the Great Hall, or in one of the guest bungalows, just as he pleases, and he must bring with him the *Codex Pappus* for final repository in the Great Hall, and he must award Mr. Moaler the following degrees—" Here again Popper consulted his notebook. "First Gnomon Knower, Far-Seeing Arbiter, Most High Steward, Grand Almoner, Intimate Counselor, Guardian of the Stone, Judge of the East and Companion of Pythagoras, which is to say, F.G.K., F.S.A., M.H.S., G.A., I.C., G.S., J.E. and C.P., the C.P. entitling him to wear the Poma. These few things, in exchange for which we live on Mr. Moaler's bounty, free from care, like those ducks, while we restore the Gnomon Society to its former eminence. What could be fairer than that? Call me a dreamer if you want to but I believe this is the beginning of a new cycle."

Mr. Jimmerson said, "Am I wearing my Poma now?"

"No, sir, you're not. Your head is as bare as I've ever seen it. Please listen to me. In La Coma you'll be able to work in comfortable surroundings for a change. Once more you'll hold an honored position in the community. Do you realize the police in this town don't even know who you are? They make it their business to know things and they don't even know your name."

"That explains it, then."

"But the Moaler Plan, you see, was no good without you. Were you alive? Able to travel? I was frantic. I tried to call. No phone. There were no replies to my letters and telegrams. I called the Burnette Police Department. The desk sergeant thought the Temple was abandoned, having been condemned by the Health Department or the Fire Department, or both, but he sent a patrolman out to investigate. The patrolman called me back collect and said he found an old man living here downstairs with two or three other people, and a pack of tramps upstairs. He said the place was a mess, he had seen nothing like it in his nineteen years on the force. I said, 'Cluttered but not nasty?' and he said, 'Nasty too. Filthy beyond description.' So here was a cop near retirement, never promoted, been out on the street the whole time, and he had never seen anything like it in all his years on the force. It was a strange report. I told Esteban to gas up the motor home and prepare for a journey north. We came blazing up the Interstate. Esteban has no sense of road courtesy at any time and when he learned that our mission was urgent he blew little foreign cars to one side and cut in ahead of emergency vehicles. Between noon and one he got up to ninety and ninety-five. He says all cops are off the road at that time. They insist on having their lunch at noon on the dot and taking a full hour. I didn't really worry too much about that because I have a deputy coroner's badge and I can usually count on professional courtesy from my fellow officers. All the way up I was wondering what I might find, and here I am and this is what I find. I find the Master here in the Red Room with the walls peeling and the floor carpeted with moldy newspapers and the trucks out there beating his brains to jelly. Over my head I hear the thumps of hoboes turning over in their fitful sleep."

Mr. Jimmerson said, "Then that explains the draft on my head. I put my Poma on and take it off three times a day. I don't wear it all the time because hot vapors rise from my head and collect in it. Usually I have it on at this time of night but I've been feeling a draft up there and it made me wonder. Now I realize that I must have forgotten to put it on that last time, at around six o'clock."

"Unless you put it on and took it off again."

"What?"

"Unless you did put it on again at six and took it off a fourth time."

"Why would I do that?"

"I don't know. A whim. Another steam buildup. I admit it sounds unlikely."

"But on and off four times a day? I would hardly have time to do anything else."

"Yes, but you see, that's another thing, your health. When you get to La Coma you can say goodbye to drafts and head colds, cap or no cap. The first thing I'm going to do is take you out to the beach for a course of sea baths in the Gulf of Mexico. No pounding surf, don't worry, just little brown rollers a foot high. We'll have you tossing a beach ball. We'll put you on a new diet and get those eyes cleared up. You'll have your glossy coat back in no time. There on the border we can get fresh eggs and Mexican range beef and yard chickens that feed on natural substances. No more of this American meat that's been pumped full of female hormones. It's a scandal how they're contaminating our food with these devilish chemicals. All over this country men are developing breasts. You haven't noticed it yourself?"

"I don't get out much these days, Austin."

"You don't have to go out. Jiggle your own and see. Just take a look at Babcock there when he bends over. I'm telling you, sir, it's a national scandal. Our soldier boys are wearing earrings and dancing with one another and drinking pink cocktails festooned with little paper parasols. A wave of foppery is sweeping over our country and it's all the work of those hormones. But let's hear what you think about all this. I know you must have some questions about Mr. Moaler. There are so many things I haven't touched on yet—his fine head of hair, his famous domino games, his deep-pouch coin purse with the snap top, his manner of eating—the way he sniffs his food just before forking it in, and the great care he takes to get a bit of cake and a bit of strawberry and a bit of cream in each spoonful. But please, don't let me give you the idea that Mr. Moaler toys with his food or lingers over it—nothing could be further from the truth. But look here, I think it's time I took some questions from the floor. High time. You'll just have to stop me with your questions or I'll rattle on here all night."

Babcock said, "Am I included in that offer?"

Popper looked at his watch. "Certainly. Fire away."

"Thank you. I have no questions but I do have a comment or two. First, the matter of the Poma. What seems to be uncertain is when the Master last took it off."

"Or why he did not put it back on at six. I understood that to be his concern."

"Yes, but it's all part of the same puzzle. There's a simple explanation. I can tell you that he took his Poma off at around three o'clock in the excitement of your arrival and simply forgot to put it on again. It was a curious lapse and I noticed it at the time."

"You may be right."

"I am right, and I have another point to make. It may interest you to know, Mr. Popper, that the new cycle has already begun. We are well into the new cycle and it has nothing whatever to do with you or Mr. Morehead Moaler or his red grapefruit. I plotted the curve myself and the Master has confirmed it."

Mr. Jimmerson said, "It's true, Austin. Those figures are sound. It's a sharply rising curve, even allowing for the Lag. Maurice worked it out on his slide rule."

Babcock was emboldened by this support. "Let me say further, Mr. Popper, how surprised I am that this Mr. Moaler would attempt to dictate terms to the Master of Gnomons. People come to the Master, he doesn't go to them. The Moaler millions count for nothing here. The Poma is not for sale and Mr. Moaler will just have to make do with his sombrero for a bit longer. We are perfectly content here in the Temple. This is and shall remain the seat of Gnomon authority. Under no circumstances can the *Codex Pappus* be removed from our archives. There is no need for any research institute, such as you mention, and certainly not in Texas.

The climate and the southern folkways down there would not suit us at all."

Popper crossed his arms and looked Babcock over anew. "Suit you? Who are you? You have no standing here that I recognize."

"For one thing I am Keeper of the Plumes. I take my duties seriously. Now, you like Texas, Mr. Popper. That's fine. It's just the place for you, a big place, offering plenty of scope for your life of sly maneuver and sudden departure. I think your work is there and I think you should leave us to our work here."

Popper turned to Mr. Jimmerson. "You allow this secretary of yours a good deal of liberty."

"Maurice is a good boy."

"Maurice is a middle-aged boy. Is a boy going to lead us into a new cycle? I can't believe you would put yourself in the hands of this rabbit secretary."

Mr. Jimmerson grinned. "Maurice has a lady friend in Chicago. I think he wants to stay close to her."

"Now we get down to it."

"He's sweet on Dolores. I believe they have marriage plans."

"I might have known there was a woman in it. I never get over it, the power of this mating business. Out there on the woodland floor there are white worms living under rotten logs, blind, deaf, barely able to move, and yet they never fail to find one another, the male and the female. Now Babcock here, he wants to get in on it too. I should have seen through this fellow and all his high-minded talk about the Temple. One minute he's Keeper of the Plumes and the next minute he's Maurice, the ace of hearts. What is she, Babcock, a plump widow with a little money put by?"

"No."

"Some hysterical old maid in a shawl? Some old loud-mouth red-headed barroom gal in tight britches?"

"I'm not going to discuss her with you. The subject is closed."

"How old is this woman anyway?"

"I don't see that it's any of your business but Dolores is about forty."

"About forty." Popper's eyes rolled upward. "Around the waist maybe. Did you demand to see a birth certificate?"

"Of course not."

"You couldn't sneak a look at her driver's license?"

"I'm not a sneak."

"They might prove to be interesting documents. Let me tell you something, Shuttlecock. I know the world and you don't. You'd do better to stay away from these crazy and desperate women who hang around barrooms half the night."

"Dolores doesn't even drink."

"As far as you know. How far is that, I wonder."

"I've known her for years."

"And you see nothing odd in that? The delayed consummation? You don't see what's happening? One thing I can still do is grasp a situation and I've seen this one too many times. This old sister has got you on a tether while she waits around for something better to turn up. She's got you staked out as the Last Chance Liquor Store and you can't even see it. Why don't you wake up? Why don't you think of someone besides yourself for a change? You would deny the Master his historic opportunity just so you can continue to carry on with this roly-poly woman in some Cicero motel room whenever you feel like it. What if it gets in the papers? It means nothing to you to see the Society's good name dragged through the mud?"

"I have better things to do than listen to this. We'll see who has the standing around here."

"Go on. Go to the kitchen where you belong. You're a pantryman if I ever saw one."

17

It was Popper who prevailed, and the appeal of the ocean bathing that swung the Master around, that and the promise that he could ride with Mr. Morehead Moaler atop the lead float in the Charro Days parade, the pair of them wearing oversize sombreros and waving to the crowd along with the dusky beauties of Brownsville. On Sunday morning they left for Texas in the camper van—Popper, Mr. Jimmerson, Maceo and Esteban—with Mr. Jimmerson lightly sedated and strapped to a bunk, and the *Codex Pappus* stowed safely in the icebox.

There was no known ceremony for this unprecedented event, the Master's withdrawal from his Temple, and so Popper, feeling the need for a formal gesture, had Ed go to the roof of the Temple and fire a small bottle rocket over the expressway. Popper watched the ascent and the dying fall from his seat in the van. He waited for the thread of smoke to break up, then said, "So be it. Let's go, Esteban." Mr. Jimmerson was under way.

Babcock and Ed were to follow later. They were to pack whatever seemed worth packing and bring it along to La Coma in a rented truck. All was haste and confusion. Things were unraveling. Babcock was being swept along. His instructions were vague. Popper had given him some money for the truck and a Skelly credit card for gasoline, and said, "You wind up things here, Babcock, and come on when you can. Make sure you get all the books. The Master will very likely want to look something up as soon as he comes around. And don't forget his army stuff. He'll be asking about his puttees and his musette bag. No need to worry, we'll get him there in fine shape. He'll think he's in a Pullman. You come on when you can and we'll look for you when we see you."

He spoke as though there had been a reconciliation. Babcock found himself listening in the same way, nodding and giving assent. But Popper was gone now and what was he, Babcock, to do about the Temple itself? How did one decommission the Temple? Who owned it? He consulted a real estate agent, who advised him to remove the walnut paneling, the giant bathtubs, the fireplace mantels, the oak doors and a few other pieces, and then burn the place for the insurance. There was adequate coverage? Babcock knew that the Master had several shoe boxes packed with insurance policies, all golden scrollwork and gray printed matter, hedges against every mishap that life might bring, but surely they were all expired, and anyway, arson was out of the question. That he had even considered it for a moment was due, he believed, to the corrupting influence of Austin Popper and to the presence of the firebug Ed. He sent the agent on his way.

All this activity had not escaped the tramps, alert to any vacuum in the making. They sensed that authority had fled. Winter was at hand. From their upstairs base they began to probe the downstairs area and to settle in those rooms where they met no resistance. They staked out claims with their dropped bags, mostly green plastic garbage bags.

Ed was no help in driving the squatters out, nor was he of any use in loading the rental truck. He did not mind driving the truck, he said, but the U.S. government had forbidden him to lift anything heavy or otherwise exert himself. He showed the note from the government doctor. Neither could the tramps be induced to work, and Babcock had to hire some boys off the street. He enticed them with signs in the yard that read: "Attention, Boys! Something New! Register Here for Free Toys!"

"Many hands make light work," he said to them, as he

organized them into a kind of bucket brigade. Their hands were small but willing. With a certain amount of horseplay and breakage, they moved the goods steadily along into the high-cube bay of the truck—housewares and books and strange Gnomon objects. Ed ate a candy bar and watched.

Down below in the boiler the rats were stirring. The busy patter upstairs had made them curious. The footfalls of the children, light and quick, made them pause and look at one another. They began to quiver and gibber. Then on a signal from their captain they poured forth from the boiler and came slithering up the cellar stairs in a column to see what was going on. In the kitchen they met a horde of cockroaches who had emerged from their dark runs, led by a big bull roach. They too had been disturbed by the new vibrations. Soon the floor was alive.

The boys threw grapefruit and books at these vermin and, caught up in the game, turned on the tramps and gave them a good pelting as well. Some of the tramps had found their way to the Red Room, where they were resting in the recliners and reading magazines before the fire when the attack came. The boys tipped them over. They went berserk. They dashed about screaming. They slid down the banisters and broke windows.

One ran into the street weeping. "That place full of rats and bums," he sobbed out to a knot of loitering young men. They were whites and Negroes about equally mixed, members of a motorcycle gang who had no motorcycles but who foraged about on foot in a shambling troop, led by the oldest male. Their regalia was made of shiny black plastic instead of black leather. They had no bike chains, but only belts as weapons. The leader, a wiry Negro, glowered. He doubled up his plastic belt and whacked it against his leg. "These old stinking winos be making our sweet little chirrens cry," he said. "I know me some bums need a good lesson."

The gang charged up the Temple steps. Babcock, seeing the two-blade propeller emblem on their caps, thought at first they were members of an aero club, young pilots who rushed serum cross-country and who searched for downed chums on weekends, but he did not think that for long. They swept past him and laid into the tramps with their belts, while kicking at the rats with their black plastic boots.

"Watch out, they hiding!"

"Here's another one!"

"A day at the zoo!"

"They going out the windows!"

One tramp, an old man in an army fatigue cap and a long army overcoat, turned in his flight at the top of the stairs and said, "Two on one is nigger fun!"

"Listen to his old GI jive!"

"Burn his ass!"

Babcock saw that all was up with the Gnomon Temple. This was the end of the line. Some of the invaders were now running through the house gathering armloads of goods. Babcock grabbed the inert Ed, who was enjoying the show, and shook him. "Go start the truck. Roll up the windows and lock the doors and wait for me." Then he went to the Inner Hall for one last check. The roaches crunched underfoot. It was like walking on the peanut hulls at Wrigley Field. A big gray tomcat was pacing about in the Hall with his tail high, giving the place yet one more Egyptian touch. The sight of so many rats appeared to make him uneasy. Babcock retrieved a yellow silk cloth and a silver bowl, whose ceremonial uses he did not know, and made his way back to the front door.

There he was intercepted by one of the gang members, who had left off bashing and seemed to be rehearsing a song. He was doing some intermediate thing between walking and dancing, to the beat of some intermediate thing between talking and singing.

"Can't do without," he said, taking a measured step.

"Can't do without." Another step.

"Can't do without." One more. "Yo' precious love."

Babcock said, "Excuse me."

"Hey, my man, who stay in this old jive house anyhow?"

"Nobody. Excuse me. I must go now."

"Naw, Slick, you got my bowl."

He snatched at the silver bowl and Babcock broke away and ran for the truck. He jumped on the running board, yelling at Ed through the glass. Ed pulled away with a jerk. They were off. The two cargo doors at the rear of the truck were swinging open and books dribbled out all down Bulmer Avenue. Babcock, holding to the mirror bracket, looked back and saw people running into the street to claim the falling prizes. When they saw that the free stuff was only books and that they had been taken in and made to look like fools, they kicked at the copies of *Hoosier Wizard* and *Why I Am a Gnomon* and shouted angry words at the receding white truck with the flapping doors.

18

On the long ride to La Coma, Babcock came more and more to doubt that Ed was really Nandor. Did they work in concert, these Three Secret Teachers, or independently? Did they even know one another? In what circumstances did they declare themselves? The answers to these and many more questions were not to be found in Ed's face.

Ed drove and Babcock sat beside him, hatless, with the Gnomon bowl in his lap. He missed his hat. His hat was his banner. He had left his pills behind too and his stomach was a blazing pool. Cold rain fell. The windshield wipers juddered back and forth. The road was a straight corridor between bleak fields of corn stubble. Babcock told Ed that if he drove carefully and obeyed orders, then Mr. Jimmerson would buy him the biggest, blackest, most earsplitting Harley-Davidson ever made.

Ed honked at female drivers. He said "woo woo" to them and made kissing noises at them. He said he enjoyed doing security work for Mr. Jimmerson, keeping nuts and gangsters out of grenade range of the Master, but that one day he hoped to marry a woman who owned a Jeep with raised white letters on the tires. He would take her home and ride around town some. "Look," the people would say, "there goes Ed in four-wheel drive, with his pretty little wife at his side." The way to get women, he said, was with a camera. Chloroform was no good, at best a makeshift. But all the girls liked to pose for the camera and became immediately submissive to anyone carrying a great tangle of photographic equipment from his shoulders. You didn't even need film. He said he had once killed a man when he was in the Great Berets by ramming a pencil up his nose and into his brain.

Babcock said, "It's the Green Berets."

"What did I say?"

"You said the Great Berets. But you weren't in the Great Berets or the Green Berets either one, Ed. I don't know why you want to say things like that. I've seen your records."

"I was in a ward with a guy named Danny who was a Green Beret."

"Yes, but that's not the same thing."

"Danny always had his nose in a book. He had a lot of books about this guy called the Undertaker who goes all over the world rubbing out hamsters and kidnappers."

"Hamsters?"

"Gangsters, I mean, and kidnappers and dope bosses. Big crooks. Danny read those books over and over again and he wouldn't loan them out to anyone else in the ward."

"I suppose you called Danny the Professor."

"We just called him Danny. You didn't want to bother him when he was off his medication. Or even when he was on it. Or when he was reading or eating or sleeping or watching TV. He didn't like for you to rap on the door when he was in the bathroom either. Are we in Texas yet?"

"No, we're still in Illinois."

"We're not even in Texas yet and I already miss the Red Room."

"I do too."

"Do you know what's going on?"

"Where?"

"Anywhere."

"No."

"Will our heads clear when we get to Texas?"

"It's hard to say, Ed. We probably shouldn't count on it."

"The road—to honor."

"What?"

"I heard somebody say that once. 'The road—to honor.' Or maybe it was the name of a TV show I saw somewhere. 'The road—to honor.' Did you ever see it?"

"I don't think so."

The truck had a governor on the engine and there was a power fade at about sixty. Babcock kept putting off the call to Dolores. Would she trip over things in her dash to the telephone? No. He felt himself caught in the Jimmerson Bog, or rather Lag. Now and then out of a silence Ed would utter in a defiant way some paradoxical truth he had once heard, or arrived at himself, one that he seemed to think was too little known or appreciated. "Fat guys are strong," he said, and "You can brush your teeth too much." He said his mother was living with a retired gangster who had some stolen red rubies hidden behind a wall socket.

The clouds were low and heavy. Ghostly white hogs rooted in the fields. The farmers of America, Babcock noticed, had stopped wearing straw hats, overalls and high-top shoes, and had gone over to the trucker's uniform of baseball cap, tight jeans and cowboy boots, this outfit having the raffish air of the pool hall. Ed said he had weighed 112 pounds in the third grade, and then in the fourth grade 130 pounds. "I was a little pink pig in grade school." He said Danny had written more than three hundred songs in several three-ring notebooks that he kept under lock and key with his Undertaker books.

At Ed's insistence they stopped at motels with marquees boasting the dreaded Live Entertainment, with howling young demons up on the bandstand playing the amplified music of Hell. Ed showed his doctor's note to waitresses and bartenders. He slapped his fingers to the rhythm of the music on the plastic pad at the edge of the bar. He fondled the pad too but Babcock had already made him surrender his razor blades. Late on Saturday night in the room he watched the long string of football scores on television and cried out, "God almighty!" and "Did you see that!" and fell back on the bed in amazement over such unexceptional scores as 13 to 7 and 10 to 0, from games involving obscure college teams he could have known nothing about. Over breakfast, which had very likely been prepared in aluminum cookware, Babcock had to listen to Ed read aloud from the two features he always sought out in a newspaper, "TV Mailbag" and "On This Day in History."

They passed through Texarkana at night. Babcock said, "Now we're in Texas."

"Which lane do I get in, Skipper?"

"I'll let you know in plenty of time, Ed. We still have about six hundred miles to go."

From the radio there came music and news. Ed talked steadily against this flow. He said he had been a Golden Gloves champion of Nebraska and that plain old Coca-Cola was the best thing to use in wiping bugs off a windshield. He said he had rather have a man coming at him with a gun than a knife. Vinyl repair had never really interested him but nursing school took too long, not to mention medical school, which went on for years. He wouldn't mind going to that school for circus clowns down in Florida or running the pony ride at a kiddieland zoo or working in a crime lab. He enjoyed his work as an investigator for Mr. Jimmerson, protecting him from creeps who would disturb his naps and waste his time, and from gangsters who wanted to kidnap him or rub him out, but what he really liked was the screech of the machine shop. What he really wanted to do was wear goggles and stand over a grinding wheel, grinding metal objects down to nearly nothing in a fountain of sparks. If he ever got his hands on any red rubies or won a big lump of money in a lottery he would use it to help poor people instead of throwing it away on women and Jeeps the way so many people did. The last time he had gone home his mother had chased him out of the yard with a Weed-Eater. Texas looked okay so far. It looked better than Chicago. He had never liked Chicago. "Downtown there at night," he said, "I was afraid every minute that some headhunter with a sock over his head was going to jump out at me with a knife and say, 'Boola magoola!' "

Babcock lay in a crouch against the door, limp, feigning sleep, numb under the pounding of Ed's conversation and the strain of looking for Skelly stations. It was another TKO for the golden gloves of Ed. But now at last the sun was out and the weather become mild. Now they could have the windows down. The skies of Texas opened up before them with glorious pink streamers that converged to a point over the horizon. Small birds were diving on a big soaring bird, harrying him.

The trip was tiring and a plunge into the unknown but Babcock found it pleasant to speculate on how future chroniclers of the Gnomon Society would deal with him and his role in this historic flight south. Then not so pleasant. What if they saw no reason to deal with him at all? It was Popper who was traveling with the Master and the *Codex Pappus*, while he, Maurice Babcock, Keeper of the Plumes, straggled along behind in the baggage cart with Ed, who at this moment was eating with hoggish noises a giant peanut log. Nandor dissembling again?

Babcock felt no lift. He felt no access of vigor or courage or understanding. If the Telluric Currents were now rising in Texas then they must be rising still farther south. He felt if anything a slight drain. His socks had collapsed too, in a lifeless heap around his ankles, and his clothes seemed to be falling apart.

They made one more overnight stop, at a small motel with a children's wading pool, which Ed soon cleared with his rubber snake and his violent splashing. He called out repeatedly for Babcock to watch this antic or that one. By midafternoon of the following day they were passing through the onion farms of the Rio Grande Valley, this place of winter crops, although to Babcock's eye it was less a valley, in the sense of a riverine depression, than a broad coastal plain. Here, Popper claimed, the Society would bloom anew. It would take hold in this warm soil and swell in the sun like a melon.

The expressway came to an end in downtown Brownsville, near the river, which was the border. Ed was preoccupied. He was comparing a government hospital he had just seen with the ones he had known up North.

Babcock said, "Don't get on that bridge, Ed."

Ed drove onto the international bridge and went past the toll booth into Mexico. Learning of his mistake, he made a U-turn in Matamoros and was back in the United States within a minute or so. Still, technically, they had been in Mexico with their truck, and a customs agent ordered them to unload everything for contraband inspection. Every article must be turned out, down to the last wad of newspaper in the last teacup. The job fell to Babcock, Ed being unable to help. Night came. It was under the floodlights that Babcock finally got everything back in the truck, minus the Master's badger-hair shaving brush, this having been seized as a suspected source of some foreign hair disease. Twice in a matter of hours Babcock had moved more than a ton of *Hoosier Wizards*.

He had never known such fatigue. He was concerned too about the late arrival. It was almost midnight before they found La Coma and the Moaler estate, long past the bedtime of elderly Gnomons. There it was at last, the Moaler mailbox, next to the golf course. On that point, at least, Popper had told the truth. But Babcock need not have worried about the late hour. Lights were still burning in the Great Moaler Hall of Gnomons.

19

"**B**ut *robbed*?" said Popper. "No, I don't think so. A bank is robbed, Babcock. A temple is plundered or looted. Just as a resignation is tendered, a complaint lodged, charges preferred. Verbs are our action words. You, a secretary of all people, should see to it that your verb always matches up nicely with your—the other thing. You should also try to learn a new word every day and then use it in conversation to fix it in your head."

"Looted then. Or pillaged or sacked, if you like."

Babcock could not understand why his arrival and his dramatic account of the last hours of the Temple should meet with such indifference. Indiana, it seemed, had been shaken off and the new life in Texas begun in earnest. They listened hardly at all—Popper, Mr. Jimmerson and Mr. Moaler, he a little man with brick-red face and a full head of fluffy white hair that looked highly flammable. He sat in a wheelchair. He was not yet wearing his Poma. On his dangling feet he wore what appeared to be Buster Brown scout shoes, size five, with bits of string molded into the rubber soles. The Master himself was even less attentive than usual. He had received the silver bowl and the yellow sash, recovered from the Inner Hall at such risk, with no sign of recognition. From time to time he sneaked a look at Babcock, as though having trouble placing him.

Popper said, "But what happened to your clothes, Babcock? You come here in your rags to make your report. It doesn't show much respect for the Master or Mr. Moaler. Have you and Ed been drinking on the road?"

"No. I don't know what happened."

Popper raised a hand. "Later, please. We can't take up any more time with that now. A political problem has come up and we can't sit around here all night discussing the failure of your buttons and zippers."

They sat in a long, low room of plastic couches and Mexican blankets and dull hues, a room less grand than the Red Room but cleaner and more fragrant, and more comfortable too in its snug way. The Great Moaler Hall was in fact a mobile home. It was a big one, some seventy feet long, with three bedrooms, but it was still a trailer with a flimsy aircraft door and not at all the great manor house that Babcock had been led to expect.

The place was cluttered with Mexican curios made of shells, stones, bones, feathers and corn shucks. There was an inflated plastic globe of the earth, which Mr. Moaler sometimes held in his lap. Atop a bookcase there was a stuffed bobcat. On the floor by Mr. Moaler's wheelchair there sat what Babcock took at first to be a stuffed dog, a small white terrier sitting in the sphinx position, head erect, paws forward, not blinking or moving. A beloved pet preserved? Texas humor? What? Then the dog turned his head. He was alive, a little dog grown unnaturally fat from some sex operation, which had also softened his nature. His name was Sweet Boy.

The guest house was compatible with the Great Hall in both form and scale. It was another, older, smaller trailer, with its own rectangular charm, set back in a thicket of thorny shrubs. Ed was there now having a late supper in the company of Maceo, Esteban and Lázaro. Lázaro was Mr. Moaler's cook and driver. Babcock did not know it yet but he too was to eat there and bunk there with the domestic staff. Farther back in that same thicket there was a third trailer, older and smaller still, where Teresita lived. She was Mr. Moaler's housekeeper, now largely retired.

There were formal expressions of regret all around about the death of the Temple, as though for some distant historical calamity, but nothing in the way of heartfelt sorrow. Popper dismissed the subject. "Well, we can't take up any more time with that tonight." He held up the registered letter. "This is the thing we must deal with now."

There was some confusion over the letter. The Master had taken it into his head that it was an invitation for him to address a session of the Texas legislature. He wished to honor that invitation. But this was a gross misreading of the letter, Popper explained to him again, watching his face all the while for some flicker of understanding, and in any case it would be demeaning for the Master of Gnomons to jump, as it were, whenever these politicos snapped their fingers.

The letter was not quite a subpoena but it was a very firm request, all but commanding "Lamar or James Lee 'Jimbo' Jimmerson and Austin Popper alias Wally Wilson of the Gnolon Society" to appear at a hearing of the Churton Committee on the following Friday in Austin. Senator Churton sought their help as he and his committee members looked into the recent infestation of the state by various cults, sects, communes, cells, covens, nature tribes and secret societies, their aim being to identify the more pernicious ones, those disruptive of public order, those who fleeced the elderly and those who made extravagant claims to truth and authority, preying on the senile, the college students and other credulous and weak-headed elements of society.

Mr. Moaler urged defiance. "Big Boy is behind this," he said. "This is his way of getting back at me for taking you in. He wants those two parking lots of mine downtown. He thinks I don't have enough sense to run my own business. If it was me I would just wad that letter up and throw it in a trash can."

Popper said, "Does Big Boy know anything that might embarrass us?"

"He knows nothing. He doesn't even know that the new cycle has begun. Big Boy knows no more about Gnomonism than"—Mr. Moaler looked around for a good example of Hermetic ignorance—"than Sweet Boy here does."

Mr. Jimmerson said, "But I don't mind answering their questions. I don't see why you and Morehead are making such a fuss, Austin. You know I have nothing in my personal life to hide. I think they are showing great consideration in allowing me to air my views there in the capital."

"They don't want to hear your views, sir, they want your hide. These people are not friendly, they're hostile. I'm thinking about your dignity. I just don't think there's any place for the Master of Gnomons in a vulgar political scrap."

Mr. Moaler said, "If it was me, Lamar, I would tell Churton and Big Boy and that whole gang up there to mind their own beeswax."

Popper thought he saw a third way. They could comply with the summons and at the same time spare the Master from an ugly political confrontation. Following the example of Ed, with his light-duty medical certificate, they could get a note from some medico excusing Mr. Jimmerson on the grounds of ill health. He, Popper, could go alone to the hearing and testify. To capture their hearts? No, that would be asking too much. But he might fend them off. He knew enough to string the senators along, and if they began to probe in delicate areas, then he, as a mere spokesman, could plead ignorance of details. It seemed much the best way to go.

20

It was late on Friday night when Popper was called to come forward and be sworn. The big hearing room with its dark wood and high windows had a desolate air. This was the tattered end of the Churton investigation. The television people had left with their blazing lights, but still the room was too warm. Only a handful of spectators remained. The panel of a dozen senators had dwindled down to just three—Churton, Rey and Gammage—all in shirt sleeves. From their raised platform they looked down on Popper with fatigue and dull disapproval.

Senator Churton, the chairman, was a thin, haggard man who smoked cigarettes and made impatient gestures with his gavel. Behind him on a stool sat Senator Junior Moaler, a big man, whose face, like his father's, was congested with blood. There was little further resemblance. Junior was a much bigger man. Here the pygmoid strain in the Moaler blood had skipped a generation. It was Junior, untroubled heir to the Moaler property until this Gnolon band had come along and settled in on his father, who had persuaded the committee to pencil in Jimmerson and Popper as last-minute additions to the witness list, to summon them and show them up for sponges and charlatans. Junior sat anxious on his campstool with a box of papers on his knees, ready to prompt the examiners with questions and feed them damaging material.

Popper was the last witness. He swore to tell the truth, then kissed the Bible, not strictly required, and took his seat with Esteban at the long table. He wore his blue western suit, with a yellow neckerchief this time, tied cowboy style, the knot to one side and the two pointed ends laid out just so.

Senator Churton said, "Thank you for coming, Mr.—is it Popper or Wilson?"

"Popper."

"Mr. Popper then. Thank you for coming and bearing with us. We're running very late. Your boss, I understand, has taken to his bed with the sniffles, or should I say, Mr. Moaler's bed. Is he feeling any better?"

"He was able to eat a little solid food last night."

"Always a good sign. Senator Moaler tells it a little differently. He tells me that this crafty old man, Mr. Jimmerson, is down there in his daddy's trailer lounging around in his shorty pajamas and eating like a hog, with a broad sheen of grease around his mouth, just smacking his big lips and looking around for more."

"I'm not surprised he called in sick," said Senator Gammage. "Eating like that at his age."

"Not true," said Popper. "And I was not aware that Senator Junior Moaler was a member of this committee."

"Big Boy is here at my request. He is acting as an advisor. All perfectly proper. His father's homestead is overrun by a swarm of mystical squatters and you wonder that he takes a personal interest? Perhaps your attorney would like to introduce himself."

"I am not represented by counsel, Mr. Chairman. This man beside me is Esteban, my security chief and director for press hospitality."

"Well and good. But let Esteban keep silent and let him keep absolutely still. All week long we've had these strange people sitting down there, a parade of stargazers, soothsayers and cranks, whispering and grimacing and blinking and suddenly shifting their feet about to some new position. These leg seizures are particularly distracting. One more thing. It's late, we're all tired and we need to wind this session up, so,

above all, keep your answers brief. Now you're the represen-
tative of this—group. What's it all about, Mr. Popper? What
are you Gnolons up to? We don't have to know your pass-
words or your secret winks and nods but we would like to get
some general idea of your mission."

"It's the Gnomon Society, not the Gnolon Society, and I
believe I have anticipated all your questions, sir, in my opening statement, if I may be permitted to read it. I have prepared
a timely and interesting—"

"No, you may not read it. No statements and no charts.
You may present any written materials you have to the bill
clerk. Just short answers to our questions, please. That's all
we want here."

"Then allow me to say, before we get into those questions,
Mr. Chairman, how much I admire the way you have handled this inquiry—the patience you showed with that last witness, Dr. John, and the fairness with which you—"

"Thank you, Mr. Popper. We need to move along. It was
your mission I was asking about. Your movement."

"Well, our mission, sir, as you put it, is simply this—to
preserve the ancient wisdom of Atlantis and to pass it on,
uncorrupted, to those few men of each new generation worthy of receiving it."

"Fair enough. More power to you. You have chapters elsewhere?"

"Yes, sir. We call them Pillars. We have Pillars in all the
fifty states and Guam."

"What about your leader? This mysterious Mr. Jimmerson? Who is he and just what is he doing here in Texas?"

"Mr. Jimmerson is the Master of Gnomons. He is in La
Coma, Texas, as the invited guest of Mr. Morehead Moaler,
himself a Gnomon of very high degree."

"How long will he be here?"

"It's hard to say. At least until we can get our hospital
project off the ground."

"What hospital is that?"

"A hospital for poor children we are planning to build in La Coma. These things take time."

"They sure do. What it really comes down to is this, isn't it, Mr. Popper? This sly old man, Mr. Jimmerson, wearing a very peculiar electromagnetic cap, has moved in, bag and baggage, with poor old Mr. Moaler for an indefinite stay, bringing with him his family, a butler, a hairdresser, four or five musicians and various sacred birds and monkeys. Is that not a fair summary of the situation?"

"No, sir, most unfair. The Master, I repeat, is an invited guest. That can be confirmed easily enough. His cap has no magnetic properties. His family did not accompany him on this trip. He does, very naturally, travel with his executive staff."

"He comes off to me as a very sinister figure. Can you tell us a little more about him?"

"I'll be glad to. Lamar Jimmerson is a decorated veteran of the Argonne campaign. He is a man of military bearing and twinkling good humor. He is clean and strong. He suffers from an occasional head cold but is otherwise a fine specimen. He runs six miles a day and maintains the physique of a thirty-year-old man. He is a gentleman. Children and animals take to him instinctively and rub up against him. He is a philosopher. He is a teacher in the great tradition of Hermes Trismegistus and Pletho Pappus. Mr. Jimmerson is the American Pythagoras."

"Quite a man. How come I never heard of him until two weeks ago?"

"Like all the truly wise men in this world, Senator, Mr. Jimmerson is unknown to the world."

"He's not some naked and scrawny sage from India, is he?"

"No, sir."

"What can you tell us about his economic theories?"

"He has none that I know of."

Senator Gammage put in a question. "Is he the one who claims that the Chinese discovered America?"

Senator Churton rapped his gavel. "Later, Senator. Your turn will come. Now tell me this, Mr. Popper. How much does this old man charge for these fraudulent academic degrees that he sells through the mail?"

"Mr. Jimmerson sells no degrees. He sells nothing."

"Are his financial records intact?"

"I believe so."

"You're not going to tell me that they were all blown away in a tornado like those records of Dr. John's, are you?"

"Our records are intact as far as I know."

Senator Moaler leaned forward for a whispered consultation with the chairman. Papers were passed. Senator Churton looked them over and then resumed his examination.

"What can you tell us, Mr. Popper, about Mr. Jimmerson's police record?"

"He has no police record."

"So you say. According to my information he was released from a maximum security prison in Arizona in June of 19 and 58 after serving seven years of a ten-year sentence for armed robbery and aggravated assault. He was going by the name of James Lee 'Jimbo' Jimmerson at the time. It says here that he played various percussion instruments in the prison band."

"That would be another Jimmerson."

"Perhaps. We do know this. You cult people are great ones for altering your names or taking new names."

"Altogether a different person."

"Perhaps. Even so, you can't deny that your man springs from that same Jimmerson family of thugs in Stitt, Arizona, can you?"

"I can and do deny it."

"I understand he practices herbal medicine. A lot of sprouts and berries in his program."

"He doesn't practice any kind of medicine."

"Hypnotism?"

"No, sir."

"Does he conduct pottery classes?"

"No, sir."

Senator Churton took a closer look at his paper and placed his finger on a word. "Or is it poetry classes?"

"He teaches neither of those arts."

"Does he claim to be in contact with spaceships that are circling the earth, communicating on a daily basis with humanoid pilots one meter tall wearing golden coveralls?"

"He makes no such claim."

"I have been told that he is a man with several rather unpleasant personal habits. I won't specify further."

"I don't know what you're talking about."

Senator Gammage broke in. "These unpleasant habits. Around the house? Out in the streets? Where?"

"Around the house," said Senator Churton. "But I would rather not specify further. You will be recognized in due course, Senator Gammage. You can put your questions then, on your own time. We'll leave that and go on to this. Now, Mr. Popper, how do you answer the charge that this cunning old man, Mr. Jimmerson, has come to Texas to work out his imperial destiny?"

"I don't understand the question."

"No? You can tell us nothing about his plans to conquer the earth and divide it up into triangular districts?"

"Mr. Jimmerson has no such plans."

"So you say. But he does maintain a chemical laboratory?"

"We have our little experiments in metallurgy."

"And in magnetism as well?"

"I believe so, yes."

"Experiments that are carried on behind locked doors, I am told, with vicious dogs patrolling the corridors. What safeguards do you have in place, Mr. Popper? What precautions have you taken to ensure that these experiments do not get out of hand and set the air afire and perhaps melt the polar ice caps?"

"None."

"Very well, then. Let's move on to this dancing school that Mr. Jimmerson runs. How is that connected to your organization? Just what goes on in those classes?"

"Mr. Jimmerson has never run a dancing school."

"It's all right here in this report, with an eyewitness account of the old man himself dancing. It says here that he appeared to be hopped up on some kind of dope."

"That report is completely false."

"Oh? And yet strong narcotic drugs do play an important part in your ceremonies, do they not? In your revels?"

"They do not."

"And lewd dances led by this man Jimmerson? Although you tell us he has never run a dancing school. I have it all right here in black and white, Mr. Popper."

"Not true. I'm afraid you have confused us with another organization calling itself the Gnomon Society. That pathetic little band is led by a man named Sydney Hen, and yes, I believe they do jig about some by the light of the moon. But we have nothing to do with them and they have nothing to do with true Gnomonism."

"Hen, Hen, Hen. Don't we have something here on Hen?" He huddled again with Senator Moaler. There was another flutter of papers. "Oh yes, here we are. Hen the co-founder. Hen in Malta. Hen in Canada. Hen in Mexico. He pops up with frequency in this sleazy tale. A fine fellow too. Both he and your man Jimmerson, it appears, have been living off the earnings of women now for many years. A pretty pair."

"A pretty unsavory pair," said Senator Rey.

"Two rival gangs," said Senator Gammage.

"More a matter for the vice squad, it seems to me, than a legislative body," said Senator Rey.

Senator Churton rapped his gavel. "Order. And when may we expect Hen's arrival in Texas, Mr. Popper? On the next bus? Don't tell me he's already here, pawing our women in Lufkin or Amarillo."

"Your guess is as good as mine, Senator. Personally, I have never clapped eyes on the man."

"You have no knowledge of his whereabouts?"

"No direct knowledge, no, sir. There are several stories going around. I have heard that he was living on a barge in Mexico, wearing a yachting cap and selling fish bait and taking in a Saturday *corrida* now and then and quoting Virgil at the drop of a hat. Another story has him dead, with his remains, a half pint of gray ashes, in the custody of his former wife, the former Lady Hen, who is now Señora Goma y Goma of Veracruz. Another one has it that his acolytes in Cuernavaca have preserved his body in a crock of Maltese honey."

"His entire body?"

"Yes, sir."

"That must be some jug."

"His entire body, intact, except for the lapis lazuli eyeballs in his eye sockets, forever staring but seeing nothing in that golden haze. I have also heard that he is in Cuernavaca in a deep trance of some two or three years' standing, and I have heard that he is not in a trance but is living alone in a small downtown hotel in Monterrey, wearing a beret, calling himself Principato and claiming to be five hundred years old. They say he looks six hundred, with his body all dried up from the desert air. They say he's all head now like a catfish and just tapers away to nothing. These are some of the rumors I have heard."

"Somewhere in Mexico quoting Virgil, if alive. Not much to go on."

"No, sir."

"Still, as long as he stays there. Does he intend to remain there in his Mexican lair, Mr. Popper?"

"As far as I know. If we can speak of the lair of a Hen."

"You mention rumors. Tell me this, if you can. What perverse joy does this man Jimmerson get from starting rumors? Rumors or hoaxes that raise hopes, so soon to be cruelly dashed. What are we to think of such a man?"

"I don't understand the question."

"Let me be specific then. The fifty-dollar jeep. The army surplus jeep, brand-new, crated and packed in Cosmoline, to be bought for only fifty dollars if you could just find the right government agency. Didn't that story originate with Jimbo Jimmerson in late 19 and 45 in Oakland, California?"

"It didn't originate with Lamar Jimmerson."

"And the kidney dialysis machine, to be given away to any community or church group that could collect some great number of old crumpled-up cigarette packs—wasn't that another of Jimbo's lies, first set on wing in a Seattle bar?"

"Mr. Lamar Jimmerson has never been to Seattle."

"Perhaps. I have nothing more at this time. Senator Rey?"

Big Boy Moaler gathered his stuff and moved down the way at a crouch to take up a new whispering position behind Senator Rey, who was sleek and thoughtful. The senator tapped his microphone with a pencil in an exploratory way, then said, "Thank you, Mr. Chairman. Yes, I do have a question or two for this witness. As you can see, Mr. Popper, I have here before me a number of Gnolon or Gnomon books. You prefer Gnomon?"

"I do."

"Why the two names? Don't you find that confusing?"

"We don't have two names."

"A number of Gnomon books, then. There are works here by Sir Sydney Hen—*Approach to Knowing, Approach to Growing, Atlantis a Fable?, Teatime at Teddy's, November Thoughts, Boyhood Rambles* and *The Universe a Congeries of Flying Balls?*, every page of them, I'm sorry to say, badly defaced by vandals with green ink. I have also collected some books and booklets that were presumably written by you, Mr. Jimmerson and this man Pappus. It's hard, really, to say. There's not much information in the front of these books, where we might normally expect to find the names of the author and publisher, the date of copyright and so on. I have here *Gnomonism Today, The Codex Pappus,* 101 *Gnomon*

Facts, Hoosier Wizard, The Jimmerson Spiral, Dungeon of Ignorance—"

Popper broke in. "*Hoosier Wizard* is the work of an outsider. I don't know *Dungeon of Ignorance*. I don't believe that's a Gnomon book."

"It's one of Dr. John's books," said the chairman.

"So it is," said Senator Rey. "I stand corrected."

"And please don't tap the mike again with your pencil. There's no need for that. The audio system is in perfect working order."

"I stand corrected and rebuked. Anyway, I have looked into these books—I won't say read them through—and I find some puzzling and disturbing things. Maybe you can help me, Mr. Popper. It could be that I just need some guidance. This man Hen, for instance. Hen and his busy pen. I don't understand him. Why all the question marks? Why all these approaches to this, that and the other thing? Why can't he ever tell us of his arrival somewhere? And why must he sink our spirits with his November thoughts when he might lift them with his April reflections?"

"Those are good questions, sir, and I only wish you could get the little trifler up here under a two-hundred watt bulb and beat some answers out of him. His books make me gag."

"You don't defend him?"

"Certainly not. No decent person could defend that trash."

"All right then, let's leave Hen and turn our attention to some of your own stuff. Here. This flat earth business. Now, do you think it would be a good thing for me at this particular point in time to go around telling people that the earth is flat in this day and age? To instruct small children in that belief discredited so many years ago by Christopher Columbus? Would that be the proper way for me to prepare our boys and girls to play constructive roles in this our modern world and to take their places in society and meet all the future challenges of the space age in whatever chosen fields of endeavor they might choose to—endeavor?"

"Well, if you sincerely believed the earth to be flat, then yes, Senator, I suppose it would be your duty to say so."

"Which is how you justify your position. You alone in your great pride are right and everyone else is wrong. The plea of every nut in history."

"I don't know what position you're talking about, sir. The Gnomon Society has never questioned the rotundity of the earth. Mr. Jimmerson is himself a skilled topographer."

"Excuse me, Mr. Popper, but I have it right here in Mr. Jimmerson's own words on page twenty-nine of *101 Gnomon Facts.*"

"No, sir, excuse me, but you don't. Please look again. Read that passage carefully and you'll see that what we actually say is that the earth *looks* flat. We still say that. It's so flat down around Brownsville as to be striking to the eye."

"But isn't that just a weasel way of saying that you really do believe it to be flat?"

"Not at all. What we're saying there is that the curvature of the earth is so gentle, relative to our human scale of things, that we need not bother our heads about it or take it into account when going for a stroll, say, or laying out our gardens."

Senator Rey, now tapping his pencil against his teeth, conferred for a time with Senator Moaler, took some papers from him and went on.

"What is this Jimmerson Spiral, or Hen-Jimmerson Spiral, that we hear so much about? Early on it's the Cone of Fate and then that symbol seems to give way to this spiral. What is this helical obsession you people have?"

"There is no such thing as the Hen-Jimmerson Spiral, Senator. You have been taken in, along with so many others, by Sydney Hen, one of the slickest operators of the twentieth century. There is only the Jimmerson Spiral. Mr. Jimmerson is the only begetter. Let me give you the background on that. When the Master first made his discovery known, Hen, an envious little man, jumped in to claim equal credit, citing the historical parallel with Newton and, who was the other one, Darwin, I believe, yes, the pair of them working independently in their own tiny cottages, and then one day, miles apart, clapping their foreheads in unison as they both hit on the idea of phlogiston at the same time. But there was a big difference. Hen, unlike Darwin, would never show his work sheets to anyone, and do you know why? Because they didn't exist."

"Yes, but regardless of whose brain the thing was first cooked up in, just exactly what is it?"

"Now there we're getting into deep waters, sir. I have never known quite how to handle that question when put to me so bluntly by a Perfect Stranger. Years ago, when I was on the lecture platform, I would handle it with a cute little story. I find that a light note sometimes helps. Very often the only way to approach these very difficult concepts is by way of allegory. We have to slip up on the truth. We are obliged to amuse our audience while at the same time we instruct them. You gentlemen will understand. All four of us have stood at the podium, may God forgive us, and addressed the public, and all of us have heard those scampering noises, the tramp of many feet making for the doors, and so we have our own little devices for holding our audience. Now this particular story is a story about three brothers. Let me tell you that story, Senator. Once there were three brothers. The first brother—"

The chairman's gavel came down in a single sharp crack of walnut. "Ask him about something else, Senator Rey, if you don't mind. He's leading you around the mulberry bush. We'll be here all night at this rate. And don't get him started on Hen again."

"Very well. We have annoyed the Chair again, Mr. Popper, so let us move on. Let us have a look at this *Codex Pappus*. I open the book at random here—or farther along—

here. Yes, this will do. We have made our way through all the numbers and triangles and here, coming upon a block of text, we think we're in for a bit of plain sailing for a change. Not so. This is what we run into. I quote:

> . . . *and thus the course of the Initiate is made clear. He must emulate Pletho, the son of Phaleres, first Hierophant of Atlantis, pride of Jamsheed, the White Goat of Mendes, who, at the River Loke, on the day of the full moon, of the month Boedromion, when the moon is full at the end of the sign Aries, near the Pleiades and the place of her exaltation in Taurus, with majestic chants and with banners bearing the images of the Bull, the Lion, the Man and the Eagle, the Constellations answering to the Equinoctical and Solstitial points, to which belong four stars, Aldebaran, Regulus, Fomalhaut and Antares, at once marking the commencement of the Sabaean year and the cycle of the Chaldean Saros, conjunctive with the colure of the full moon, bearing in his left hand the four signs or cardinal points, and forsaking the northern regions and the empire of night, and taking his leave of the Three Secret Teachers, Nandor, Principato and the Lame One, goes to slake his thirst at the sign of the Ninth Letter, or Hierogram of Nomu, in the Circle of the Twelve Stones at the base of the Third Wall. . . .*

"And on and on. Now, that Initiate's course is far from being clear to me. Can you give us some idea of what all that means, Mr. Popper?"

"It doesn't mean much of anything in a surface reading like that."

"That's what I would have said too. So much sawdust. I'm surprised to hear you admit it."

"I acknowledge it freely enough. A lot of that is just filler material in the oracular mode to put P.S. off the scent."

"P.S.?"

"Perfect Strangers. Those who are not Gnomons. Others, outsiders. P.S. or A.M. Perfect Strangers or the Ape Men."

"But to what purpose? Apes we may be, but why throw dust in our eyes? Can you explain?"

"Sure can. I thought it would be obvious. We do it to protect our secret knowledge. We don't know whose hands those books might fall into, Senator, and so we are obliged to put a lot of matter in there to weary and disgust the reader. The casual reader is put off at once. A page or two of that and the ordinary man is a limp rag. Even great scholars, men who are trained and well paid to read dull books, are soon beaten down by it. The wisdom is there but in order to recognize it and comprehend it you must have the key. That key is transmitted by word of mouth and only by word of mouth from one Gnomon to another in a closed circuit."

"So if I had the key I could understand this Choctaw."

"If you had the key, Senator, you could read that book with profit. You couldn't fully understand it unless you had the key to that key."

"What, another key?"

"These are our methods. In this way we have kept our mysteries inviolate for sixty thousand years."

"More like sixty years," said Senator Gammage, in that bass organ note that had caused so many cheap radio speakers in west Texas to shudder and bottom out. "Will the senator yield?"

"For the moment."

"Thank you. This won't take long."

Big Boy moved his campstool again, to a new prompting position behind this third and final examiner.

Senator Gammage squared up the stack of papers before him in a bit of stage business. Then he looked over his glasses at Popper for a silent, challenging minute or so, but in the end it was the senator who broke off and looked away, from Popper's unwavering smile.

"Let me say first that what struck me about those books is how slow they start. Maybe it's just me but I thought they started awfully slow."

"It's not just you," said Senator Churton.

"No, I noticed the same thing," said Senator Rey. "You get hardly any sense of movement or destination."

"Well, I wasn't sure. I thought it might be just me."

"No," said Senator Churton.

"I'll tell you something else about those books," said Senator Rey. "I was a happier man before I read them."

"What?" said Senator Churton.

"He said those books made him uneasy," said Senator Gammage.

"They didn't have that effect on me."

"Me neither. Your sensitive Latino, I guess."

"That's not quite what I said."

"Close enough. May I continue, please, with this witness? Now, Mr. Popper, we have heard about Hen and we have heard about Mr. Nickerson, this cunning, grinning old man with feathers around his mouth, and we have heard—"

"It's Mr. Jimmerson."

"Jimmerson, yes, we have heard about him too, and we have heard about your Society and your literature, but we haven't heard much about you personally. I have some odds and ends here that need clarification. Perhaps you could help me."

"I'll do what I can."

"Thank you. Do you present yourself to the public as a petroleum engineer?"

"Petroleum consultant."

"I see. Are you an American citizen?"

"I am indeed. First and last."

"I ask that question because there seems to be some mystery surrounding your origins and your early years. Suddenly you just appear on the scene, a grown man."

"I am an orphan, Senator. I had to make my own way as a

child, but I am no less a good citizen for that. I am also an outspoken patriot. My friends tell me I go too far at times but I can't help it, it's always been Fifty-four forty or Fight with me. I'm too old to change now."

"According to my information you sat out the war in a small upstairs room on Grant Avenue in San Francisco, playing fan-tan with one James Wing, and emerging only for the Victory Ball."

"My military work was confidential and, much against my wishes, remains so to this day. It will all come out in thirty years."

"Is Austin Popper your true name?"

"Yes, sir. It's not one I would have chosen."

"You say that man Esteban is your security chief. Is he armed?"

"He's well armed."

"You fear some attack in this chamber?"

"We have our enemies."

"But you did not always travel in such style, did you? With attendants and a briefcase. I'm thinking now of your years on the road as a bum."

"I was a tramp, yes, sir. I was down and out. I've never tried to conceal that."

"A drunken bum?"

"Yes, sir."

"Calling yourself Wally Wilson?"

"I believe I did use that name at one time."

"Sleeping in haystacks? Stealing laundry off clotheslines and hot pies from the windowsills of isolated farmhouses? Leaving cryptic hobo marks scrawled on fence posts and the trunks of trees?"

"No, sir, I was very much an urban tramp. No haystacks or barns for me. Mostly I walked the city streets wearing cast-off clothes, with overcoat sleeves hanging down to my knuckles. I did live in a box once for about a week. I went from a Temple to a box, so steep was my fall."

"A big crate? A packing case of some kind?"

"A pasteboard box."

"Under a viaduct in the warehouse district of Chicago?"

"No, sir, it was in a downtown park in one of our eastern cities."

"A long box you could stretch out in?"

"A short one. Mr. Moaler lives in what I would call a long box. Mine was very compact. When it snowed I had to squat in it all night with my head between my knees like a yogi or a magician's assistant. Then when morning came I had to hail a policeman or some other early riser to help get my numb legs straightened out again."

"More a stiff garment than a house."

"Yes, sir."

"Hunkered down there in your box, slapping at imaginary insects on your body. Your only comfort a bottle of cheap wine in a paper sack. Supporting yourself with petty thievery, always on the run, with Dobermans snapping at your buttocks. Not a pretty picture."

"It was cheap rum."

"The clear kind?"

"The dark kind."

"As an urban bum, Mr. Popper, did you often stagger into the middle of busy intersections with your gummy eyes and make comical, drunken attempts to direct traffic?"

"No, sir. In my worst delirium I never interfered with the flow of traffic. I never drank any hair tonic either."

"Senator Moaler informs me that you once got mixed up with some left-wing women."

"The senator is correct. But I was a passive figure in that affair."

"You blame it on the rum?"

"They dragged me in off the street. I was too weak to resist. I was a stretcher case."

"What street was this?"

"A side street in one of our great eastern cities."

"How many left-wing women?"

"Three. I didn't know what it was all about. I thought at first they felt sorry for me. I thought they were just three jolly bachelor gals with short hair, bowlers or rock hounds, who went on motor trips together to our national parks and our regional festivals, and on pilgrimages to the boyhood homes of popular singers."

"This was not the case?"

"No, sir, very different. A very different kettle of fish. Let me tell you what happened. They took me in and hosed me down and disinfected me. Then they powdered me all over and dressed me in a loose white shirt and loose white trousers, held up with a piece of twine. It was a kind of Devil's Island outfit and could have done with some touch-up ironing. Then they locked me in a windowless room that had a mattress on the floor."

"What was the purpose of all this?"

"At first I thought it was merely to instruct me in their doctrines. They explained to me why it was necessary to transform this country into the likeness of one of those countries where they can arrest you for laughing in bed. Padlock the churches, bludgeon the dogs, gas the poets—they outlined the entire program for me. They also tried to do something called 'raising my consciousness.' This was a fairly humorous business, their fumbling efforts to break down my natural human resistance to nonsense and falsehood. But it was a soft berth, I was in out of the wet and so I said nothing. I went mute. I fell into a long silence."

"A long silence, Mr. Popper?"

"Long for me, sir. Then they seemed to lose interest in that part of it and they left off lecturing me. No more political workshops. Except now and then they would pop their heads into my room at night and shout one of their beliefs at me. 'It's all blind chance!' they would shriek, and 'We're animals and we perish utterly!' and 'No more private gardens!' But mostly they just let me feed and sleep. I ate well. I had

Popper said, "It looks like a fellowship hour."

"Where is the waterfall, Austin? Did we pass it?"

"It's down there in the woods somewhere. This is just what I was counting on, sir. We can meet with these fellows on an informal basis before you give your address."

"Is that the falls I hear? I expected a different kind of noise. I never dreamed that Rainbow Falls would whir."

"That's just some mixing machine at the bar, sir, a little cocktail engine of some kind. Here, let's make the most of our opportunity. Let's wake some of these old bozos up."

Popper took the Master in tow and they went forth to mingle and ingratiate themselves. The first man they disturbed said, "Go back where you came from, fatty." The next two were a bit more friendly, mistaking Mr. Jimmerson for the stage magician who was to perform at the banquet that night. Another one asked to know the name and address of his hatter.

Soon, however, his identity became known. This was the mystical old bird from Burnette who, not even a member of the bar, dared to run for public office. This was the turbulent old fellow from the north who wanted to shut down all the nursing homes and quarter all the old folks with their sons and daughters. The word spread and the lawyers began to mutter.

"What is he doing here?"

"Who invited him anyway?"

"I like his nerve!"

"The gall of some people!"

"What a crust!"

"What a getup!"

"He comes here in his nightgown and tarboosh!"

"The very idea!"

"Of all the nerve!"

"Take a look at the other guy!"

"I thought I had seen everything!"

whatever I wanted whenever I wanted it—big T-bone steaks with onions and potatoes, oyster stew, deviled eggs, the end cut of prime rib with horseradish, doughnuts by the dozen, double-X whipping cream on my corn flakes, five or six meals a day."

"New potatoes?"

"No, sir, big Idaho bakers split lengthways and filled with pats of butter. No baloney or chicken franks or other jailhouse grub. It was like a dining car on a train—I wrote out my own orders. Just before turning in at night I had the girls bring me a short stack of buckwheats with sausage links and a glass of cold milk with ice spicules just beginning to form in it. They provided me with a certain amount of rum too."

"What did you make of all this?"

"I didn't know what to make of it but I suspected it would end badly."

"How long did it go on?"

"I don't know. I lost track of time. I had no radio and they wouldn't let me see any newspapers."

"You could have scratched off the passing days on the wall with a nail or a pin—six vertical strokes and then a long diagonal stroke to close out the week."

"I had no pointed instruments. They took my pencil stub away after each meal order. But it was long enough to fatten me up. I grew fatter and sleeker. At night those women would come with their brushes and soft rags and baby oil to curry me and buff me. They ran their hands over my expanding belly. They poked my hams with their fingers. Then they would stand back and look at me and whisper among themselves with their arms folded. Finally it dawned on me. I saw what their game was, from a dropped word or two. I'm slow but I get there, usually around dusk. I saw in their eyes that they meant to cook me. My room was a fattening pen. They were preparing me for a sacrificial barbecue. They meant to eviscerate me and stuff me with celery and roast me, sir, as a symbol of something they hated—men, tramps in their freedom, people of cheerful mien, white Anglo-Saxon Protestants from the heartland, I never knew. Perhaps all four, or even something else. On that point they were never clear."

"No one would miss you. A bum with no connections. No one to inquire. The few people who knew you wouldn't greatly care. These women could spit you and baste you at their leisure. A symbolical porker. Not a bad plan."

"It was a good enough plan."

"A sweet plan. And yet you managed to escape."

"Yes, but there again my role was a passive one. Late one night, perhaps as late as midnight, they came to me with burning candles, very solemn, their faces painted white, and led me into their living room and had me sit in the middle of the floor. They sprinkled meal and blood on my head while muttering something, some kind of Communist maledictions. They began to sway their heads and hum or sing. Then they snuffed out the candles on top of my head and joined hands and began to dance around my obese form."

"Dancing in their bowling shoes?"

"Barefooted."

"But singing? I thought those old Red gals were all business."

"Singing or keening. It wasn't what you and I would call a song. It wasn't an expression of joy. These weren't the Andrews Sisters. It was some kind of Marxist sabbat and I knew my hour had come. Then suddenly, in my despair, I found my voice again. I began to talk, through a nasal obstruction I had at the time. I started talking and before I knew it the afflatus was on me and I couldn't stop talking. I gave those women amusing anecdotes and bits of Gnomon lore. I recalled vivid scenes from childhood. For some reason this annoyed them. It put them in a rage and all at once these Amazons broke off their dance and tied me up in a bedsheet, bagged me if you will, and proceeded to beat me with brooms for what seemed like twenty minutes before rolling me down the stairs and out into the street, where I got pavement burns

on my knees. They just sent me sprawling out there on the
concrete, which is a good name for that stuff."

"Then what?"

"They left me there. Right there on the street where they
had found me."

"That was it?"

"Yes, sir."

"So instead of slitting your throat and broiling you over
a bed of coals they just put this sheet job on you. I don't
get it."

"Neither do I, Senator. I can only surmise that I did something or said something inadvertently to queer their spell, to
contaminate the rite, somehow rendering myself unfit for im-
molation. That's just my guess."

"Or it could be that they simply turned squeamish when it
got down to the nut-cutting. The squeals and gouts of blood.
They shrank from it."

"Those three? No, sir, I don't think so. Certainly not Ca-
milla."

"If you ask me he was pretty darn lucky to get away with
just those strawberries on his knees," said Senator Rey.

"They got fed up with all his chatter," said Senator Churton. "Can't we go a little faster here?"

"One more question and I'm done," said Senator Gammage. "You have testified here under oath, Mr. Popper, that
this old Indiana buzzard, Mr. Chickering, or Mr. Jimmerson,
whatever you want to call him, this old Grand Dragon of
yours, has never set foot in Seattle, Washington. We have
you on the record there. But Senator Moaler has provided me
with incontrovertible evidence that your man was in fact living there in 1959 and 1960. Chuck Jimmerson was the name
he was using then. He was working as the host on a local
television program called *Your Pet Parade,* as if you didn't
know. Thousands upon thousands of people saw Chuck ca-
vorting with small animals and playing the fool on that show
and you have the gall to come here and state under oath that

Jimmerson never set foot in that city. Would you now like to change your testimony?"

"No, sir. That would be another Jimmerson."

"All those thousands of people are mistaken?"

"It's not the same person."

"So you keep telling us whenever we manage to throw a bit of light into some dark corner of this man's life. It's always somebody else. Well, I give up. We're not getting anywhere with this fellow. You can have this witness back, Senator Rey, and welcome to him."

Senator Rey had no chance to speak. The chairman moved quickly into the opening, switching off all the microphones except his own, and hammering the proceedings to a close *sine die.*

Big Boy Moaler had done his worst and he wondered if it had been quite enough. He thought not. It might have been a different story if his two witnesses had shown up. Where were they? This Popper or Wally Wilson fellow had lost a few tail feathers but no blood to speak of. These Gnolons were well dug in. He supposed he must count himself lucky that the other faction, that Hen force, had not settled in on his father as well.

Popper himself, while thinking he might have done better, was in general agreement with Big Boy, that the attack had largely failed, leaving the Gnomon Society in no immediate danger of eviction. He knew nothing about Texas trailer law but he suspected that there was no really effective way of removing a person from a trailer in the Rio Grande Valley without the use of firearms or tear gas.

21

Professor Golescu and Judge Pharris White arrived in Austin on Sunday, too late to testify at the Churton hearing. Notified late, they arrived late. The two men, who were unknown to one another, had flown to Texas at Senator Moaler's urging and at their own expense, both eager to bear witness against Popper. Golescu came from his Auric Laboratories in Sacramento, and Pharris White, a retired hearing commissioner, called Judge by courtesy, from his home in Baltimore.

No one met them at the airport and there were no messages for them at their hotels. Big Boy Moaler, their sponsor, could not be located. They walked the dead Sunday streets of Austin, actually brushing against one another at a downtown newsstand, and then went back to their rooms to wait for Monday morning.

On Monday they had no better luck. They learned, working separately, that Senator Moaler had left the state on a duck-hunting trip. Senator Churton was tracked down to his home in Lufkin but he refused to come to the telephone. His wife advised them that the senator was taking no more calls concerning the recent hearing, and that he was particularly taking no calls from people who identified themselves as professors, judges, scribes, swamis, commanders or masters of this and that. She had never heard of Austin Popper. The hearing was over. Send letters if they must but don't call again.

This was enough for Golescu. He packed his bag in haste

and returned at once to Sacramento and his greenhouse, explaining to his wife, June, and their often divorced daughter, Ronelle, back home again herself, that it had all been a trick, a ruse to make him show his head, a scheme engineered by Popper and the Gnomon Society to humiliate him once again, so late in life, to frighten him and show that he, Cezar Golescu, was still under their eye. They wanted to silence him. They wanted him to shut up about Mu and stop showing the seal. Their tentacles were everywhere. Moaler was one of them and no doubt Churton too. They never slept. Nothing was hidden from the Gnomon host. They were capable of anything—fraud, slander, vandalism, murder, a criminal assault on Ronelle, anything at all. They would rip your tongue out. They knew no law but their Master's decrees and his mad whims.

Bulldog White did not give up so easily. He called the state capitol again and again but could raise no one beyond the switchboard operator. It was the holiday season, she told him, and the office workers were sometimes away from their desks on these festive days. The telephone approach, he decided, was unsatisfactory. Moaler was in his Arkansas duck blind and Churton was incommunicado, hiding behind his wife. All the secretaries at the capitol seemed to be caroling. He gathered his papers and put on his down-filled vest, his blue parka, his blue muffler, his blue knit cap and his rubber overshoes and went out into the springlike weather.

First to a newspaper office, where he thought he might get some straight answers. What he did not know, for all his years in public life, was that newspapers do not welcome direct, unsolicited communication from the public, that they hide their street addresses and telephone numbers in dark corners of inside pages, when indeed the information is printed at all, that they make onerous demands of letter writers so as to discourage the traffic and that they treat as pests those citizens who walk in off the streets with inquiries, or even with news.

The newspaper people took White quickly in tow and put him in a small holding room for troublesome callers and told him to wait. He waited. They checked on him at long intervals through a peephole, until it became clear that he was not going to leave without a poke or two from the cattle prod. An adolescent sports reporter was sent in to deal with him. The boy knew nothing about Popper or the Churton hearing. He had no idea who Lamar Jimmerson was or where he might be located. The newspaper files were not open to the public; he did know that. "Look," he said, taking White's elbow and guiding him to the door. "Why don't you take this up with your preacher? Here's a complimentary copy of today's paper for you."

"Are you trying to tell me that Popper is still not in custody?"

"I don't know."

"He's taken a powder again?"

"I just don't know, sir."

"You don't know much, if I may say so."

"No, sir. Right this way."

Pharris White found himself out on the street again. He wandered about town in a thoughtful mood, turning over in his head the major allegations he had brought against the Gnomon Society in his brief. It was a solid piece of work. It was watertight. A passerby, taking him for an old bundled-up street vendor, asked to buy a paper. White accepted the man's coin and allowed him to take the paper without understanding the transaction.

After lunch he went to the capitol grounds. He walked the corridors and tunnels of the state buildings, a round blue figure on the prowl. He looked in on jolly office parties. Slabs of fruitcake were thrust at him and he was directed here and there. Late in the afternoon he managed to corner a woman who worked on the Senate clerical staff. She agreed to listen to him.

"I can give you a few minutes," she said. "Let's go to Room 61-B, where we won't be bothered."

She took him to another isolation cell, barren but for a wooden table and two molded plastic chairs. She ushered him quickly to his seat and said he need not take off his big coat or his mukluks.

This time he was determined to establish his credentials early and fully. He showed the woman his certificate of merit from the postal union, awarded for three years of perfect attendance at union meetings. He showed her his Gnomon card, laminated in plastic, the ghostly VOID still just visible, and his FBI ring and a letter of guarded praise from the Attorney General and some newspaper clippings in which his name appeared. He presented her with a photograph of himself in his magistrate's robe, a chubby monk in black, standing before a wall of law books all of identical size and binding, and extending, the viewer could only guess how far, beyond the borders of the photograph in every direction. He signed it: "Best wishes to a fine woman from Judge Pharris White."

Then down to business. He laid out before her on the bare table the brief he had drawn up against the Gnomon Society, Jimmerson, Popper *et al.*, along with the yellowing warrant for Popper's arrest he had carried about for so long.

"It's all here," he said. "Chapter and verse, going back to 1942. Jimmerson's misfeasance and Popper's crimes against the people. Get Popper and you've got Jimmerson. Bag one and you bag the other. You may object that Popper is only the front man, and up to a point I can agree with you, but I think you may underestimate how much the old man has always relied on Popper. I also have here Jimmerson's ceremonial baton. His so-called Rod of Correction. Look at it. A little rod you couldn't correct a dwarf with. It will make an interesting exhibit."

The woman informed him that these names meant nothing to her and that in any event the Churton hearing was concluded.

"What you must do is separate them," White went on. "First put Popper away and then get Jimmerson on the stand and sweat him. Drag him out of his palace, impound his bank accounts, seize all his secret books and then sweat him good. Trip him up and catch him out. Ask him about his women and his financial intrigues. Ask him about those perforated white shoes he had on in Washington in June of 1942, the kind barbers used to wear. He's an old man and can be easily confused and made to weep and blubber by a good lawyer. Nobody knows how old he really is. You see me as an old man but Jimmerson was already an old man when I was a young man. Even then he was high-handed and arbitrary. It's Master Lamar Jimmerson, you see, who has ultimate control over the Gnomon secrets and I can tell you from personal experience, madam, that there is nothing fair about the way he exercises that control. The lower and middle ranks of the Society get nothing but crumbs. All the real stuff is held back for a privileged few at the top. This is not well understood by the public."

The woman informed him that no more testimony was being taken by the Churton Committee. No more appointments were being made for meetings with committee members. No transcript of the hearing was available and she was unable to give him the addresses of Mr. Jimmerson and Mr. Popper. She herself was not empowered to take depositions. She would, however, be pleased to pass these documents along to the senators for their consideration.

"Turn it all over to you? Here? The Rod too?"

"I will see that they get it, sir."

"I was given to understand that I might serve this warrant personally."

"I will see that it gets in the proper hands."

"I'm not sure you appreciate how strong this material is. How comprehensive."

"I will bring it to the chairman's personal attention."

"Do you question my integrity?"

"No, sir."

"It doesn't disturb you to know that these two men are continuing to make improper use of their secret knowledge?"

"We would have to get back to you on that, sir."

He had not foreseen this, that his vengeance would be wreaked at an administrative level in Room 61-B, in chambers as it were, with the judge on the wrong side of the table, appearing as humble petitioner with cap in hand. He knew he could not expect from the law a hasty determination. He knew, none better, that the law was largely a matter of papers drifting leisurely about on top of heavy tables in dismal rooms like this, but still the proposal had caught him off guard. Could the woman be trusted? She seemed to be efficient. She was clean. They had not been bothered here in this room. She had been truthful about that.

He pushed himself back into the plastic chair. This chair, the guest chair, was tilted slightly forward and waxed, so that the sitter could maintain his seat in it only through a constant bracing effort of the legs. The weaker the legs, the shorter the visit.

"I won't be here tomorrow," the woman said. "Or the rest of the week. Of course, you can always mail it to us if you like. It's up to you."

But it wasn't up to him. His knees were quivering and he was sliding forward again. He felt the papers slipping from beneath his fingertips. The woman was pulling them across the table ever so slowly, her eyes elsewhere. She was disarming him. Pharris White surrendered them without another word, so forceful was the woman's will in this special room of hers. She thanked him on behalf of Senator Churton for his "valuable input." When he was gone she took an express elevator to the basement and went to a closet and dropped the brief and the crumbling warrant into a deep box where letters, telegrams, books, tracts, poems, manifestos and other supplementary reading matter were stored, soon to go up the flue. She kept the brass rod, to be placed with the other little loose treasures in her desk drawer, and went back to her party.

22

Mr. Jimmerson and Sir Sydney Hen sat on the beach looking out at the Gulf of Mexico. They sat in deck chairs, not talking much, with their toes burrowing idly in the sand. They looked at the water but they did not plunge into it. There were woolly clouds overhead. A breeze came off the whitecaps, fresh but not sharp, nothing at all to the December blast off Lake Michigan. Many years ago the two Masters of Gnomonry had gazed thus in dumb wonder at another enclosed sea, with the cries of sea birds all around them.

Mr. Jimmerson said, "I am a swimmer but I am not a strong swimmer."

Hen said, "I don't fear the water but I do respect the water."

Hen had lost some of his fire. With his floppy hat and his chalky white face and his sunken eyes and his lipstick he looked like an old villain from a cowboy movie of the 1920s. There was froth in one corner of his mouth. Laughing now made him foam a little.

Once again Mr. Jimmerson said, "You're looking well, Sydney."

"Thank you, Lamar, I quite agree. I feel good too. I seem to expand when Christmas comes round. I bloom at this time of year like the poinsettia."

"With the solstice."

"Yes."

"So many of them. The years have flown."

"I quite agree. Night is gathering."

"But I would have known you in a vast crowd of old men."

"You were always alert, Lamar. It's true enough, though, I haven't let myself go. Laughing keeps me young and fit. Oh, one says that, but no, my real secret is eating things in season. Grapes, melons, exquisite plums that drop to the touch. Vine-ripened tomatoes, blood red, right at their peak, and avocados just as they come in. When nuts come in I eat nuts, and a lot of nuts, and when nuts are out of season I never touch them."

"A regiment of old men."

"My dear fellow, you were always on the qui vive."

"It was all so long ago, Sydney. The World War was just—"

"Ages. Who would have guessed then that our old bones would one day be cast up on this Texas littoral? Not I."

"But you know, it doesn't seem so long ago."

"My dear boy, yesterday."

This was the same Sydney Hen who had once called Mr. Jimmerson "a toad with no jewel in his head" and his followers "a cabal of ribbon clerks," and yet not the same. It was a new, agreeable Hen. He had come to La Coma for a visit from Saltillo, Mexico, his current home, traveling by second-class bus with his current companions, the Gluters, Whit and Adele. He used his Christmas money from sister Fanny to pay for the trip.

So it had come at last, the reunion of the two Masters, and it had all been arranged so simply, through the good offices of the Gluters and Mr. Morehead Moaler, and brought off with so little fuss, given the historic nature of the event and Hen's love for ceremony.

The Gluters, whose present job it was to make a flutter around Sir Sydney, had been in the counseling profession in California before retiring to Mexico. They were not culture-bound, they said, but rather citizens of the world. They were people oriented. They preened themselves over their handling of this Hen-Jimmerson affair, to Babcock's annoyance.

Whit Gluter, with his operatic laugh, hearty and unconvincing, said, "It was all so easy!" and Adele Gluter, striking a pose in her long peasant skirt, fists on hips, said, "Why didn't somebody think of this before, for crying out loud!"

Babcock explained to them that the pace of these things could not be forced. There was no occasion for boasting. The Gnomonic Cycle came around in its own good time, Gluters or no Gluters. As it happened, a new cycle was beginning, and consequently here were the two Masters, face to face again. It was not an occasion for crowing.

The formal meeting, with its promise of drama, took place in Mr. Moaler's trailer. The silver bowl was the centerpiece. Resting on a tripod, it was filled with alcohol, which was set afire. Hen wore a white gown with a red rose embroidered on one sleeve and a strange red animal on the other. It was some fierce heraldic beast clawing its way upward. Mr. Jimmerson's gown was unadorned and a bit tight. Each man wore his Poma, as did Mr. Moaler, newly proclaimed Judge of the East and Companion of Pythagoras. There was no embrace, only a fraternal handshake across the blazing bowl, and the two Masters found little to say to one another at first, but neither was there any unpleasantness.

The solemn Babcock, the indifferent Maceo, the beaming and nodding Mr. Moaler and the grinning Gluters, Adele and Whit, all stood back a little way in respect, and the better to behold the scene, and would have stood farther back had the trailer walls allowed. They applauded the handshake. Whit Gluter took photographs.

Popper knew nothing of these events. He lay in a hospital bed in San Antonio with a plastic tube in his nose. Esteban had dozed off at the wheel on the long drive back from Austin and the van had smashed into a guardrail. Popper, troubled by a dream about dancing white rats, woke for an instant in midair as he was flung from his bunk, only to be knocked cold in the fall. He cracked some ribs. Esteban walked away with cuts on his knees and a little blood running down into his socks.

The days passed. Hen extended his visit. He and Mr. Jimmerson got on better and better. Here on the beach they had even enjoyed a laugh together. They were waiting for the cloud cover to break and night to come. Mr. Jimmerson wanted to show Hen the stars. You couldn't see them from Burnette, only the moon, and the morning star now and then, because of the overpowering glow of Chicago, but here each night the whole staggering business was arrayed overhead in icy clarity. He was pleased with the thought of starlight from deep space striking his bare head after so long a journey, of his skull as the apex of countless triangles of stellar rays. In his moist brain, at the point of decussation, where the rays crossed, who could say what seething processes were going on. The starry spectacle was a common enough sight in the highlands of Mexico, and even more glorious, but Hen, now so agreeable, made no mention of it as he joined in the spirit of the outing. They would sit here together and ponder the two immensities of sea and sky.

More fishermen passed by them, tramping across the sand with rods and buckets, heading in for the day. Hen nudged Mr. Jimmerson and again they laughed. The laugh was on the fishermen. Earlier in the afternoon a noisy party of these surf casters had walked heedlessly by, passing within inches of the magisterial feet, but taking no notice. Hen said, "The silly billies don't even know who we are. They think we're just two old turtles out here sunning ourselves." Then he and Mr. Jimmerson could not help but laugh at the innocence of those men who would never know of their close brush with the two world Masters.

The two Masters did not go to the beach every night to look at the stars and strain to hear the Pythagorean music, so very hard to pick up over the sloshing noises of the Gulf, and all but impossible if the wind was up—if the wind was up you could pack it in for the night, as far as listening to the music of the crystalline spheres went—and Mr. Moaler did not go to the beach at all. The sand sticking to his wheelchair tires, the salt spray smearing his eyeglasses—this was not for him. What Mr. Moaler enjoyed was a good long game of dominoes, a series of games, with a little chat along the way about Atlantis or the Three Secret Teachers or how ancient peoples might have moved their big blocks of stone around, though not so much chat as to interfere with the flow of play. He liked steady play, with a short break at 10:15 p.m. to catch the weather report on television, and a longer one at around 1 a.m. for coffee and banana pudding. Mr. Moaler did not have cymbals on his wheelchair but he did have a bicycle bell, a thumb bell, and when he rang it three times play was ended for the night.

Hen and Mr. Jimmerson regarded all such games as a waste of time and of one's vital powers but Mr. Moaler was, after all, their host, and so they agreed to humor him and sit in on a few of these sessions. As their play improved, as they became quicker at adding up the little white spots and more adept at sliding the bones around, their resistance gave way and they came to look forward to these games. They too became keen on dominoes, on the variation called Fives or Sniff. Mr. Jimmerson said he didn't know what he had been missing. Hen said, "I think Pythagoras would approve. He tells us that everything is numbers and this is certainly true of Sniff!" Soon they stopped going to the beach. Almost every night the three elderly men could be found in the trailer, playing dominoes and talking until the early hours, with Babcock or Whit Gluter or one of Mr. Moaler's local friends making a fourth at the table.

Babcock welcomed these invitations to the big trailer, as he welcomed every opportunity to escape his own dormitory trailer. Life in the Red Room had been odd but trailer life was odd too. The built-in furniture was fixed in place for all time, welded or nailed into place, so that no woman without an acetylene torch or a crowbar could ever rearrange it. Just going in and out was odd. One moment you were altogether outside the trailer and the next moment you were altogether inside the trailer, with no landing or foyer to soften the passage. Once inside there was the smoke to contend with, from Maceo's cigar and from the cigarettes of Ed and Esteban and Lázaro, who lay about like Chinamen in an opium den, puffing away, watching game shows on television and listening to droning Mexican polkas on the radio. Ed, if that was who he truly was, was still lying low, as Ed. He did no work, he slapped on things to the beat of Mexican accordion music and he laughed and egged them on when Esteban and Lázaro shouted curses at one another. There was a running quarrel between the two that sometimes flared up in an ugly way. At other times they could be great pals, very playful, as when they teased Babcock and locked him out of the trailer and made grotesque faces at him with their noses and lips pressed against the windows.

Such conditions made it hard for Babcock to concentrate on his studies. Work on the new autobiography had bogged down. He had trouble finding essential papers and books. These materials were now all jumbled up outside in a big pile with the Temple furnishings. There was no place to store the stuff and it remained on the ground where it had been dumped, and heaped up into a mound about eight feet high, and covered, after a fashion, with clear plastic sheets. The sheets were anchored all around with rocks and books but they had a way of blowing loose in the night and flapping feebly over the summit of the Temple goods. It was a pyre awaiting the torch.

Teresita's trailer, the smallest of the Moaler fleet, was dark and quiet and would have been ideal for Gnomonic study but for the Gluters, who had been assigned sleeping quarters there. The old lady, Teresita, kept to herself, licking her trading stamps and sticking them into booklets. She went out in the morning to feed her two geese and to sweep the ground outside her door, this last business being almost involuntary.

Something in her Mexican blood drove her, sick or well, to make those choppy broom strokes against the hard bare earth. In the evening she fed her geese again and tended her two flower beds, enclosed within two car tires. She glowered at Babcock but asked no questions. He found he could work in her trailer tolerably well, until the Gluters moved in. After that there was no peace.

A guest bed was available but the Gluters chose to sleep on the floor of Teresita's little sitting room, on straw mats that they carried about with them, rolling them out at night and rolling them up again in the morning and stowing them away in their ancient suitcase. The Gluters were drawn to the floor. All their counseling sessions, they said, were conducted with everyone sitting cross-legged on the floor. In the afternoon there was more of this tatami rolling, when they had their naps, followed by sitting-up exercises. Adele directed the calisthenics. All through the day they were in and out of the trailer, with Adele's pigtail bouncing, and in and out of their big suitcase, forever buckling and unbuckling, with Whit, in a snarl of belts, trying hard to please but often getting things wrong.

It was an old black leather suitcase of crinkled finish, on each side of which was painted, with little skill, their name, thus: "THE GLUTERS," in a green enamel that did not quite match the fine patina on the hinges and fittings. Babcock wondered about the quotation marks. Decorative strokes? Mere flourishes? Perhaps theirs was a stage name. Wasn't Whit an actor? The bag did have a kind of backstage look to it. Or a pen name. Or perhaps this was just a handy way of setting themselves apart from ordinary Gluters, a way of saying that in all of Gluterdom they were *the* Gluters, or perhaps the enclosure was to emphasize the team aspect, to indicate that "THE GLUTERS" were not quite the same thing as the Gluters, that together they were an entity different from, and greater than the raw sum of Whit and Adele, or it might be that the name was a professional tag expressive of their work, a new word they had coined, a new infinitive, *to gluter*, or *to glute*, descriptive of some new social malady they had defined or some new clinical technique they had pioneered, as in their mass Glutering sessions or their breakthrough treatment of Glutered wives or their controversial Glute therapy. The Gluters were only too ready to discuss their personal affairs and no doubt would have been happy to explain the significance of the quotation marks, had they been asked, but Babcock said nothing. He was not one to pry.

The Gluters annoyed him in many ways, not least with their insinuations that Hen stood just a bit higher in rank than Mr. Jimmerson. They dared to speak to the Master in a familiar way. They presumed to comment freely on the Telluric Currents, or on anything else. A nuisance, then, these Gluters, but Babcock could not in fairness blame them for the present state of things here at the new Temple, where nothing was going forward.

The Master never looked anything up these days and he kept putting off work on the new book. He seldom spoke of the Lag. There was little mention of Pletho. His only interests seemed to be dominoes and his afternoon cone of soft ice cream and the nightly weather news on television—the actual weather did not interest him, just the news. Each day more papers blew away from the Gnomon pile, lost forever, so many papers that the blizzard was remarked on by golfers out on the links who found strange pages stuck to their legs, and by other residents of La Coma, a town notable for its blowing paper.

No, the blame lay with Hen. It was Hen who had put a chill on things with his shrugs and smiles. Gnomon talk bored him. He professed not to understand the Jimmerson Lag. He treated these matters in a jocular, dismissive way and could not be engaged in serious discussion of any subject other than that of fresh fruit and goat's milk. He said over and over again that he no longer bothered to write books or, a much greater release, read them. "So very tiresome," he said. "Such rubbish. Even the best of them are not very good. Far too many people expelling gas in public these days. Don't you agree, Morehead?" He seemed to suggest that Lamar Jimmerson and others would do well to follow his example.

With so little to do, Babcock took to lingering in bed under heavy medication, sunk in waves of smoke and accordion music that never died. And even there, in his own bed, he could not get away from Whit Gluter and his lank wife, Adele. There was an intercom system that connected all the trailers in the Moaler compound, and Adele used it frequently. She came on at all hours in a hissing blast of static, calling for Whit, telling Whit to report in, asking if anyone had seen Whit, passing on urgent messages for Whit. And, likely as not, Whit would be there, in the bunkhouse trailer, though he did not always respond to the calls. He would be talking to Ed or Lázaro or, at bedside, to Babcock, telling of the Gluter travels in Mexico—so many miles by bus, so many by train, exact figures, the bargain meals, the bargain rooms, the colorful villages, their names.

Whit's delivery was clear, for he had once been a movie actor before he married Adele and became a counselor, specializing in portrayals of informers, touts, pickpockets, eavesdroppers, treacherous clerks and the like, city sneaks of one stripe or another. He was a friendly fellow with a ready laugh, as became a counselor, but with his dark moods too. One morning, in a lull between bus stories, he began to squirm and dart his eyes about as he lapsed for a moment into one of his weasel screen roles. He said, "Uh, look here, have you been making eyes at Adele?"

Babcock could not have been more surprised had Whit suddenly burst into song. "No, of course not. What gave you that idea?"

"This, uh, note. Adele found it in her tatami."

Babcock read the note, which ran:

Adell
I could go for you baby in a big way. How about it?
Burn this.

                                                    Maurice

"I didn't write this note, Whit. You can see that's not my handwriting."

"Well, I didn't know. I couldn't be sure. I wouldn't want you to think you could break our marriage up."

Later that same day Adele herself came by. She came to take Whit away for his nap. It was time to roll out the mats again. She stared at Babcock, already at rest. She stood over him, gathering her thoughts, then said, "You have no business looking down your nose at us. Oh, I know what you've been thinking. I'm not dumb. I know what you've been saying. The Gluters are silly. The Gluters are not refined people. I know what you've been saying behind our backs. You think I haven't heard it all before? From people like you? The Gluter woman is a hussy. Adele walks with too confident a stride. Even my gait is found offensive. Adele this and Adele that. Her hair. Her clothes. Whit is foolish. The Gluters are vulgar. Whit is henpecked. The Gluters could do with a bath. Well, what do you know about it? You know nothing whatever about our professional standing. How many radio talk shows have you been on, Mr. Know-it-all? You know nothing about the hundreds of interesting articles we have written or the thousands of successful encounter sessions we have conducted, helping people to expand and grow in many different directions and live their lives to the fullest, or even what personal goals we may have set for ourselves this year. Yes, and I've caught you ogling me, and let me tell you something, mister, you can just put those ideas right out of your head. I've told Whit about it and I've also complained to Sir Sydney. You think Whit is henpecked? It might surprise you to know that Whit sometimes spanks me with one of his sandals. How do you like that, Mr. Babcock? So you can just keep your love letters to yourself, thank you. No, we will not have an affair. You will never hold me in your arms. You and I, Mr. Babcock, will never go stepping out together and I want you to get that through your head once and for all. If you think you're going to break our marriage up you've got another think coming."

This was Adele, roused. Babcock said nothing.

23

Whit's photographs of the reunion turned out to be dark splotches. There was to be a reenactment of the Masters' handshake, to be captured this time on fresh film, before the big dinner on Christmas day.

Popper came rolling in the day before Christmas, in a wheelchair. The chair was a windfall. His roommate at the hospital, an old man, had died, and Popper had bought the man's chair from the distraught widow. He gave her five dollars and said he would take it off her hands. There was nothing wrong with his legs, he could walk well enough, but he liked the idea of making an entrance on high spoked wheels. He would come home wounded in action. Esteban would push him up the ramp and into the trailer, and there he would sit hub to hub with Mr. Moaler, with a knitted shawl over his knees and his hands formally composed in his lap.

So he arrived, to warm greetings from Mr. Jimmerson and Mr. Moaler. They plied him with questions about his injuries but showed only mild interest in his account of the Senate hearing, now such a remote event. Popper, sensitive to his audience, cut short the account, saying that the senators, after hearing the truth of the matter, had given him a unanimous vote of thanks for bringing Mr. Jimmerson to Texas.

"Junior had scared the fool out of everybody with a lot of wild tales about us. People were fainting. Women passing out and children crying. Well, Big Boy had to eat those words. You can bet I set the record straight, and pretty fast too. On the day I left Austin the Christmas shoppers on the streets

237

were talking of nothing else but Lamar Jimmerson and how he had been misunderstood."

"And what did Junior say?"

"Junior didn't know what to say, Mr. Moaler."

Mr. Moaler smiled at the picture in his head of his son, the big fellow, checked and sputtering. "And what repercussions may we expect?"

"None. We're clear. All is well."

The two wheelchairs in such narrow quarters made for a traffic problem. Popper maneuvered his chair about in a clumsy manner. "Watch out for Sweet Boy's tail," said Mr. Moaler. "And his paws. Watch out for my curios. Watch out for the tree." This was the Christmas tree. All the lights on it were blue.

Hen and Babcock were not so pleased to see Popper, nor was Popper pleased to find that Hen had taken his bed. He had been informed of Hen's descent on La Coma but not fully informed, it being his understanding that the visit was to be a flying one of only two or three days. He was greatly surprised to find Hen still here, and, to cap it off, wallowing in his, Popper's, sheets.

"He hasn't left? Sydney Hen is here now? You're not serious!"

"He's back there having his lunch."

Popper rolled himself down the corridor to the end bedroom. Hen was in bed eating greedily from a tray, not fruits of the season but meat loaf and fried potatoes. Adele was seated beside him with pad and pencil. She was there to jot down the words that came to him in his poetic flights, these to be picked over later for gems, such as were suitable for inclusion in the new book he was putting together on the sly. Adele also had a moist towel at the ready for dabbing the tomato sauce off his fingers and chin.

Popper looked at Hen, taking him in. The two men had never met and now they took each other in, shadows become at last sagging flesh. Hen was wearing his Caesar wig with the curly bangs, and Popper his Texas promoter wig, which was a swelling silver pompadour.

"Hen? I'm Austin Popper."

"Popper. Well, well. Lo the bat with leathern wing."

"What do you think you're doing here?"

"Austin ruddy Popper. Augustine writ small. Yes, I daresay you are Popper. You look like Popper. That narrow eye."

"You look like some devilish old diseased monkey."

"Charming. But we shall just have to bear with one another's infirmities, Popper. I with yours and you with mine."

"You've made yourself at home, I see."

"Oh yes, I've become quite fond of my room here. My little nest. A poky little room but oh so comfy. Like a snug cabin on ship or a luxury train. Morehead is very kind. I grow tired of travel."

Adele said, "Should I turn to a fresh page and get this down, Sir Sydney?"

"No, my dear, I think not."

"If I may dab. A red drop there."

"Too kind."

"About to fall."

"Most considerate."

Popper said, "It's time for you to move on, Hen. Back to your hole in Mexico. You're not welcome here. There's no place for you here in our program. You're in my bed. This is not your room. This is my room and I mean to have it back."

"Oh pooh. Do you hear that, my sweet? He makes threats from a wheelchair."

"What have you done with my things?"

"I had your man take them away."

Popper wheeled about and went back to Mr. Jimmerson and Mr. Moaler to present his case. Mr. Jimmerson, who was thinking of turtle riding in the open sea, did not follow the complaint in all its detail but he did say that this squabbling on Christmas Eve was unseemly and that surely some sleeping arrangement satisfactory to all parties could be worked out.

"Lamar is right," said Mr. Moaler. "There's plenty of room for everyone. Plenty of trailers and plenty of warm beds for everyone to lie down in. And if not, we'll *make* room. Let's not spoil our Christmas with a quarrel."

That night they saw Christmas come in at the dominoes table. Popper sat in on the game. He and Hen observed a wary truce. At midnight Mr. Moaler rang the thumb bell on his chair and they broke off play. There were Christmas greetings all around, followed by coffee and banana pudding and some friendly chat.

Mr. Moaler, taking care to get a bit of banana and a bit of yellow pudding and a bit of vanilla wafer in each spoonful, said it was interesting that cattle were mentioned upwards of 140 times in the Bible, but that the domestic hen, a most useful fowl, was mentioned only twice, and the domestic cat not at all. Mr. Jimmerson said that Sydney's recent mention of the turtle had made him think of something he had seen many years ago, and that had been much on his mind lately. It was an old newsreel showing a young man astride a swimming sea turtle. A giant turtle, with his flippers, such odd limbs, flapping smoothly away in the water. The young rider was laughing and waving at the camera. He would be quite old now and Mr. Jimmerson wondered if he retained his good humor and his gleaming teeth and his love for water sports. He wondered where the fellow might be today. Probably gumming his food well inland, said Hen. He went on to say that the domestic dog came in for a good deal of unfavorable mention in the Bible. Popper said that so far tonight no mention at all had been made of the deer, and yet his antlers, shed and regenerated once a year, were thought to be the fastest-growing of all animal substances.

They stayed up for the late weather report—"Winds light and variable"—and exchanged another round of good wishes. "Let's all look our best tomorrow," said Mr. Moaler, with a curious smile. "That is, later today. I have a little something in mind. An interesting announcement to make. Let's all look our best."

With that they turned in. Popper slept on the plastic couch, in the blue glow of the Christmas tree.

Adele, who had a way of getting wind of things, came on the intercom early in the morning to say that everyone was to wear his good clothes to the dinner today. She repeated the message at intervals, sometimes adding, "Let's keep to schedule."

Lázaro was up early too, basting the turkeys, as was Maceo, who had charge of cakes and pies. Teresita prepared the gumbo. This dish, a soup dense with shrimps and hairy and mucilaginous pods of okra, was a Moaler tradition on Christmas morning. Whit loaded his camera, in a darkened bathroom this time.

Popper had Esteban take him out for a drive in the van. He wanted to get away from Adele's voice and all the bustle. On sharp turns the right front tire rubbed against the crumpled fender. They cruised the residential streets and watched with delight the little children wobbling along on their new Christmas bikes and skates. They went to Brownsville and looked over Mr. Moaler's downtown parking lots. No revenue today, no cars, but still the recorded message played endlessly over a loudspeaker, warning those who would park there without paying that their cars would most certainly be towed away, at any hour of the day or night, Sundays and holidays not excepted, at great expense to the trespassers.

Popper said, "This is the greatest business in the world, Esteban. You do absolutely nothing but collect money."

But he wondered if these two weed lots could continue to support Mr. Moaler's expanded household. Would he be announcing sharp cutbacks at the dinner today? Or what? Something to do with the Society? Would he proclaim himself Master?

Esteban said, "Why don't we go back to Corpus, boss?"

"No, I'm just not up to it. I'm tired of all that chasing around. I'm tired of jabbering. I haven't had a drink in five years. Your brewers, your vintners, your distillers, they don't even exist for me anymore, and I try to put a good face on things, but the fact is, Esteban, that I'm still not getting enough air to my brain. The truth is that my powers are failing and I can't cut it any longer. You saw how they worked me over up there at Austin."

Babcock had no Christmas morning duties to perform either. He poked at the pile of Gnomon goods with a stick, looking for his stenotype machine, as a survivor pokes the rubble after a tornado in search of a favorite shoe. The light winds had disturbed the covering sheets again, leaving the mound exposed. The rain and sun had been at work. Alternately soaked and baked, the mass was dissolving, blending and settling into a lumpy conglomerate, something like fruitcake. Around the base there lay exfoliating copies of *Hoosier Wizard*.

Babcock's eye ranged over the big trailer. This was the new Temple, or rather Great Hall. It seemed an unlikely place for one to await apocalyptic events, but then what would be a likely place? He noted that the Hall was growing on him. The stark lines had become pleasing, the horizontal values, the very human scale. It was a Temple that could be hauled away in the night by anyone with a two-inch ball on his car bumper, but then Temples of marble and granite did not last either, as he had reason to know.

"Hey, what do you think Mr. Moaler's announcement will be?"

This from Ed, who had slipped up behind him. Ed was apprehensive.

"I don't know."

"Lázaro thinks he may kick some of us out. Or all of us."

"I don't know anything about it, Ed. We'll just have to wait and see."

Babcock thought he did know what the announcement

would be but it was not the kind of thing you could discuss with Ed, who, he knew now, was not Nandor. He had seen it coming. He had felt it coming, this climacteric, this revelation that Mr. Moaler was himself the Lame One, and that Mr. Jimmerson and Sir Sydney were Nandor and Principato, or Principato and Nandor. It was all falling together. He could see now the necessity for the flight south. It was nothing less than the coming together of the Three Secret Teachers.

Adele served Hen his cup of gumbo and his cup of cocoa in bed, and advised him to wear his green silk gown for the reenactment of the Masters' handshake. The gown was of oriental design, with ample sleeves that covered the hands when joined in front, Chinese fashion. There were white four-pointed stars scattered about over it, representing Ptolemy's fifteen fixed stars of the first magnitude.

Adele said, "The green makes a stronger statement and will help to offset Mr. Jimmerson's thicker presence. Your super-tall green Poma will help to diminish him somewhat too."

Hen nodded. He was brooding over Mr. Moaler's interesting announcement. When would it come? Before dinner? After? During? With ding of spoon on glass? What could it be? Interesting to whom? Something to do with the Lag? A recent dream? A vision? A program of compulsory physical exercise? A day trip on a motor launch?

He waved off the gown chatter. "Yes, but what news, Adele? What do you hear about this announcement or proclamation?"

"Ed told Whit that Mr. Moaler thinks there are too many people living here and that he's going to turn some of us out."

"On Christmas day?"

"Ed didn't know when. He got it from Lázaro."

"And who was Lázaro's source?"

"I have Whit working on that now."

"Babcock, you think?"

"I wouldn't think so. He never knows anything."

"Popper?"

"That would be my guess. Through Esteban to Lázaro to Ed."

"Or Popper directly to Lázaro to Ed."

"Or through Maceo to Lázaro."

"They confide?"

"They confer. Over their pots."

"Nothing about a boat ride?"

"No, sir."

"But who is to go? Who is to be given the black spot?"

"Whit is working on that now. Shall I lay out the green silk?"

"Yes, my dear, and then you can draw my tub."

24

Adele too chose to make a green statement, with her sea-green terry-cloth coveralls, cinched in at the middle with a pirate's black belt, for the occasion of this extraordinary conclave at Rancho Moaler. Mr. Jimmerson called her Juanita. Never good at sorting women out, he had thought Adele and Teresita to be the same person, though they were nothing at all alike, and he addressed them both as Juanita. Now he saw them together for the first time and was confused. Teresita wore different hues of black.

All were crowded into the big trailer or Great Moaler Hall, and all were spruced up, faces scrubbed, Ed with clean boots, Babcock in borrowed necktie, Maceo in his old tan suit and long pointed tan shoes, Esteban in his frilly white guayabera shirt, Hen resplendent under a green spire, a Merlin hat. Mr. Jimmerson's original Poma looked squat and crude in comparison. Still the eye was drawn to it.

Again the two Masters clasped hands across the burning bowl, before rapt faces. Popper did not lead the applause but he did join in. Whit took shots from different angles. He said, "Hold it, please. That flame is so faint and I want to make sure I get it in." He wanted to catch a blue wisp, seemingly unsupported, on his color film.

Sir Sydney was on edge, unnaturally animated, talking too much and laughing too readily under the tension of waiting for Mr. Moaler's announcement. He said, "Do you know, Lamar, there really is something to this stuff. There were times when I thought I might be deluded. There were moments when I wondered if my condition might not be a pathological one, but now I'm convinced that old Papa Pletho was really on to something."

Mr. Jimmerson said, "It's too bad that Fanny and Jerome can't be here to share in this."

"Yes."

"I don't believe you have any children, do you, Sydney?"

"Oh no, it wouldn't have done for me. I spared the world the late-life spawn of an aesthete and a socialite. I didn't want to foist off some rotten, helpless, exotic kid on the world. It would never have done. Out of the question. It must all end with me. The Hen line must die with me in what I had hoped would be a Wagnerian finish."

A whiff of sage came from the corn-bread dressing and there were other pleasant smells from the long buffet table. Mr. Moaler struck a green note himself, with a Gnomon sash across his body, which was like that of an Eagle Scout or a South American president. When the ceremony was done and the congratulations had trailed off, he rang his thumb bell. The guests looked at one another and became very still, like Sweet Boy. They steeled themselves. Breathing was suspended. *Here it comes.* Mr. Moaler offered a long prayer of thanksgiving for their many blessings, but made no announcement.

"Amen," said Popper. "After all, we still have our—I started to say our health. But we do still have our wits about us and we still hold our ancient secrets inviolate and we have our Society intact, lean and strong, under the generous patronage of Mr. Morehead Moaler."

There was applause for Mr. Moaler. He stopped it with a raised hand. "Time to eat," he said. Plates were prepared and served to the two Masters, and to Mr. Moaler and Popper in their wheelchairs, the four of them sitting *en banc*. Then the others formed a line and served themselves.

Adele said, "No need to overload your plate like that, Ed. There's plenty of food. You can come back."

Hen helped Mr. Moaler tuck his napkin, showing that he was not too proud to perform such small offices. "A lovely dinner, Morehead. Do you know, I believe I'm recovering some of my old form, thanks to you and your kindness."

"Good food," said Mr. Jimmerson. "Give me the dark meat every time and you can have your white meat."

Popper said, "Did you hear that, Maceo? Lázaro? Teresita? The Master's compliments. Mine too. A real dining experience. How about it, everyone? Can't we show a little appreciation for our cooks?"

More applause.

Outside there was a rustling noise, which, to Babcock, reminded of that last terrible day in the Temple, sounded like many thousands of cockroaches on the march. Again the guests looked at each other with alarm, in the way of the Atlanteans, when they first heard the rumbling on their single day and night of misfortune. What now? There was a rush for the windows, such that the Great Hall tilted a bit. Outside they saw a magnificent new mobile home, yellow, with pitched roof, being towed in under the palm trees and brushing against the dead fronds. This was Mr. Moaler's surprise. He had bought a new trailer.

His red face was glowing under his Poma. "How do you like it?" he said. "That's your eighty-foot Cape Codder with cathedral roof and shingles of incorruptible polystyrene. It's the top of the line. The Cape Codder is built with sixteen-inch centers and will never sag in the middle like those cheaper models with twenty-inch centers. The furniture is done in indestructible Herculon and there are two master bedrooms for our two Masters. Plenty of room for everybody. By day we'll study or do whatever we please and every night we'll play Sniff."

There were more cheers for Mr. Moaler, on this day of cheers and goodwill. Even Popper, who never laughed, was moved to laugh a little. Another trailer! And the suggestion that there were still more where that one came from! A Gnomon panzer formation in the Moaler grove! It wasn't the Temple of the old days but it was better than being breathed on by Dean Ray Stuart!

Hen, exultant, foaming, almost weeping, said, "I think I'll grow tomatoes by day, Lamar. The Better Boy variety for preference, in this sand. Yes, a little garden for me. How about you?"

"It's study for me, Sydney."

Babcock remained standing at a window but he was not looking at the long yellow flanks of the new Temple. He could feel the Telluric Currents. The pulsing made him a little dizzy. The surge and ebb. He saw what must be done. The flame was faint indeed and he had much work to do. He need no longer take account of the thoughtless multitude in the cities of men or of the three elderly gamesters at their table in their conical caps. He had often suppressed the thought but now he knew in his heart that he himself was a Master and that Maurice Babcock was to be Master of the New Cycle.

Whit said, "What a wonderful Christmas!"

Ed, who no longer missed the Red Room, said, "This is the best party I've ever been to!"